P9-AEU-600

HARDY BOYS

UNDERCOVER BROTHERS™

PAPERCUTZ™

THE HARDY BOYS GRAPHIC NOVELS AVAILABLE FROM P

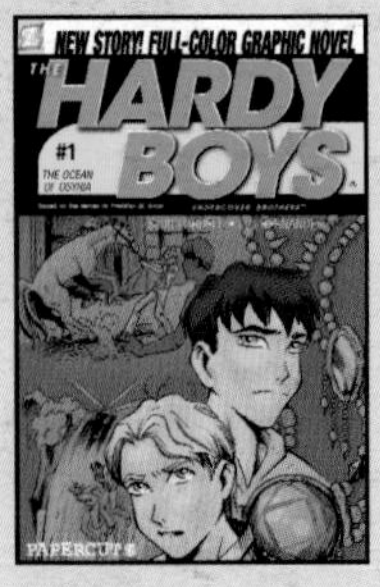
NEW STORY! FULL-COLOR GRAPHIC NOVEL
THE HARDY BOYS
#1
THE OCEAN OF OSYRIA
PAPERCUTZ

Graphic Novel #1
"The Ocean of Osyria"

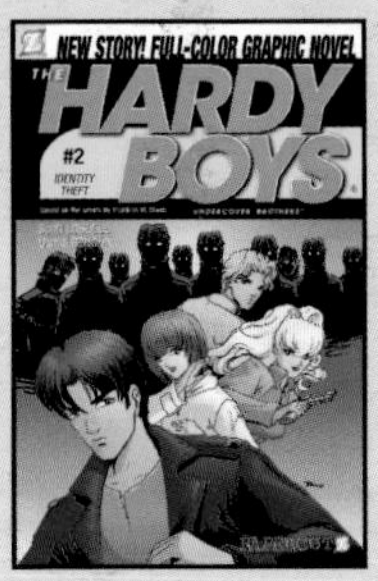
NEW STORY! FULL-COLOR GRAPHIC NOVEL
THE HARDY BOYS
#2
IDENTITY THEFT
PAPERCUTZ

Graphic Novel #2
"Identity Theft"

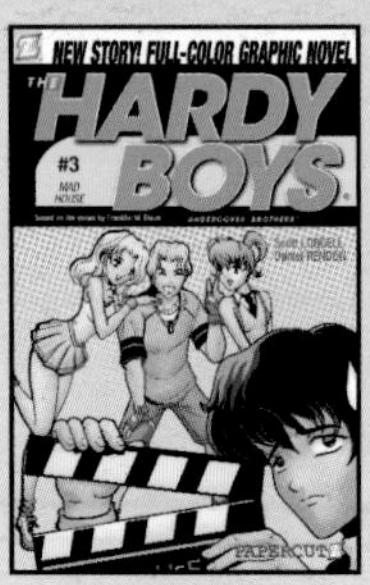
NEW STORY! FULL-COLOR GRAPHIC NOVEL
THE HARDY BOYS
#3
MAD HOUSE
PAPERCUTZ

Graphic Novel #3
"Mad House"

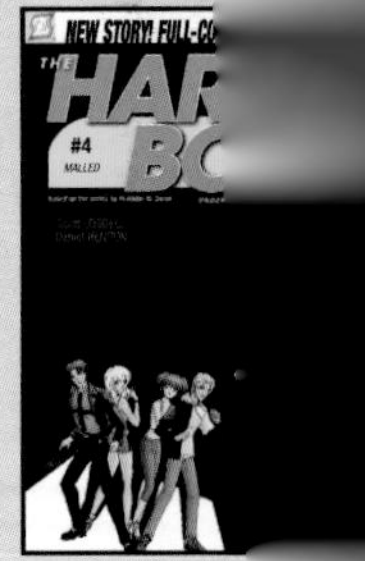
#4
MALLED

Graphic No
"Mallec

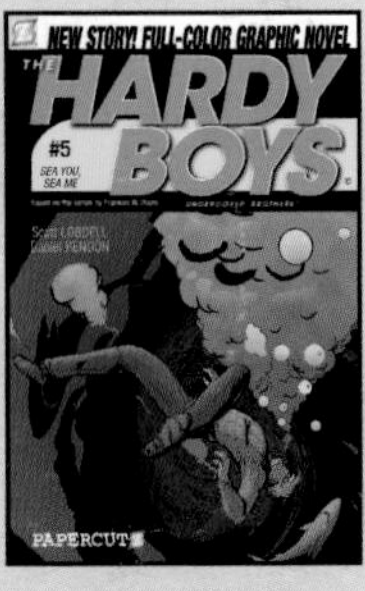
NEW STORY! FULL-COLOR GRAPHIC NOVEL
THE HARDY BOYS
#5
SEA YOU, SEA ME
Scott LOBDELL
Daniel RENDON
PAPERCUTZ

Graphic Novel #5
"Sea You, Sea Me!"

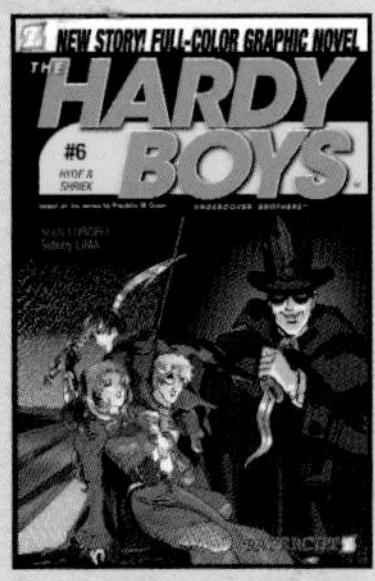
NEW STORY! FULL-COLOR GRAPHIC NOVEL
THE HARDY BOYS
#6
HYDE & SHRIEK
PAPERCUTZ

Graphic Novel #6
"Hyde & Shriek"

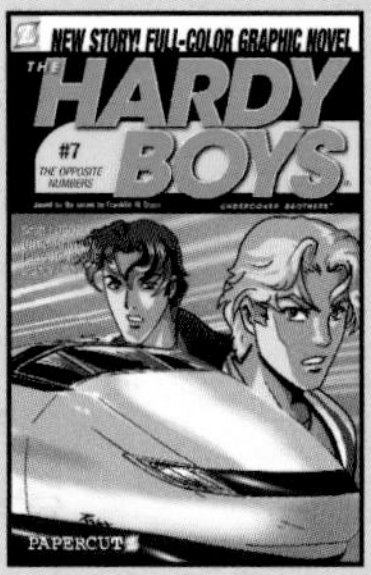
NEW STORY! FULL-COLOR GRAPHIC NOVEL
THE HARDY BOYS
#7
THE OPPOSITE NUMBERS
PAPERCUTZ

Graphic Novel #7
"The Opposite
Numbers..."

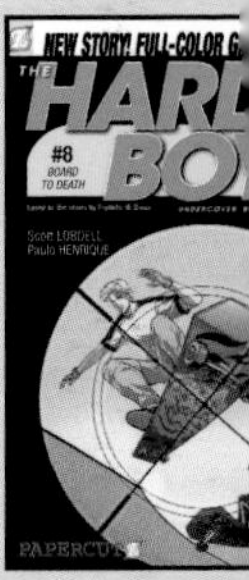
#8
BOARD TO DEATH
Scott LOBDELL
Paulo HENRIQUE
PAPERCUTZ

Graphic Novel
"Board To Dea

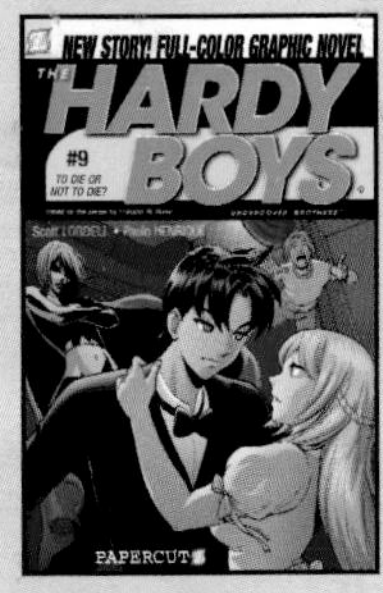
NEW STORY! FULL-COLOR GRAPHIC NOVEL
THE HARDY BOYS
#9
TO DIE OR NOT TO DIE?
Scott LOBDELL • Paulo HENRIQUE
PAPERCUTZ

Graphic Novel #9
"To Die Or
Not To Die?"

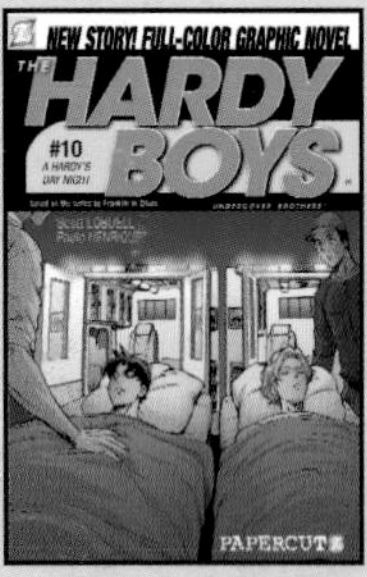
NEW STORY! FULL-COLOR GRAPHIC NOVEL
THE HARDY BOYS
#10
A HARDY'S DAY NIGHT
PAPERCUTZ

Coming in September:
Graphic Novel #10
"A Hardy's Days Night"

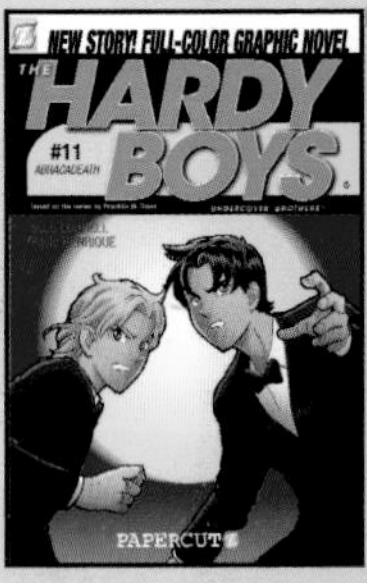
NEW STORY! FULL-COLOR GRAPHIC NOVEL
THE HARDY BOYS
#11
ABRACADEATH
PAPERCUTZ

Coming in December:
Graphic Novel #11
"Abracadeath"

$7.95 each in paperback, $12.95 each in hardcover. Please add $3.00 for postage and handling for the first book, add $1.00 for each additional book. Please make check payable to NBM Publishir

Send to: **Papercutz, 40 Exchange Place, Suite 1308, New York, NY 10005** • www.papercutz.co

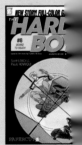

THE HARDY BOYS

#9

UNDERCOVER BROTHERS™

To Die Or Not To Die?

SCOTT LOBDELL • Writer

PAULO HENRIQUE • Artist

Based on the series by
FRANKLIN W. DIXON

PAPERCUT Z™

New York

To Die Or Not To Die?
SCOTT LOBDELL — Writer
PAULO HENRIQUE — Artist
MARK LERER — Letterer
LAURIE E. SMITH — Colorist
JIM SALICRUP — Editor-in-Chief

ISBN 10: 1-59707-062-9 paperback edition
ISBN 13: 978-1-59707-062-1 paperback edition
ISBN 10: 1-59707-063-7 hardcover edition
ISBN 13: 978-1-59707-063-8 hardcover edition

Published by arrangement with Aladdin Paperbacks,
an imprint of Simon & Schuster Children's Publishing Division.

Printed in China

10 9 8 7 6 5 4 3 2 1

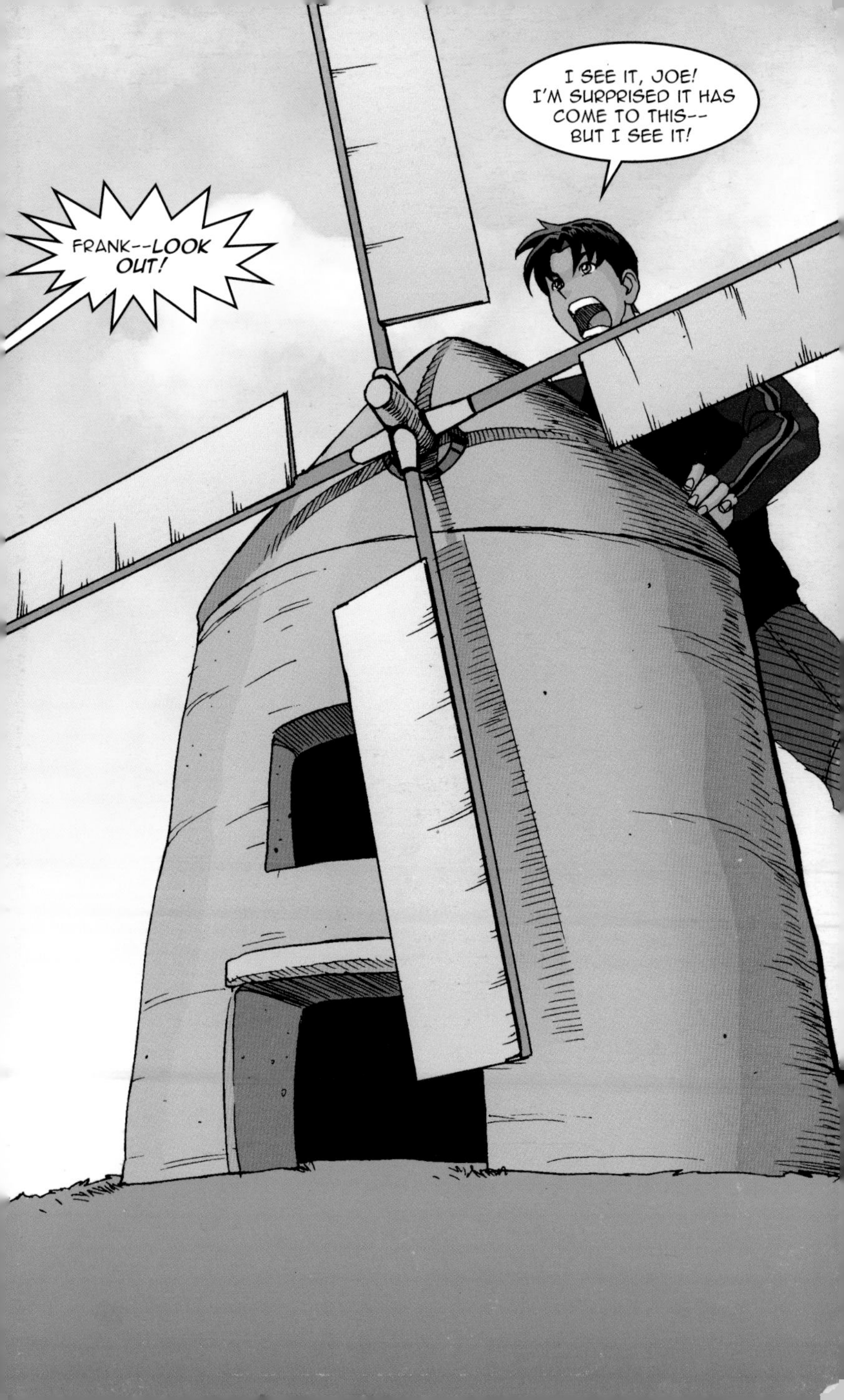
FRANK--LOOK OUT!
I SEE IT, JOE! I'M SURPRISED IT HAS COME TO THIS-- BUT I SEE IT!

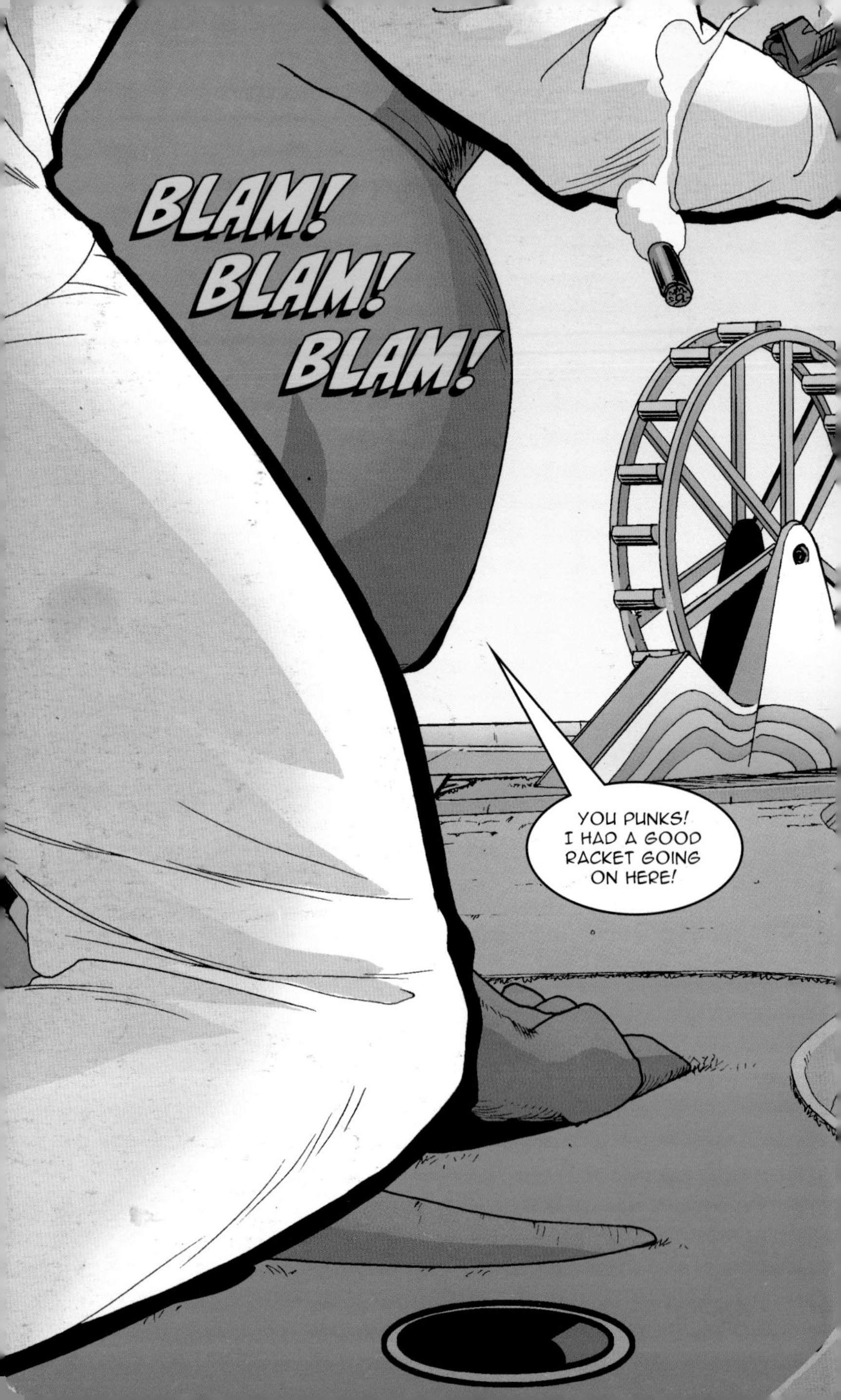
BLAM! BLAM! BLAM!
YOU PUNKS! I HAD A GOOD RACKET GOING ON HERE!

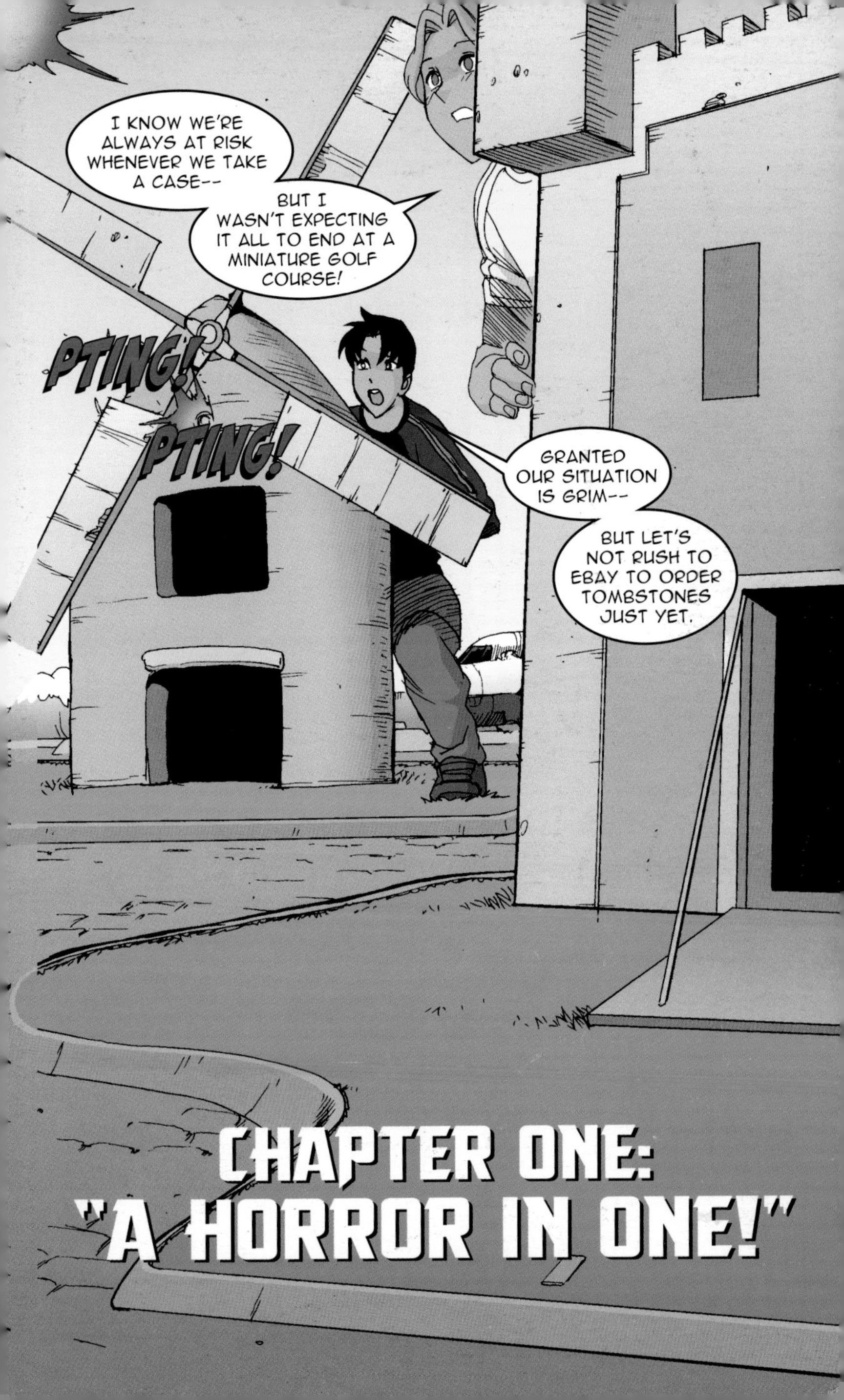
I KNOW WE'RE ALWAYS AT RISK WHENEVER WE TAKE A CASE--
BUT I WASN'T EXPECTING IT ALL TO END AT A MINIATURE GOLF COURSE!
PTING!
PTING!
GRANTED OUR SITUATION IS GRIM--
BUT LET'S NOT RUSH TO EBAY TO ORDER TOMBSTONES JUST YET.
CHAPTER ONE: "A HORROR IN ONE!"

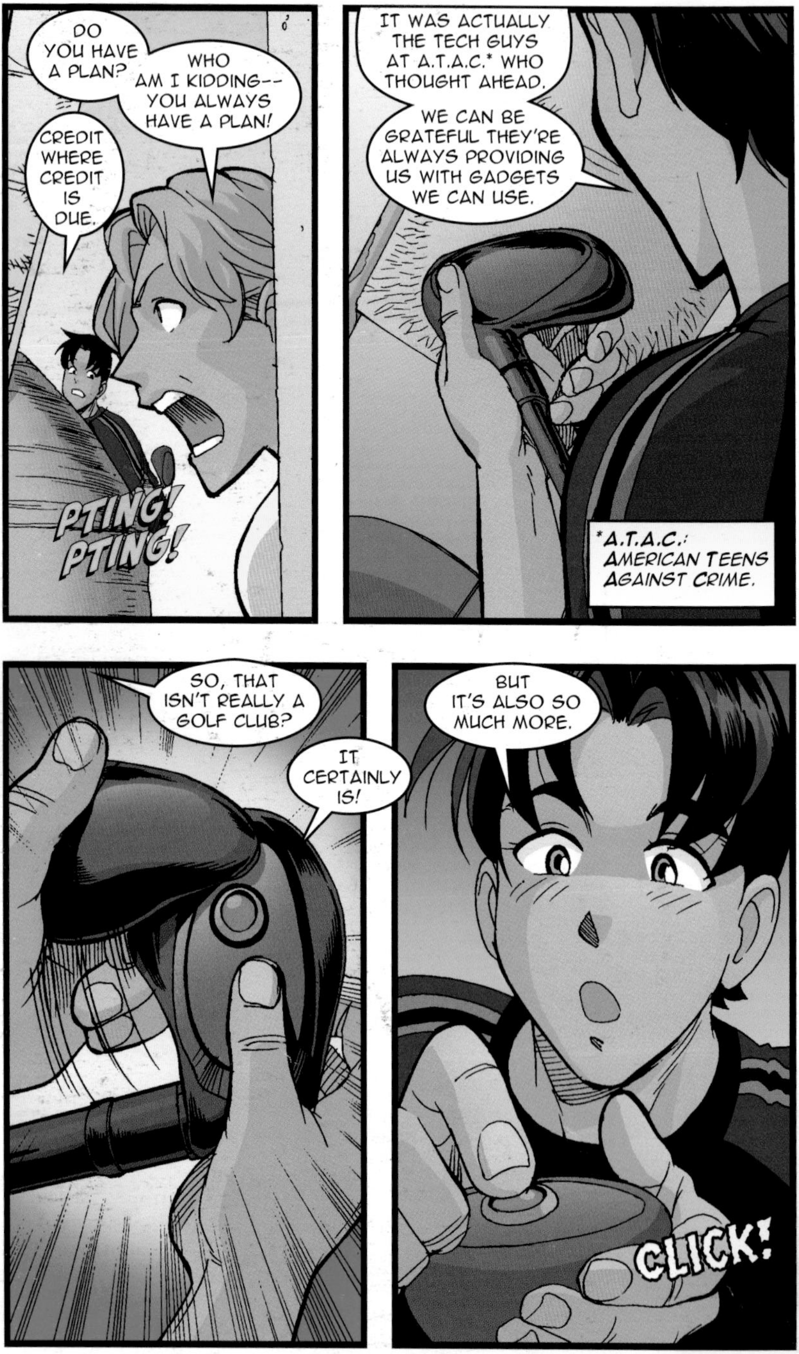
DO YOU HAVE A PLAN?
WHO AM I KIDDING-- YOU ALWAYS HAVE A PLAN!
CREDIT WHERE CREDIT IS DUE.
PTING! PTING!
IT WAS ACTUALLY THE TECH GUYS AT A.T.A.C.* WHO THOUGHT AHEAD.
WE CAN BE GRATEFUL THEY'RE ALWAYS PROVIDING US WITH GADGETS WE CAN USE.
*A.T.A.C.: AMERICAN TEENS AGAINST CRIME.
SO, THAT ISN'T REALLY A GOLF CLUB?
IT CERTAINLY IS!
BUT IT'S ALSO SO MUCH MORE.
CLICK!

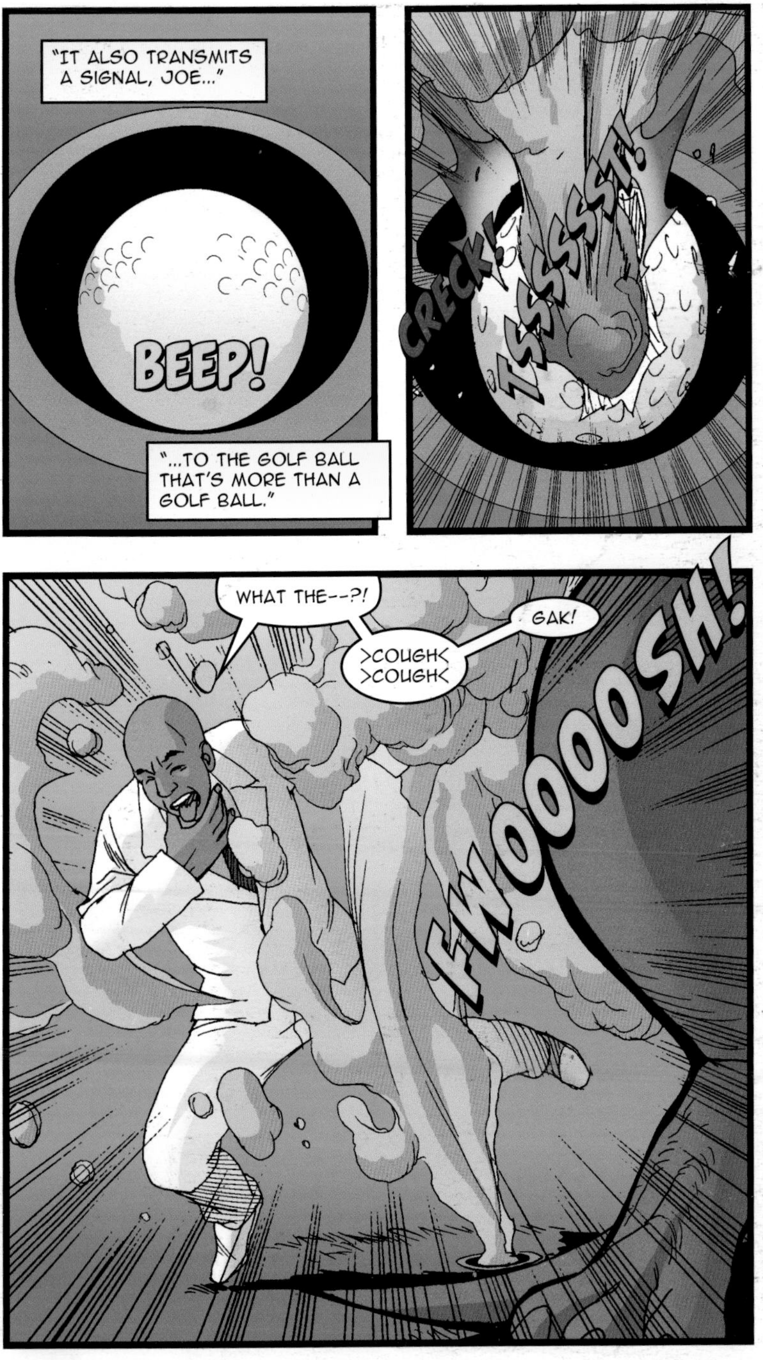
"IT ALSO TRANSMITS A SIGNAL, JOE..."
BEEP!
"...TO THE GOLF BALL THAT'S MORE THAN A GOLF BALL."
CRECK!
TSSSSSST!
WHAT THE--?!
>COUGH<
>COUGH<
GAK!
FWOOOOSH!

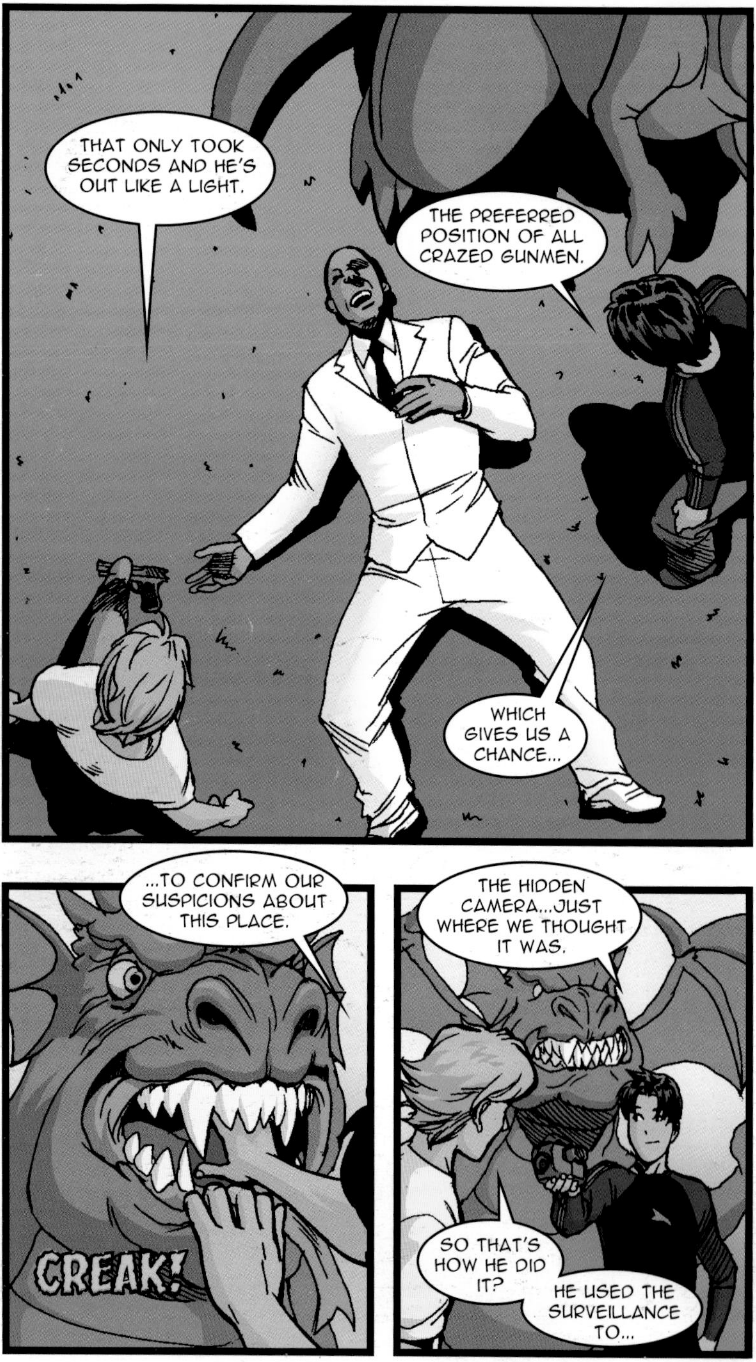
THAT ONLY TOOK SECONDS AND HE'S OUT LIKE A LIGHT.
THE PREFERRED POSITION OF ALL CRAZED GUNMEN.
WHICH GIVES US A CHANCE...
...TO CONFIRM OUR SUSPICIONS ABOUT THIS PLACE.
CREAK!
THE HIDDEN CAMERA...JUST WHERE WE THOUGHT IT WAS.
SO THAT'S HOW HE DID IT?
HE USED THE SURVEILLANCE TO...

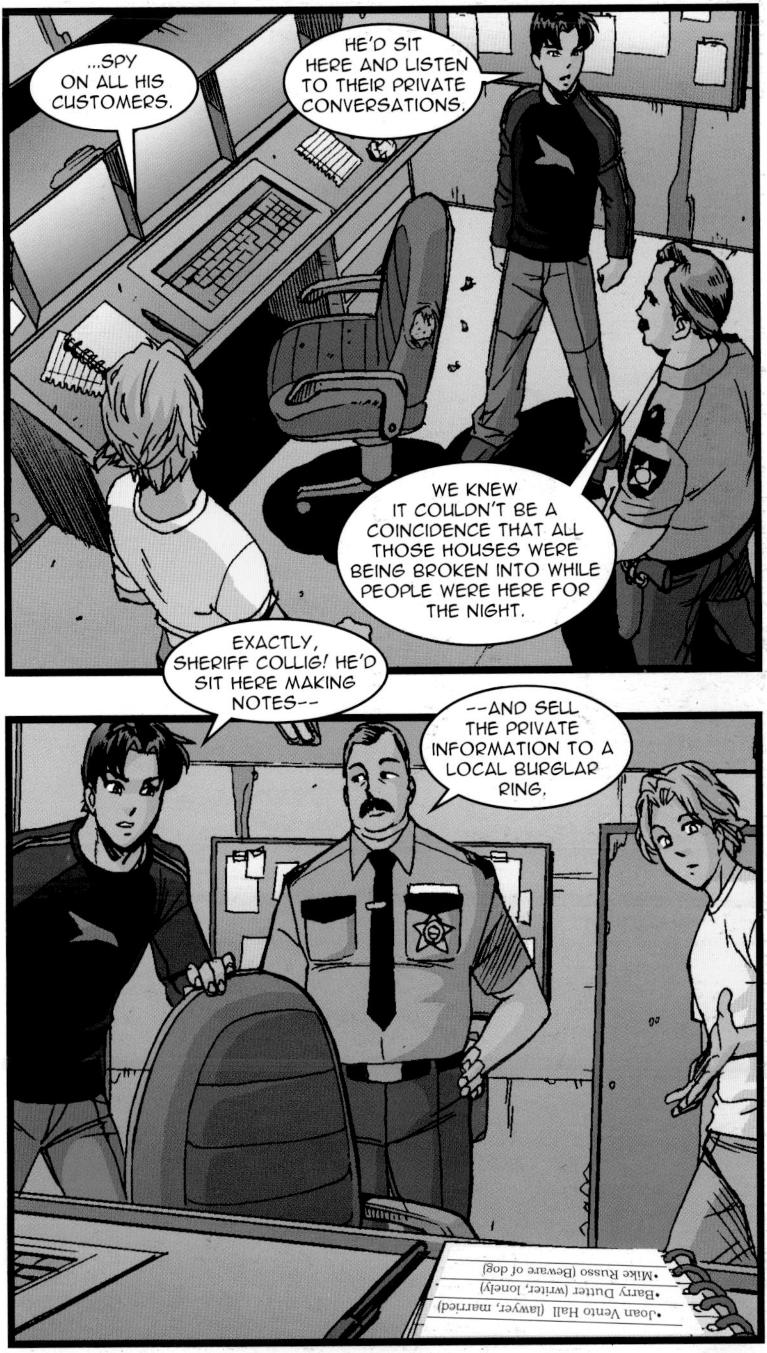
...SPY ON ALL HIS CUSTOMERS.
HE'D SIT HERE AND LISTEN TO THEIR PRIVATE CONVERSATIONS.
WE KNEW IT COULDN'T BE A COINCIDENCE THAT ALL THOSE HOUSES WERE BEING BROKEN INTO WHILE PEOPLE WERE HERE FOR THE NIGHT.
EXACTLY, SHERIFF COLLIG! HE'D SIT HERE MAKING NOTES--
--AND SELL THE PRIVATE INFORMATION TO A LOCAL BURGLAR RING.
•Mike Russo (Beware of dog)
•Barry Dutter (writer, lonely)
•Joan Vento Hall (lawyer, married)

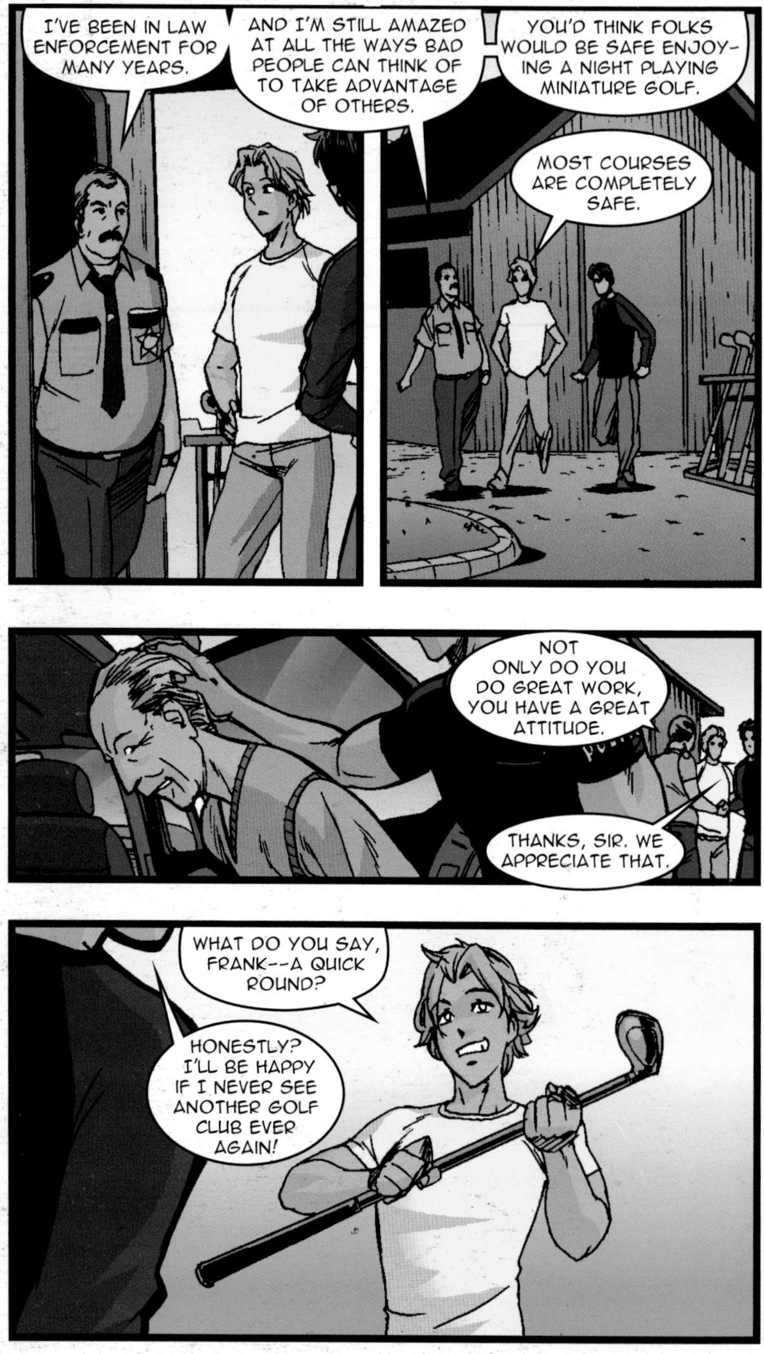
I'VE BEEN IN LAW ENFORCEMENT FOR MANY YEARS.
AND I'M STILL AMAZED AT ALL THE WAYS BAD PEOPLE CAN THINK OF TO TAKE ADVANTAGE OF OTHERS.
YOU'D THINK FOLKS WOULD BE SAFE ENJOYING A NIGHT PLAYING MINIATURE GOLF.
MOST COURSES ARE COMPLETELY SAFE.
NOT ONLY DO YOU DO GREAT WORK, YOU HAVE A GREAT ATTITUDE.
THANKS, SIR. WE APPRECIATE THAT.
WHAT DO YOU SAY, FRANK--A QUICK ROUND?
HONESTLY? I'LL BE HAPPY IF I NEVER SEE ANOTHER GOLF CLUB EVER AGAIN!

CHAPTER TWO: "ALL THE WORLD'S A STAGE"

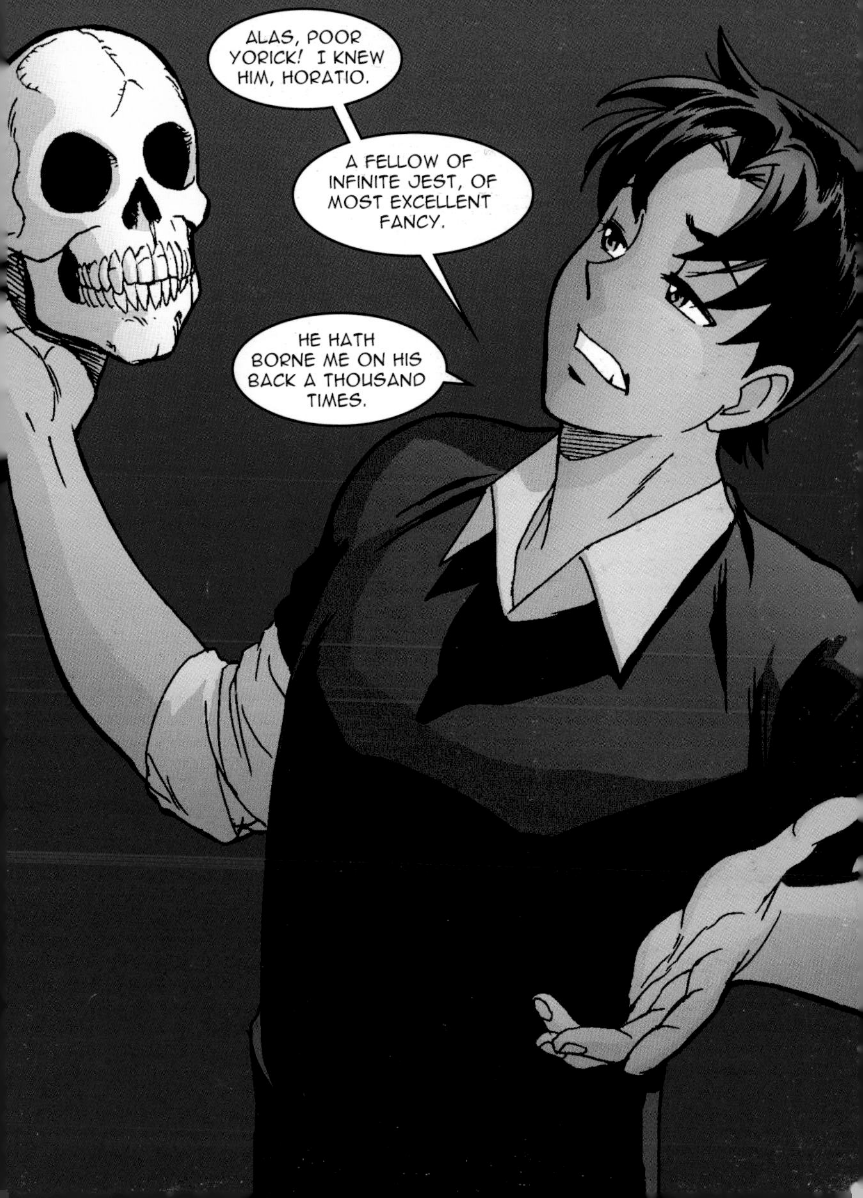
ALAS, POOR YORICK! I KNEW HIM, HORATIO.
A FELLOW OF INFINITE JEST, OF MOST EXCELLENT FANCY.
HE HATH BORNE ME ON HIS BACK A THOUSAND TIMES.

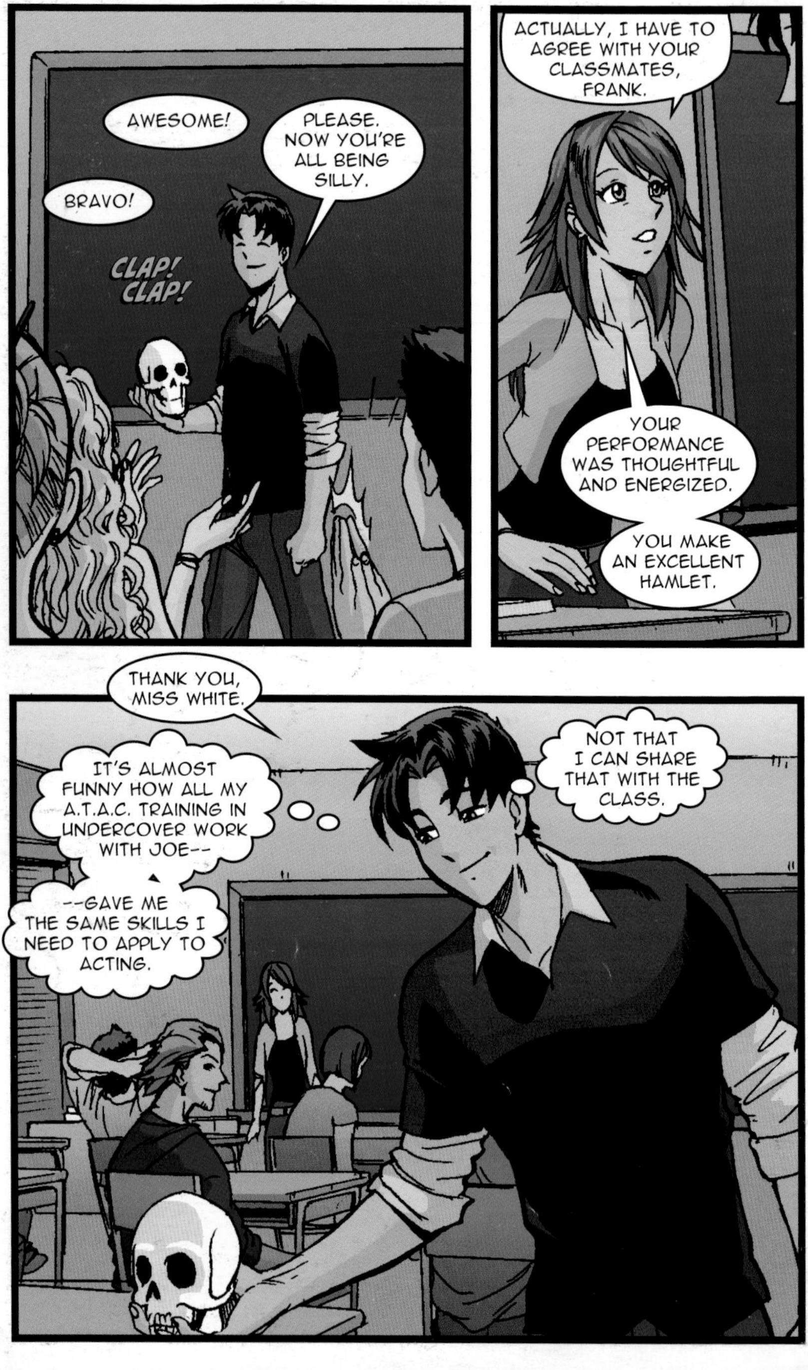
AWESOME!
BRAVO!
CLAP! CLAP!
PLEASE. NOW YOU'RE ALL BEING SILLY.
ACTUALLY, I HAVE TO AGREE WITH YOUR CLASSMATES, FRANK.
YOUR PERFORMANCE WAS THOUGHTFUL AND ENERGIZED.
YOU MAKE AN EXCELLENT HAMLET.
THANK YOU, MISS WHITE.
IT'S ALMOST FUNNY HOW ALL MY A.T.A.C. TRAINING IN UNDERCOVER WORK WITH JOE--
--GAVE ME THE SAME SKILLS I NEED TO APPLY TO ACTING.
NOT THAT I CAN SHARE THAT WITH THE CLASS.

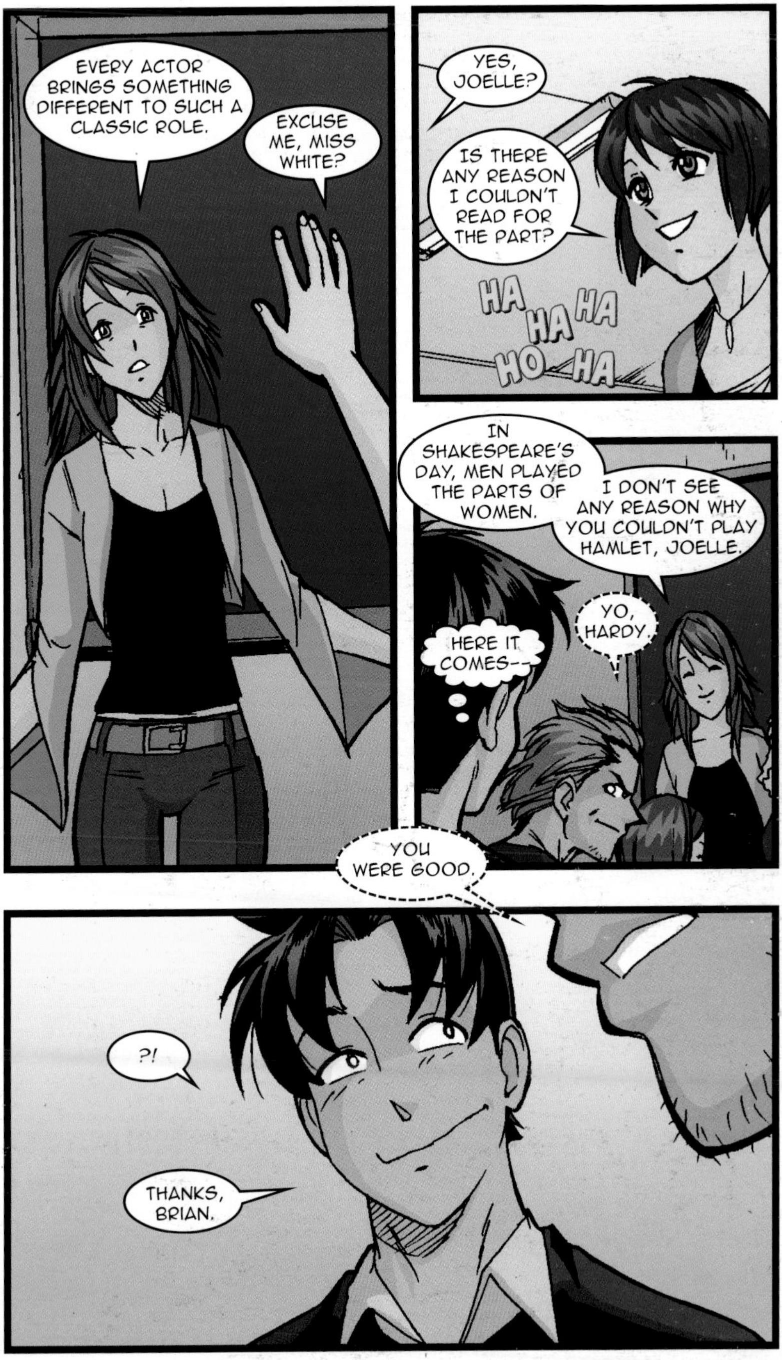
EVERY ACTOR BRINGS SOMETHING DIFFERENT TO SUCH A CLASSIC ROLE.
EXCUSE ME, MISS WHITE?
YES, JOELLE?
IS THERE ANY REASON I COULDN'T READ FOR THE PART?
HA HA HA HO HA
IN SHAKESPEARE'S DAY, MEN PLAYED THE PARTS OF WOMEN.
I DON'T SEE ANY REASON WHY YOU COULDN'T PLAY HAMLET, JOELLE.
YO, HARDY.
HERE IT COMES--
YOU WERE GOOD.
?!
THANKS, BRIAN.

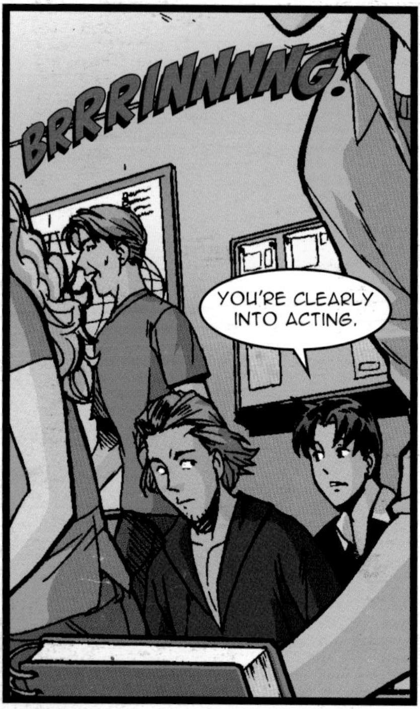
BRRRINNNNG!
YOU'RE CLEARLY INTO ACTING.

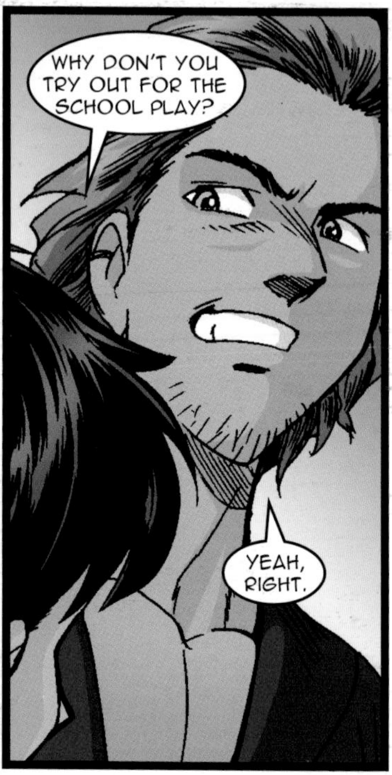
WHY DON'T YOU TRY OUT FOR THE SCHOOL PLAY?
YEAH, RIGHT.

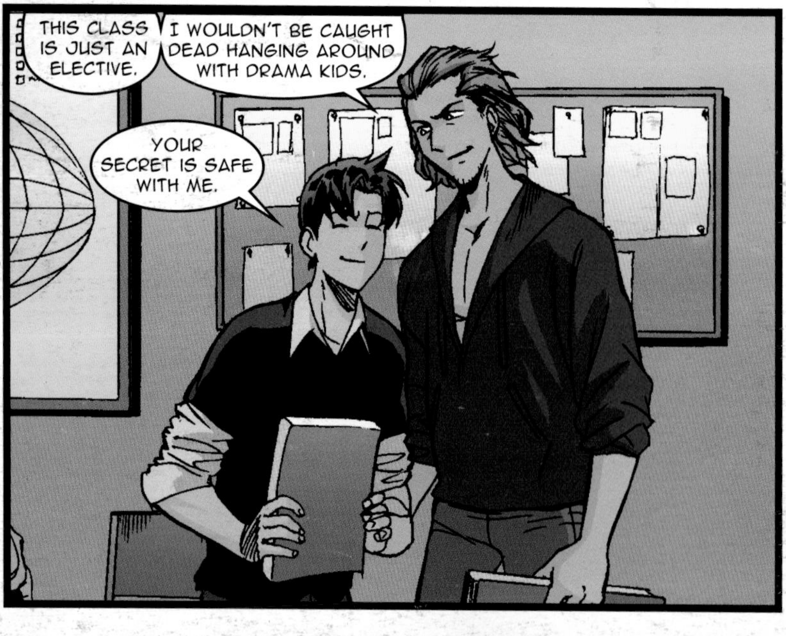
THIS CLASS IS JUST AN ELECTIVE.
I WOULDN'T BE CAUGHT DEAD HANGING AROUND WITH DRAMA KIDS.
YOUR SECRET IS SAFE WITH ME.

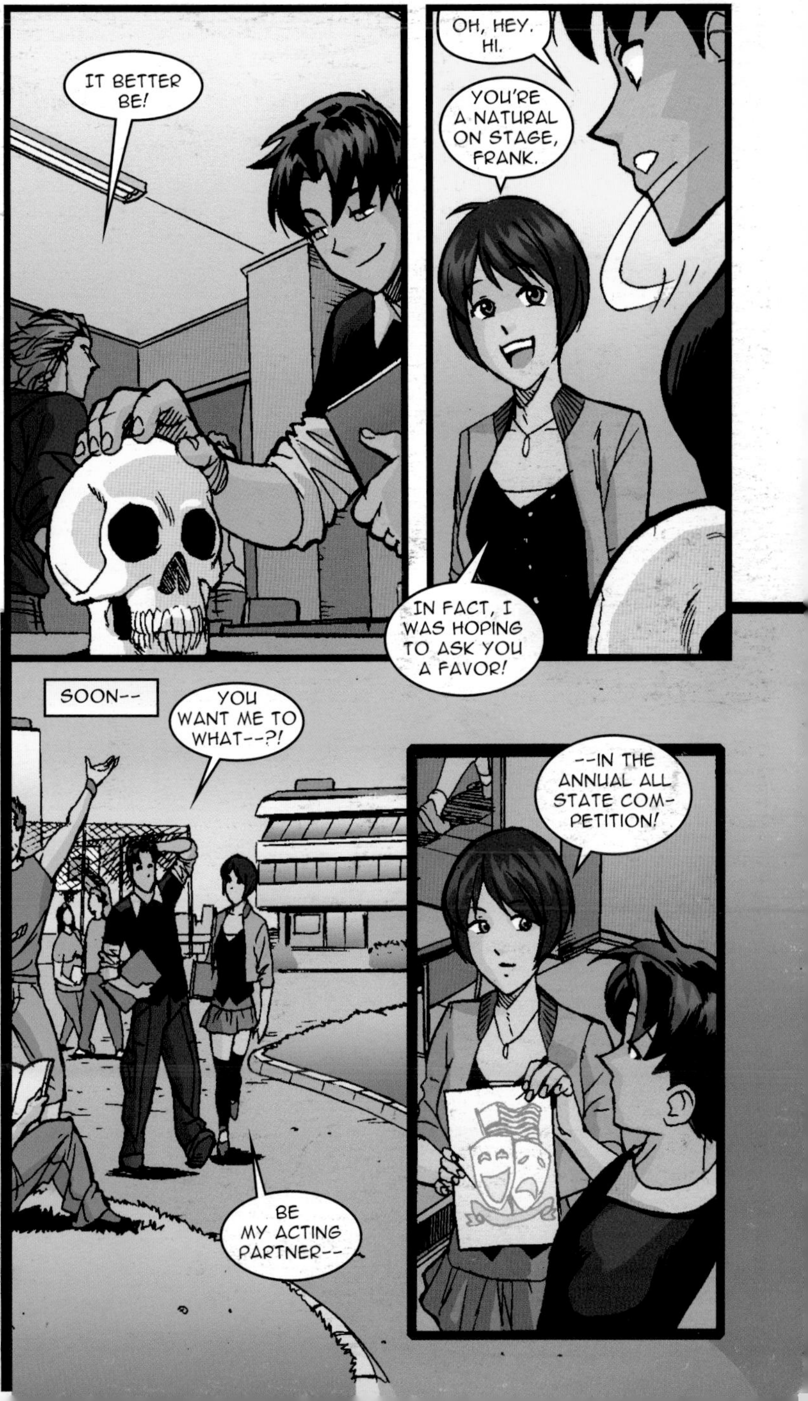
IT BETTER BE!
OH, HEY. HI.
YOU'RE A NATURAL ON STAGE, FRANK.
IN FACT, I WAS HOPING TO ASK YOU A FAVOR!
SOON--
YOU WANT ME TO WHAT--?!
BE MY ACTING PARTNER--
--IN THE ANNUAL ALL STATE COMPETITION!

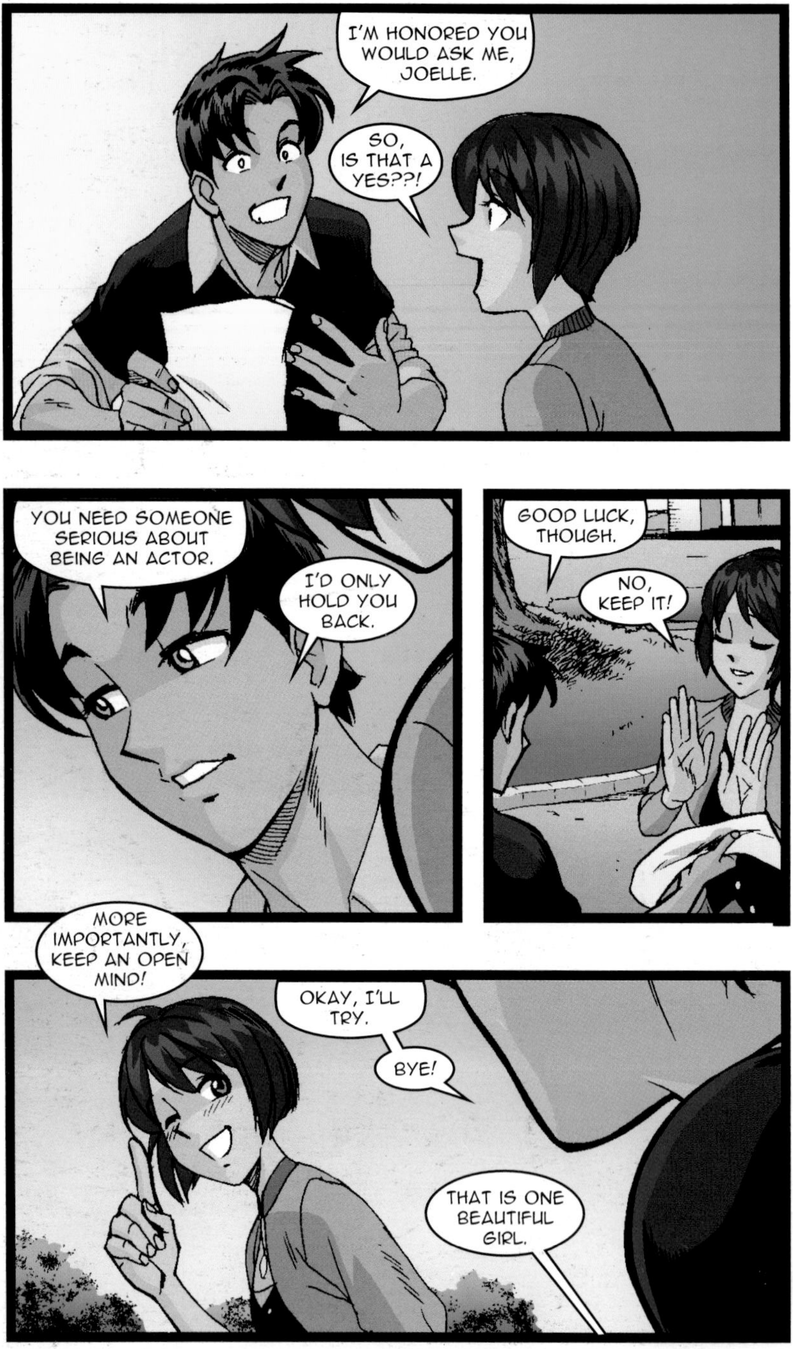
I'M HONORED YOU WOULD ASK ME, JOELLE.
SO, IS THAT A YES??!
YOU NEED SOMEONE SERIOUS ABOUT BEING AN ACTOR.
I'D ONLY HOLD YOU BACK.
GOOD LUCK, THOUGH.
NO, KEEP IT!
MORE IMPORTANTLY, KEEP AN OPEN MIND!
OKAY, I'LL TRY.
BYE!
THAT IS ONE BEAUTIFUL GIRL.

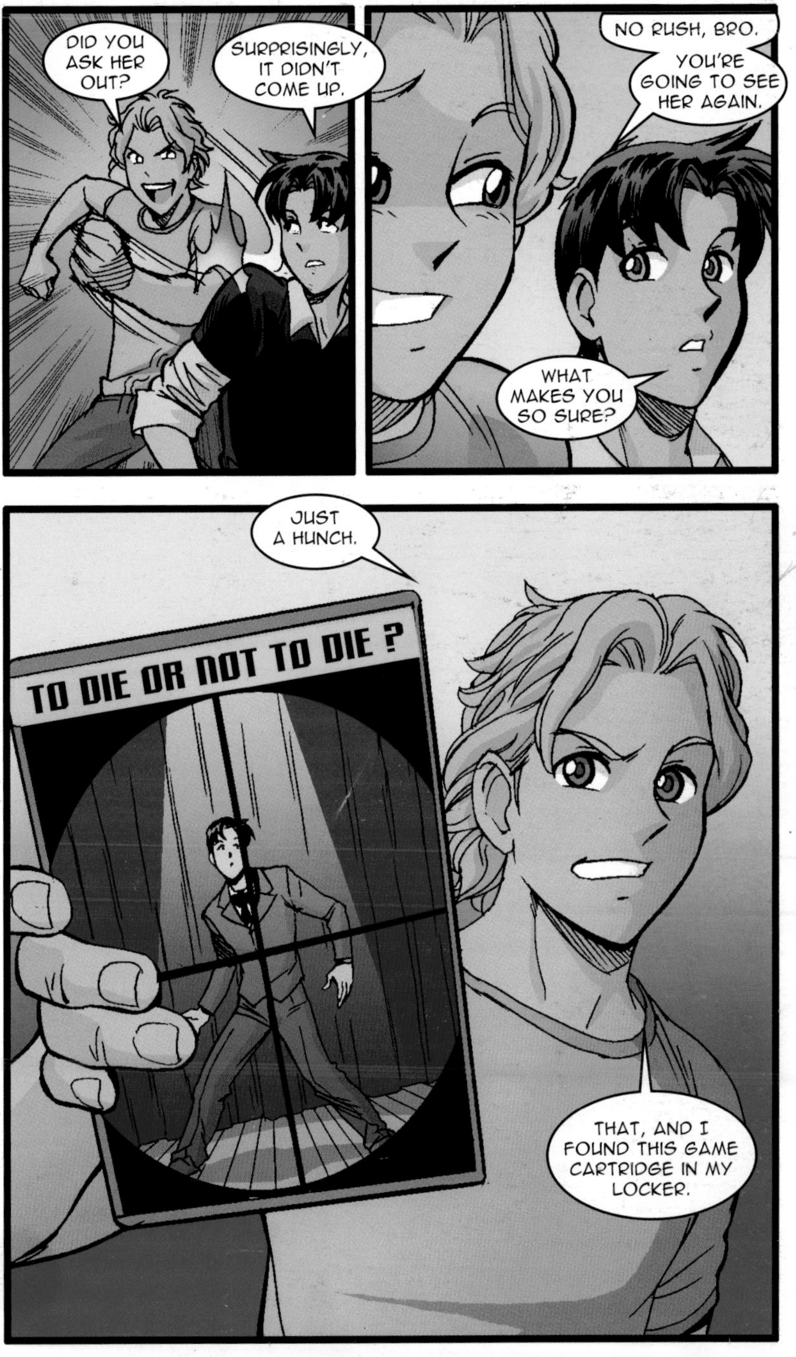
DID YOU ASK HER OUT?
SURPRISINGLY, IT DIDN'T COME UP.
NO RUSH, BRO.
YOU'RE GOING TO SEE HER AGAIN.
WHAT MAKES YOU SO SURE?
JUST A HUNCH.
TO DIE OR NOT TO DIE ?
THAT, AND I FOUND THIS GAME CARTRIDGE IN MY LOCKER.

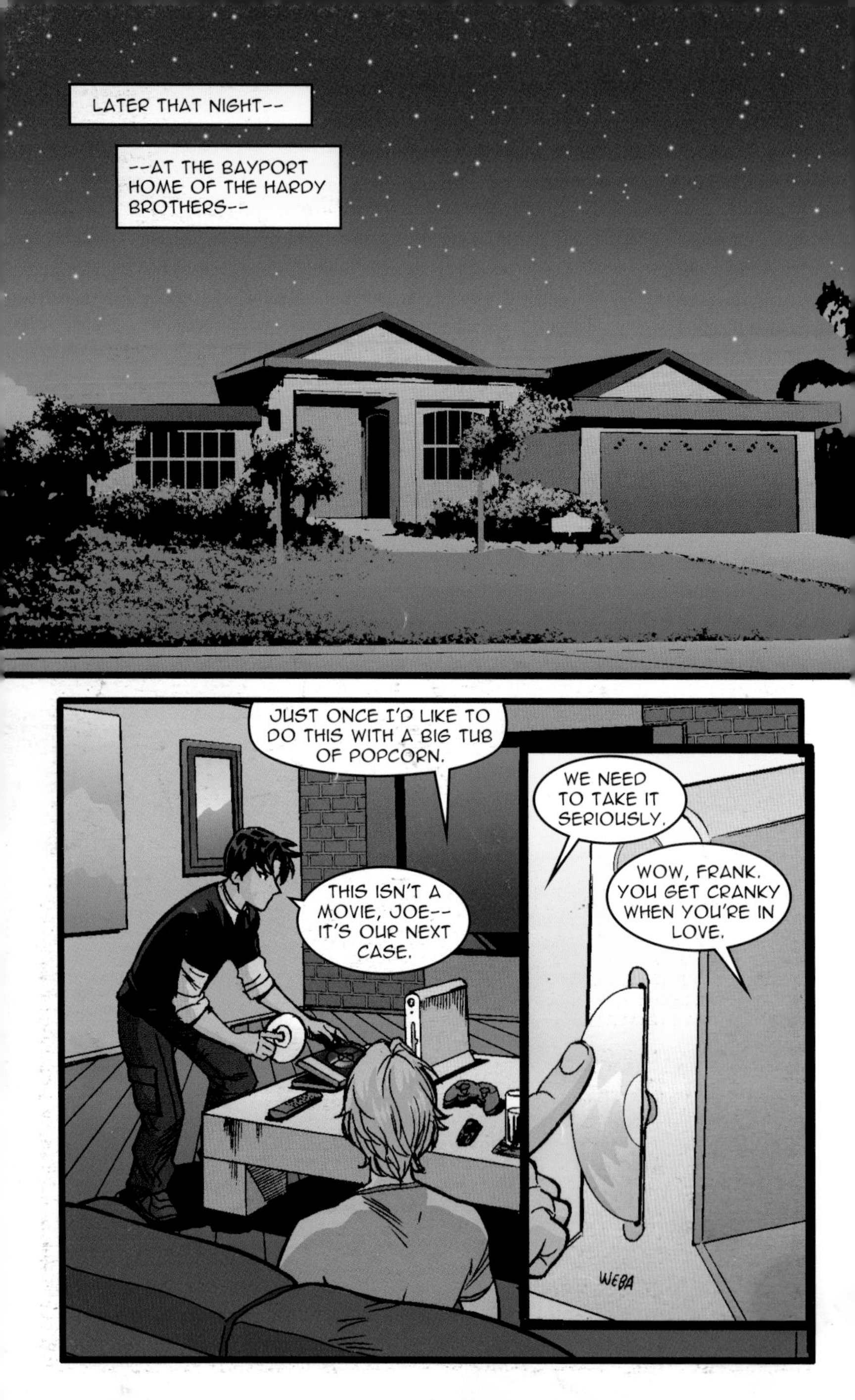
LATER THAT NIGHT--
--AT THE BAYPORT HOME OF THE HARDY BROTHERS--
JUST ONCE I'D LIKE TO DO THIS WITH A BIG TUB OF POPCORN.
THIS ISN'T A MOVIE, JOE-- IT'S OUR NEXT CASE.
WE NEED TO TAKE IT SERIOUSLY.
WOW, FRANK. YOU GET CRANKY WHEN YOU'RE IN LOVE.
WEBA

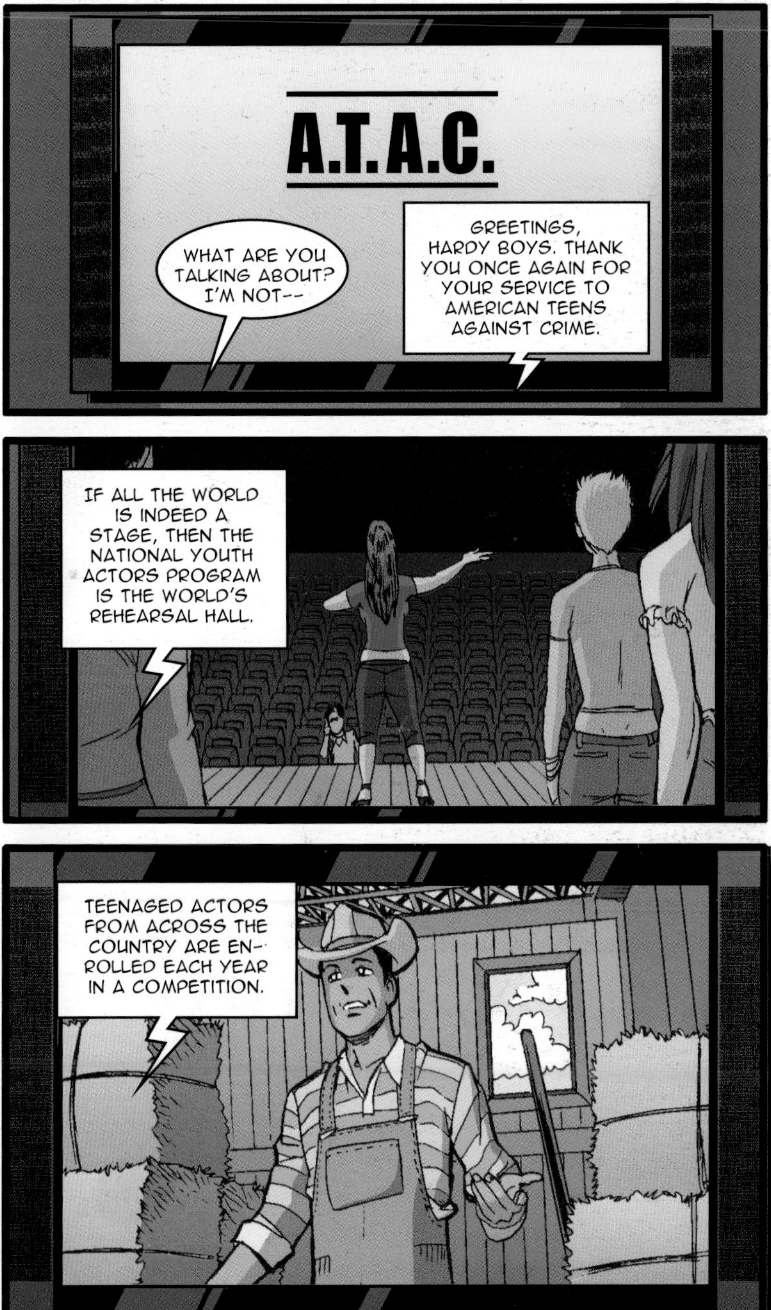
A.T.A.C.
WHAT ARE YOU TALKING ABOUT? I'M NOT--
GREETINGS, HARDY BOYS. THANK YOU ONCE AGAIN FOR YOUR SERVICE TO AMERICAN TEENS AGAINST CRIME.
IF ALL THE WORLD IS INDEED A STAGE, THEN THE NATIONAL YOUTH ACTORS PROGRAM IS THE WORLD'S REHEARSAL HALL.
TEENAGED ACTORS FROM ACROSS THE COUNTRY ARE EN-ROLLED EACH YEAR IN A COMPETITION.

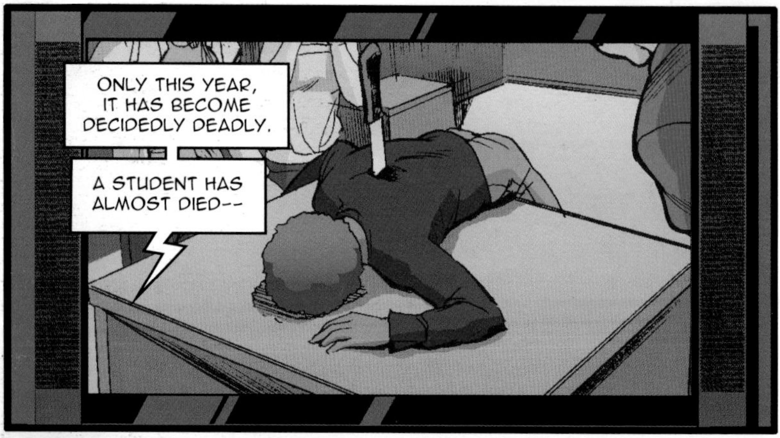
ONLY THIS YEAR, IT HAS BECOME DECIDEDLY DEADLY.
A STUDENT HAS ALMOST DIED--

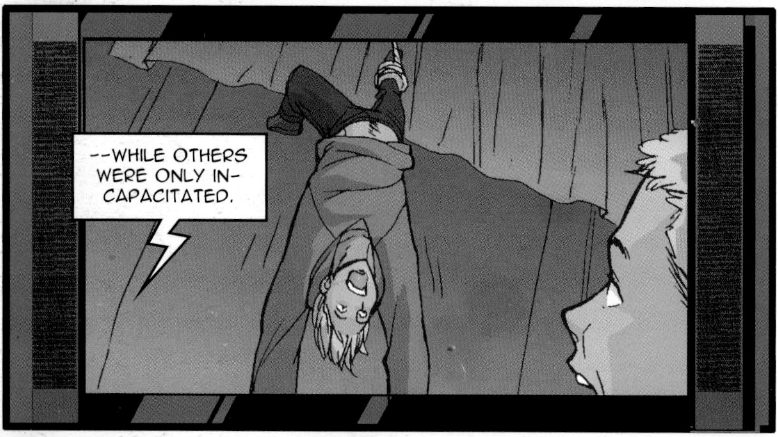
--WHILE OTHERS WERE ONLY IN-CAPACITATED.

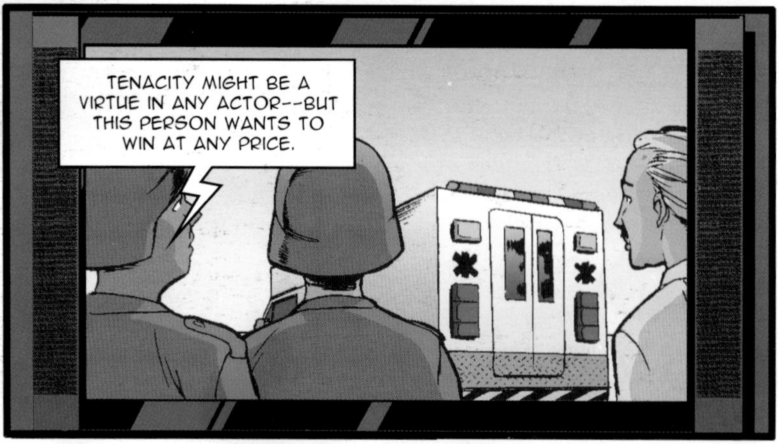
TENACITY MIGHT BE A VIRTUE IN ANY ACTOR--BUT THIS PERSON WANTS TO WIN AT ANY PRICE.

ONE OF YOUR FELLOW STUDENTS HAS EARNED A SPOT IN THE CONTEST.
HER NAME IS JOELLE RINKER, AND WE WANT YOU TO ENSURE HER SAFETY--
--WHILE YOU SUSS OUT THE PERSON RESPONSIBLE FOR THE CRIMES.
FRANK? ARE YOU COOL WITH THIS?
I MEAN, MAYBE YOU'RE TOO CLOSE TO THIS CASE? WE CAN--
I'LL BE FINE, JOE.WE BETTER GET PACKED.

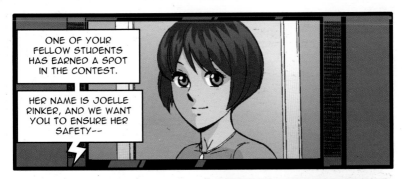

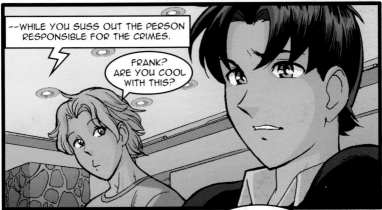

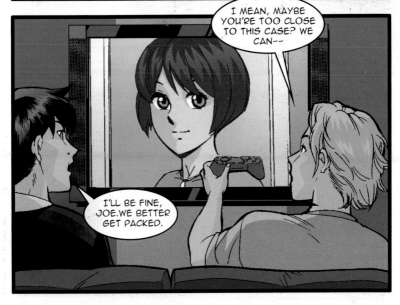

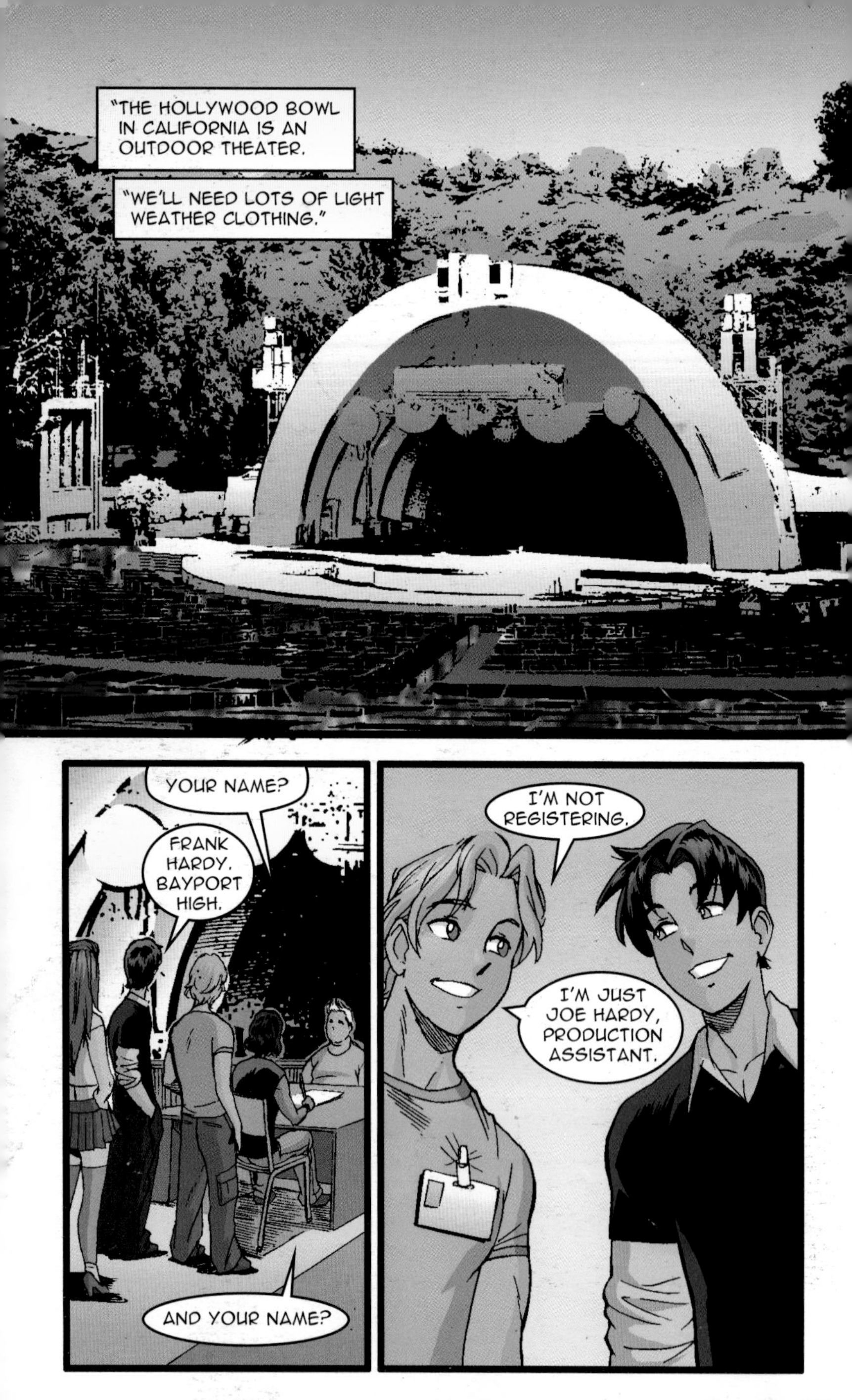
"THE HOLLYWOOD BOWL IN CALIFORNIA IS AN OUTDOOR THEATER.
"WE'LL NEED LOTS OF LIGHT WEATHER CLOTHING."
YOUR NAME?
FRANK HARDY, BAYPORT HIGH.
AND YOUR NAME?
I'M NOT REGISTERING.
I'M JUST JOE HARDY, PRODUCTION ASSISTANT.

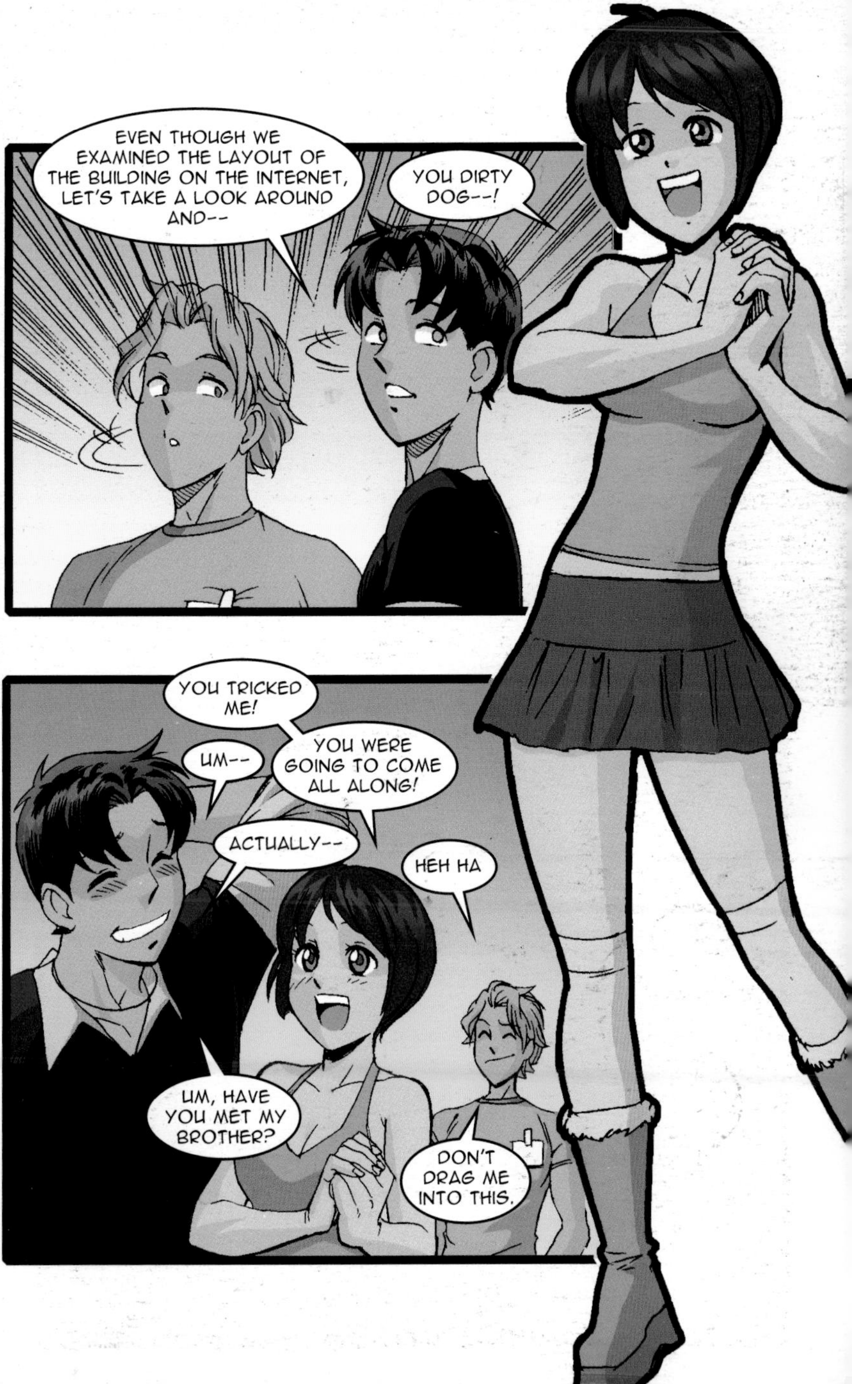
EVEN THOUGH WE EXAMINED THE LAYOUT OF THE BUILDING ON THE INTERNET, LET'S TAKE A LOOK AROUND AND--
YOU DIRTY DOG--!
YOU TRICKED ME!
UM--
YOU WERE GOING TO COME ALL ALONG!
ACTUALLY--
HEH HA
UM, HAVE YOU MET MY BROTHER?
DON'T DRAG ME INTO THIS.

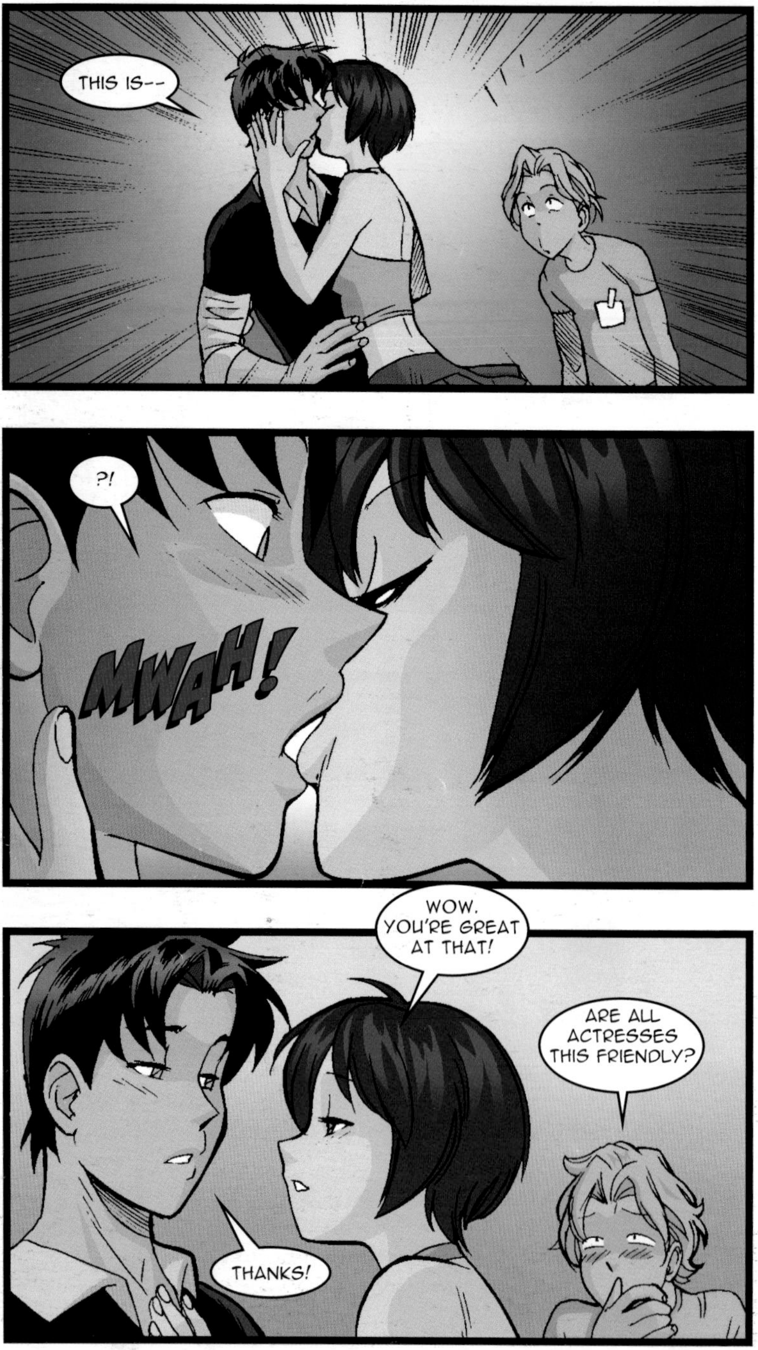
THIS IS--
?!
MWAH!
WOW. YOU'RE GREAT AT THAT!
THANKS!
ARE ALL ACTRESSES THIS FRIENDLY?

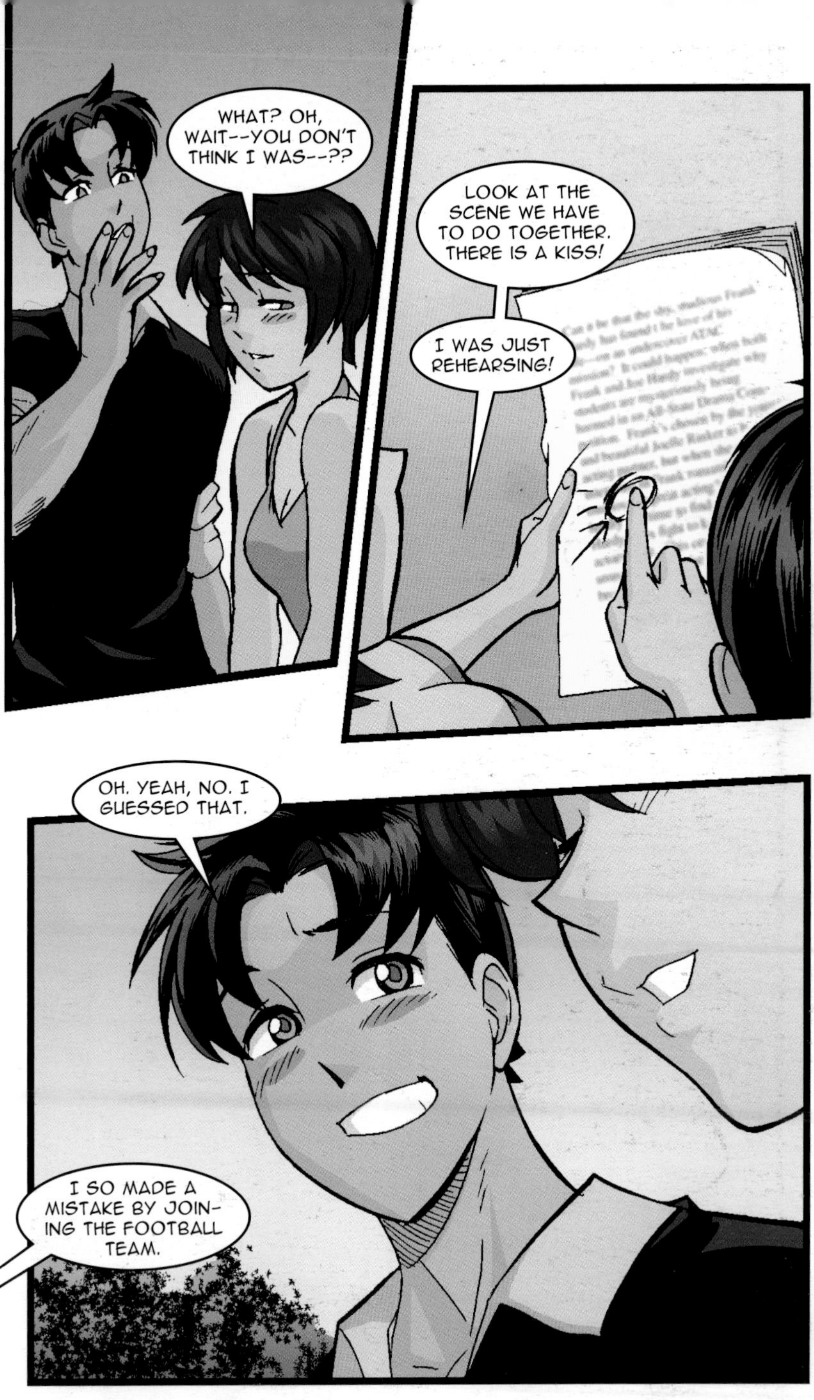
WHAT? OH, WAIT--YOU DON'T THINK I WAS--??
LOOK AT THE SCENE WE HAVE TO DO TOGETHER. THERE IS A KISS!
I WAS JUST REHEARSING!
OH. YEAH, NO. I GUESSED THAT.
I SO MADE A MISTAKE BY JOINING THE FOOTBALL TEAM.

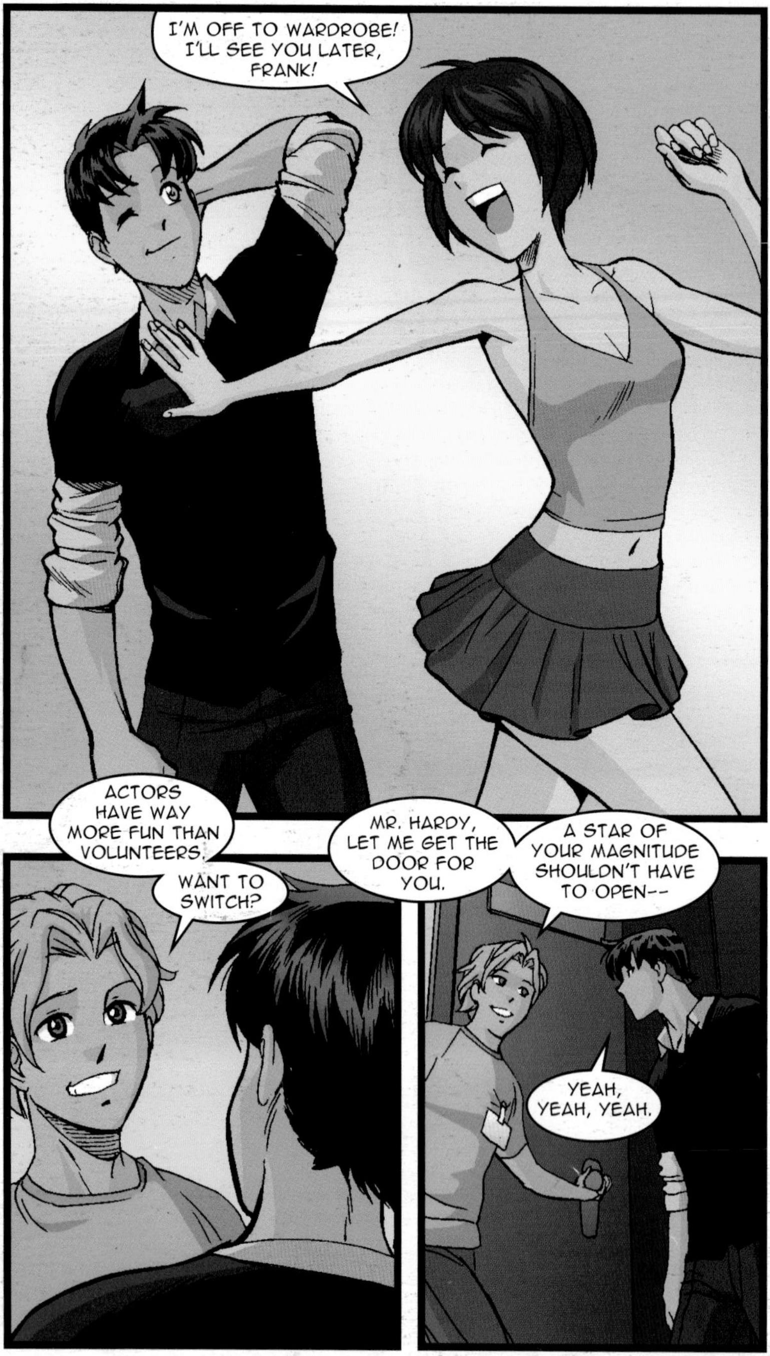

I'M OFF TO WARDROBE! I'LL SEE YOU LATER, FRANK!
ACTORS HAVE WAY MORE FUN THAN VOLUNTEERS.
WANT TO SWITCH?
MR. HARDY, LET ME GET THE DOOR FOR YOU.
A STAR OF YOUR MAGNITUDE SHOULDN'T HAVE TO OPEN--
YEAH, YEAH, YEAH.

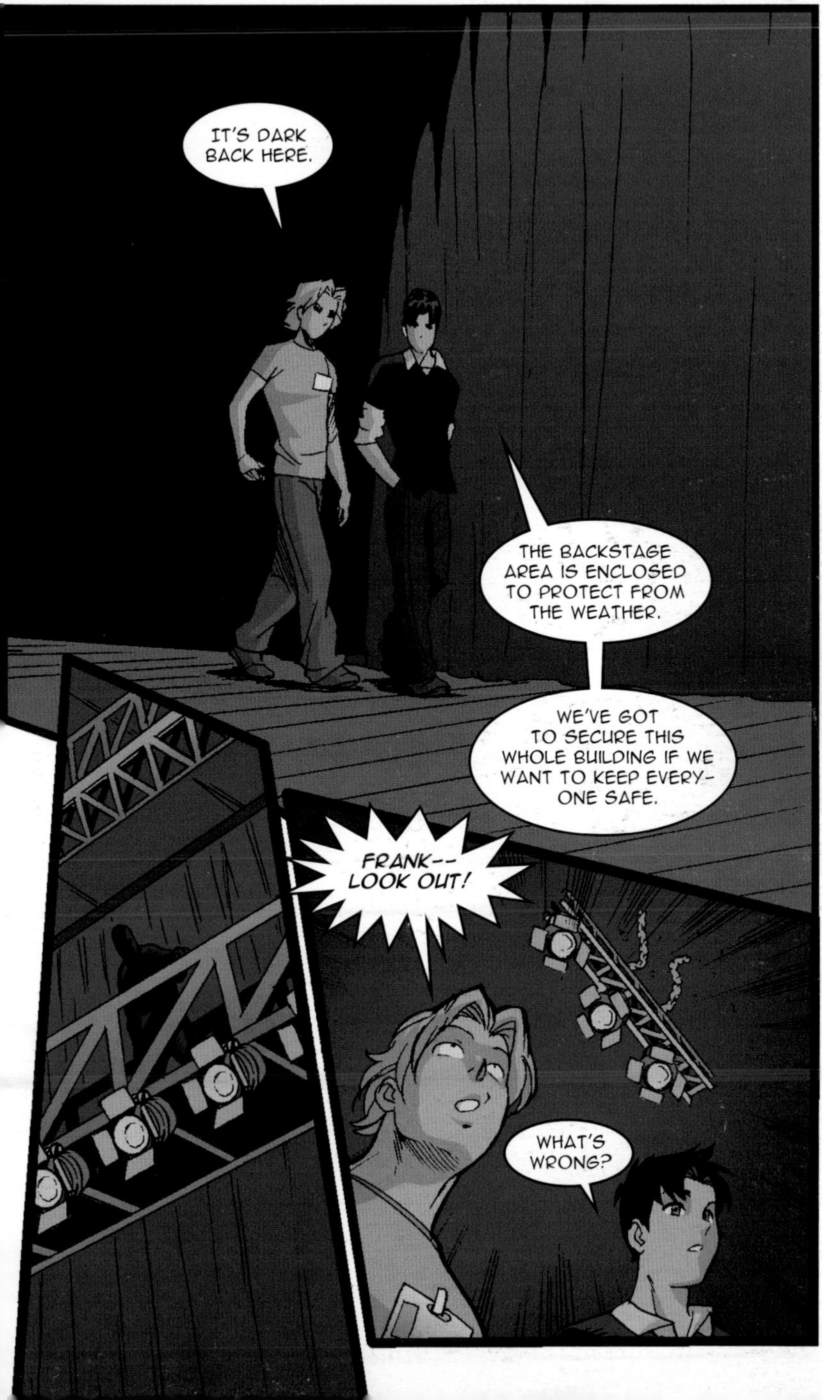
IT'S DARK BACK HERE.
THE BACKSTAGE AREA IS ENCLOSED TO PROTECT FROM THE WEATHER.
WE'VE GOT TO SECURE THIS WHOLE BUILDING IF WE WANT TO KEEP EVERY-ONE SAFE.
FRANK-- LOOK OUT!
WHAT'S WRONG?

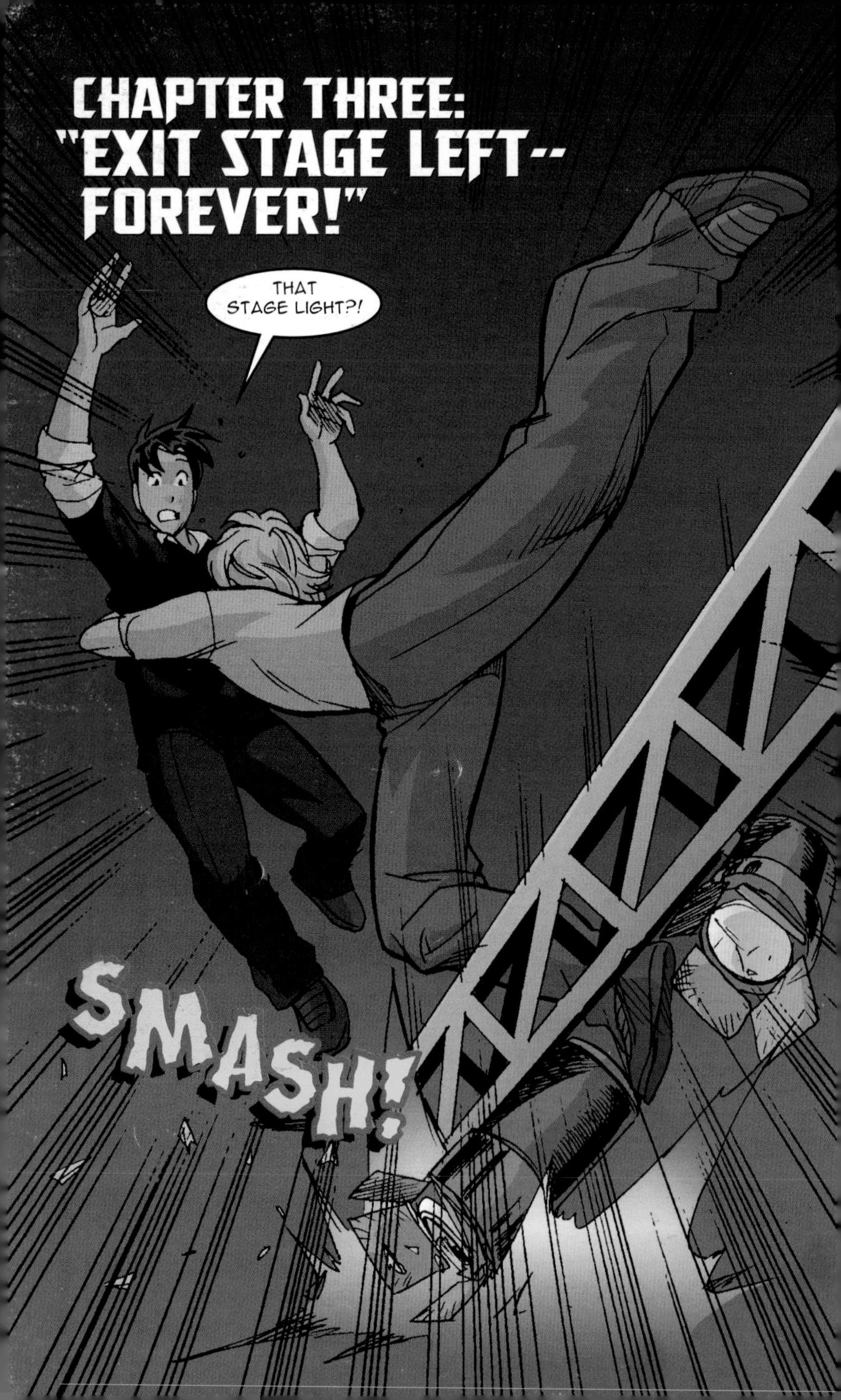
CHAPTER THREE:
"EXIT STAGE LEFT--
FOREVER!"
THAT STAGE LIGHT?!
SMASH!

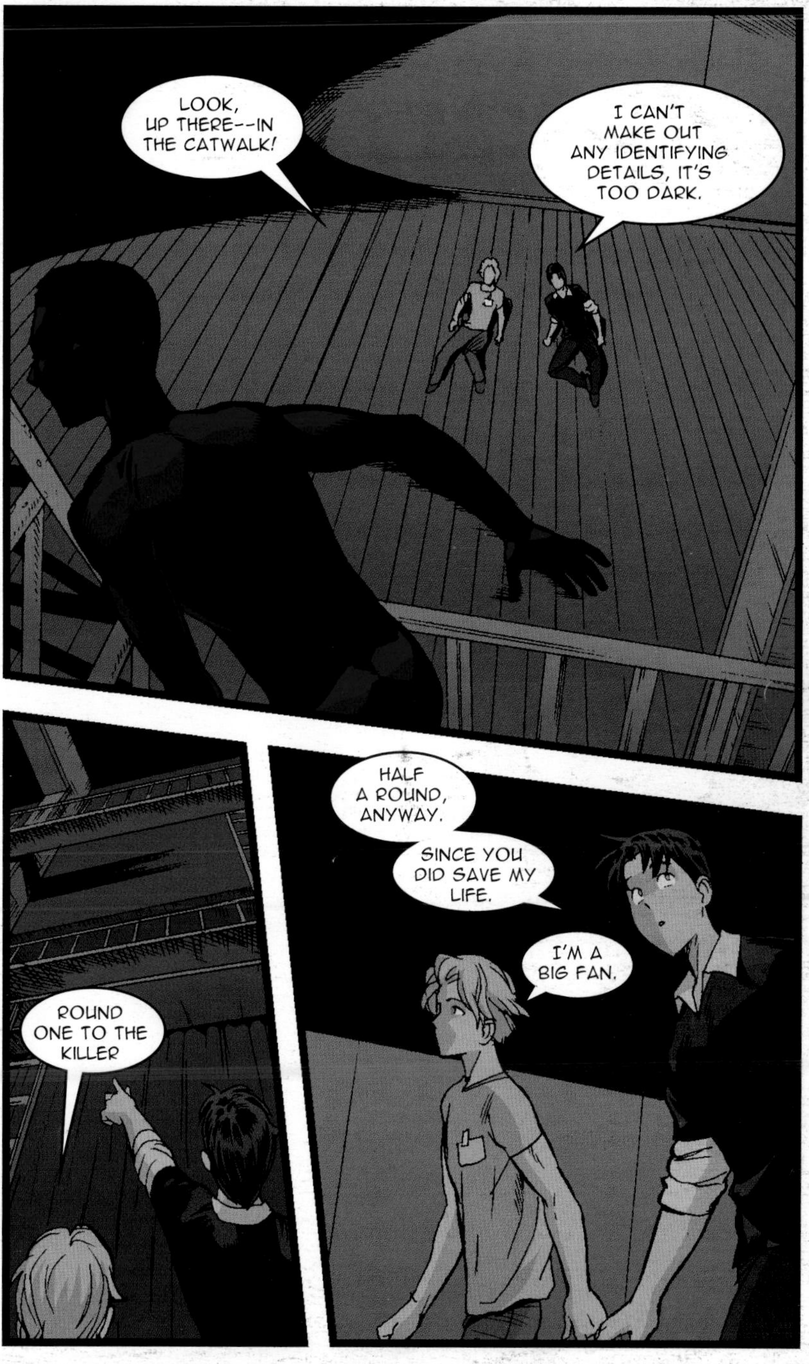
LOOK, UP THERE--IN THE CATWALK!
I CAN'T MAKE OUT ANY IDENTIFYING DETAILS, IT'S TOO DARK.
ROUND ONE TO THE KILLER
HALF A ROUND, ANYWAY.
SINCE YOU DID SAVE MY LIFE.
I'M A BIG FAN.

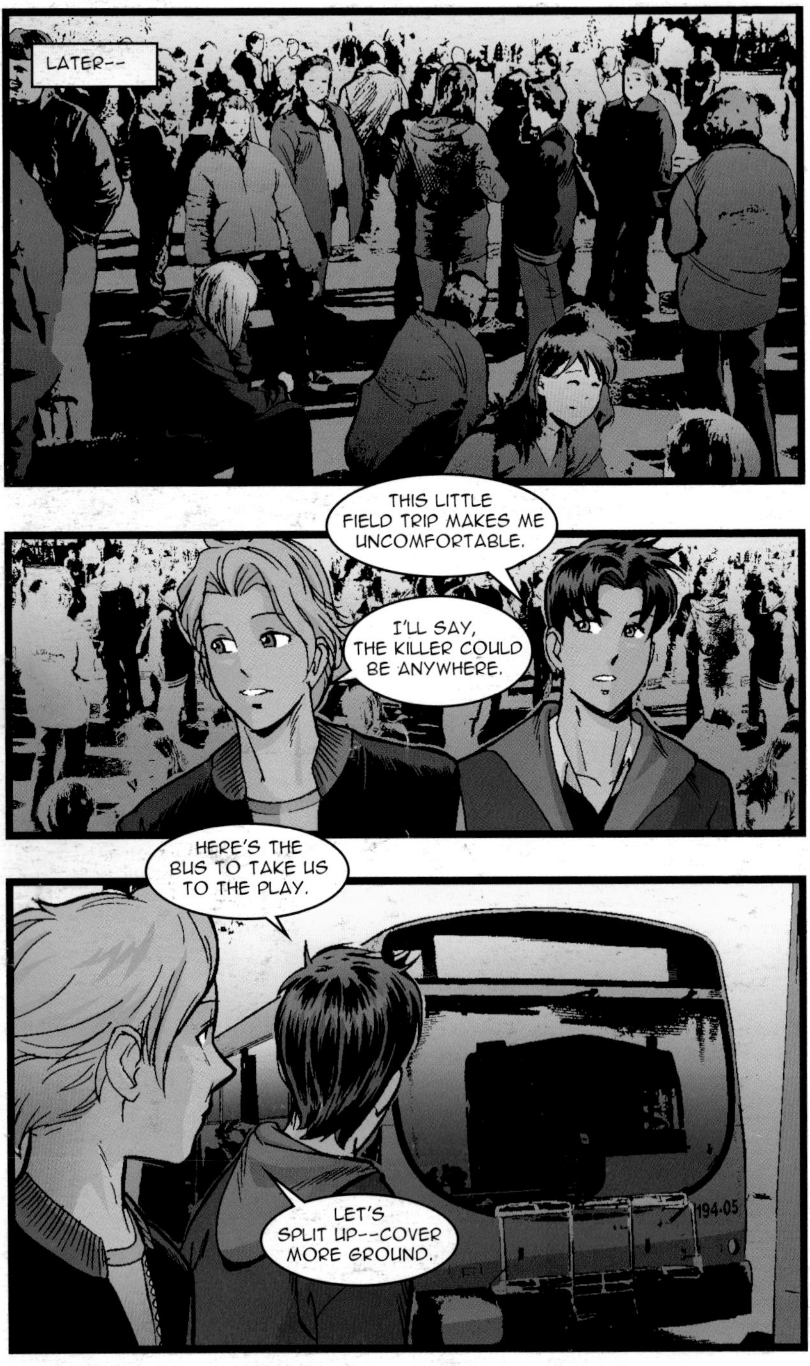
LATER--
THIS LITTLE FIELD TRIP MAKES ME UNCOMFORTABLE.
I'LL SAY, THE KILLER COULD BE ANYWHERE.
HERE'S THE BUS TO TAKE US TO THE PLAY.
LET'S SPLIT UP--COVER MORE GROUND.
194-05

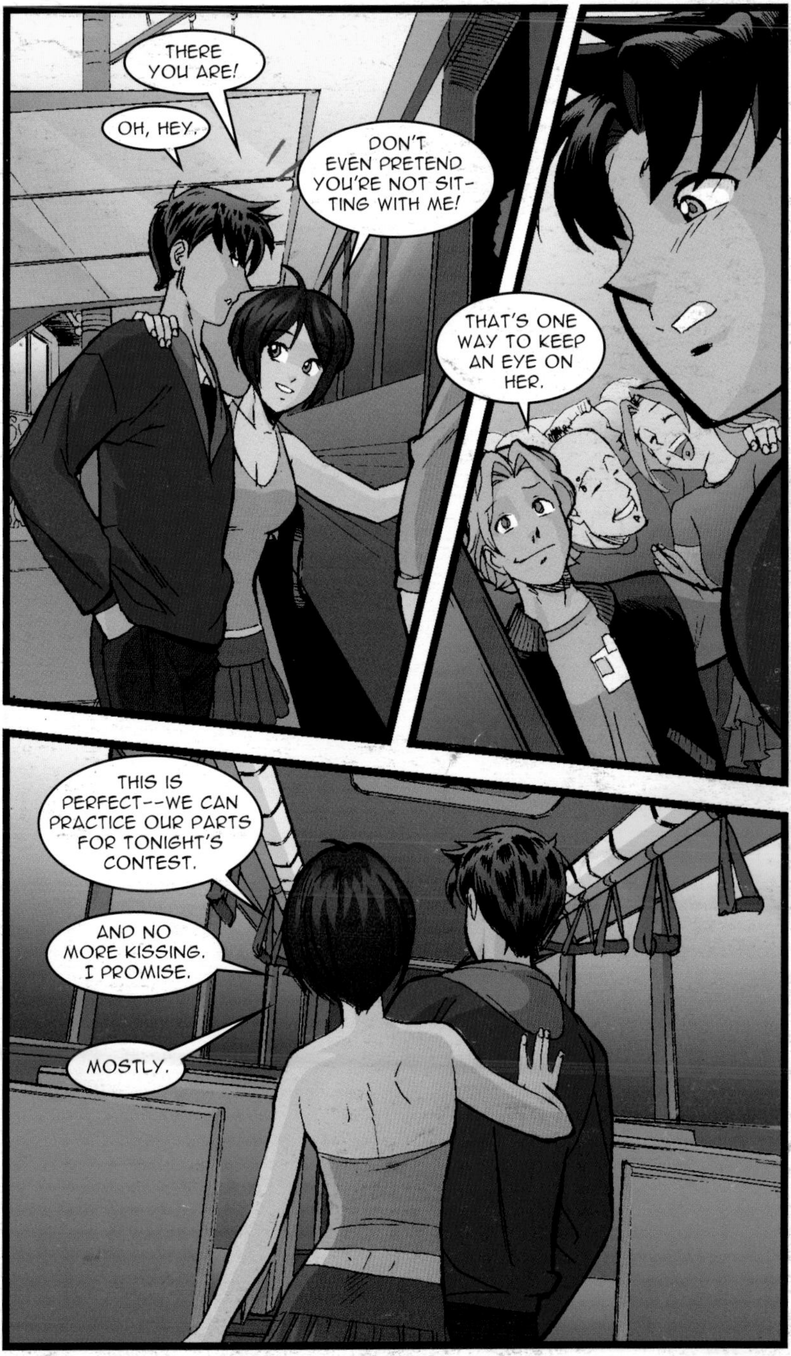
THERE YOU ARE!
OH, HEY.
DON'T EVEN PRETEND YOU'RE NOT SIT-TING WITH ME!
THAT'S ONE WAY TO KEEP AN EYE ON HER.
THIS IS PERFECT--WE CAN PRACTICE OUR PARTS FOR TONIGHT'S CONTEST.
AND NO MORE KISSING. I PROMISE.
MOSTLY.

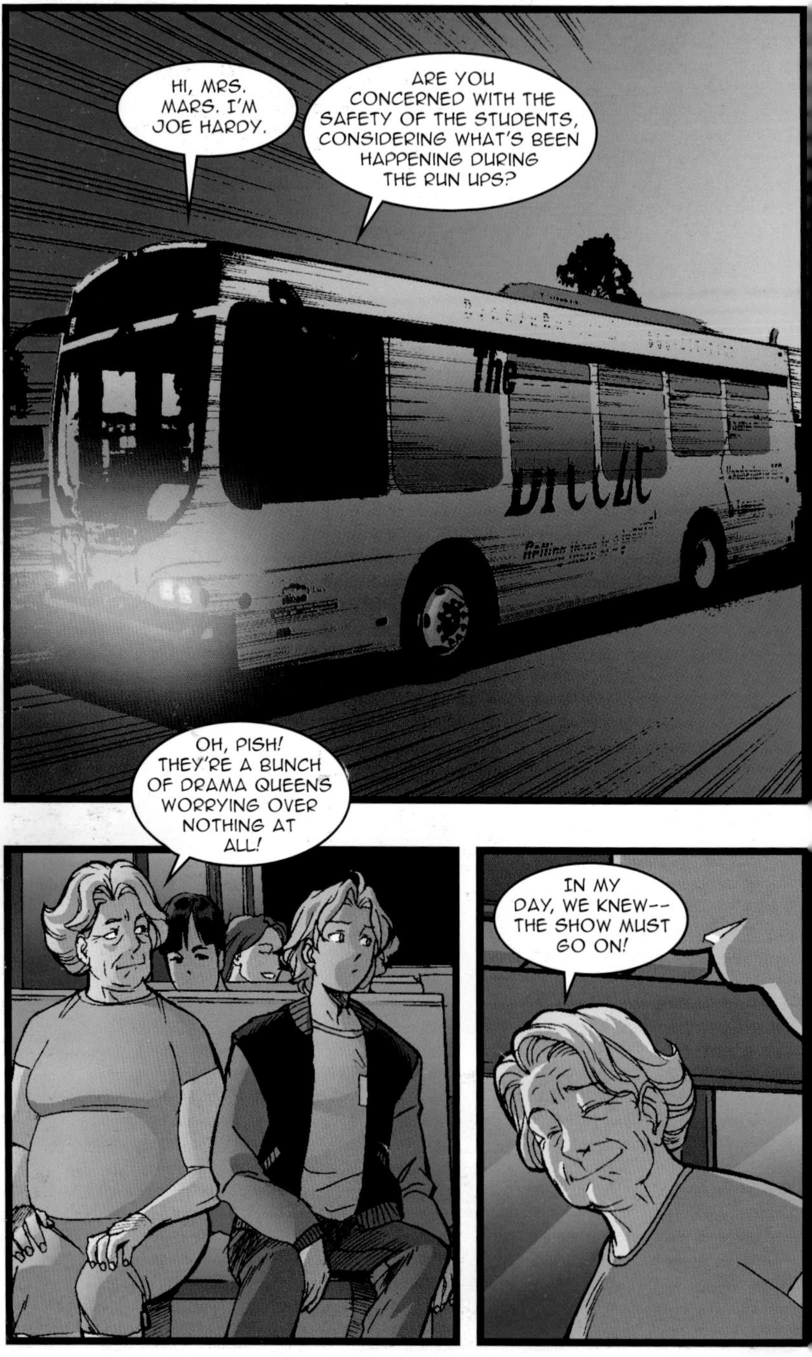
HI, MRS. MARS. I'M JOE HARDY.
ARE YOU CONCERNED WITH THE SAFETY OF THE STUDENTS, CONSIDERING WHAT'S BEEN HAPPENING DURING THE RUN UPS?
The
OH, PISH! THEY'RE A BUNCH OF DRAMA QUEENS WORRYING OVER NOTHING AT ALL!
IN MY DAY, WE KNEW-- THE SHOW MUST GO ON!

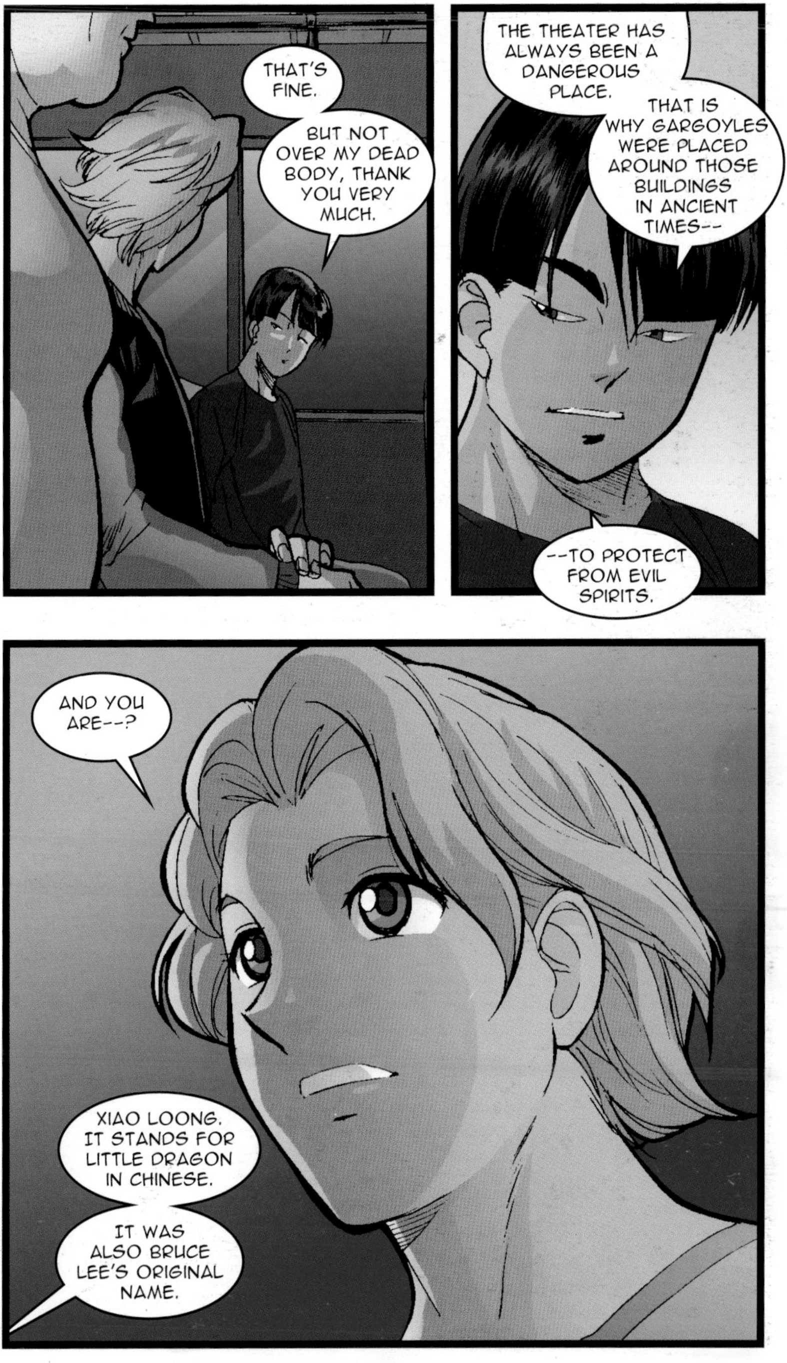
THAT'S FINE.
BUT NOT OVER MY DEAD BODY, THANK YOU VERY MUCH.
THE THEATER HAS ALWAYS BEEN A DANGEROUS PLACE.
THAT IS WHY GARGOYLES WERE PLACED AROUND THOSE BUILDINGS IN ANCIENT TIMES--
--TO PROTECT FROM EVIL SPIRITS.
AND YOU ARE--?
XIAO LOONG. IT STANDS FOR LITTLE DRAGON IN CHINESE.
IT WAS ALSO BRUCE LEE'S ORIGINAL NAME.

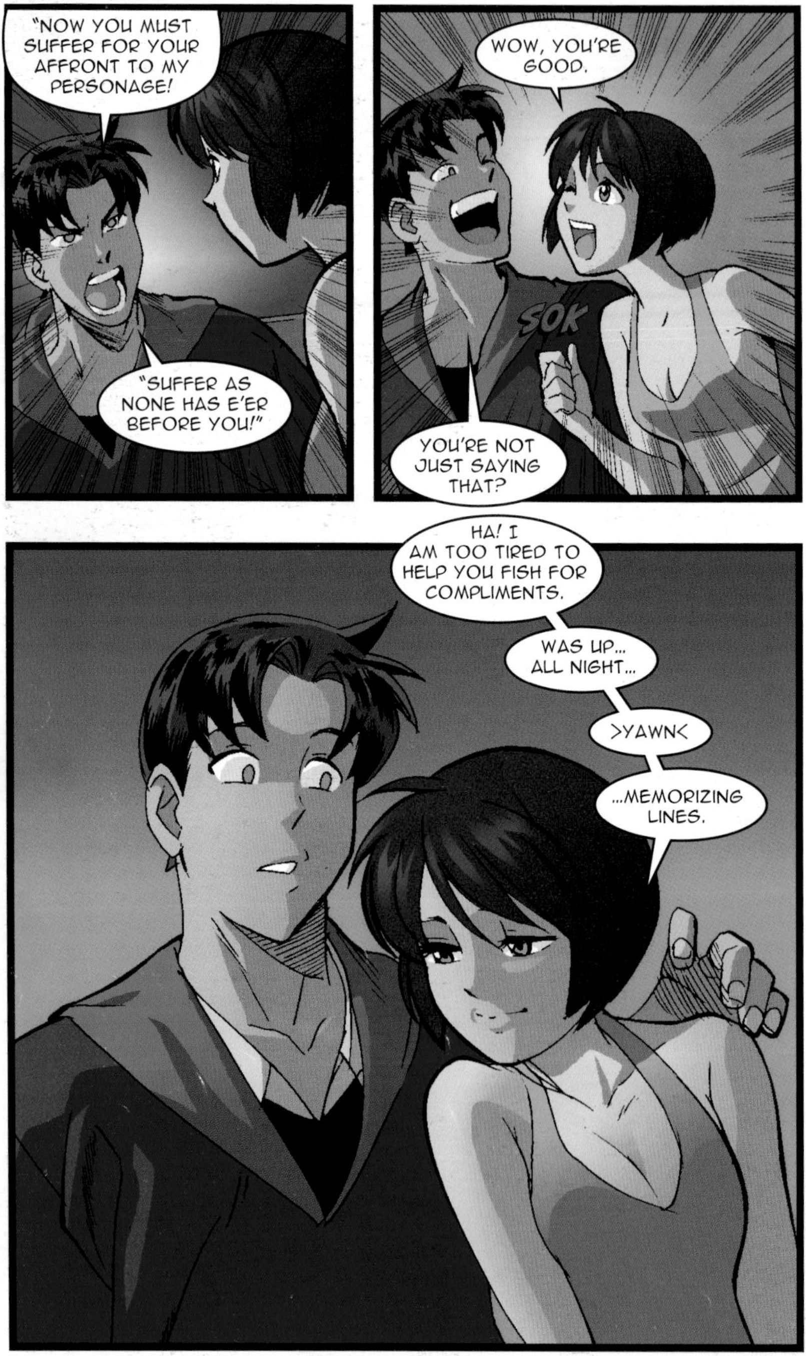
"NOW YOU MUST SUFFER FOR YOUR AFFRONT TO MY PERSONAGE!
"SUFFER AS NONE HAS E'ER BEFORE YOU!"
WOW, YOU'RE GOOD.
SOK
YOU'RE NOT JUST SAYING THAT?
HA! I AM TOO TIRED TO HELP YOU FISH FOR COMPLIMENTS.
WAS UP... ALL NIGHT...
>YAWN<
...MEMORIZING LINES.

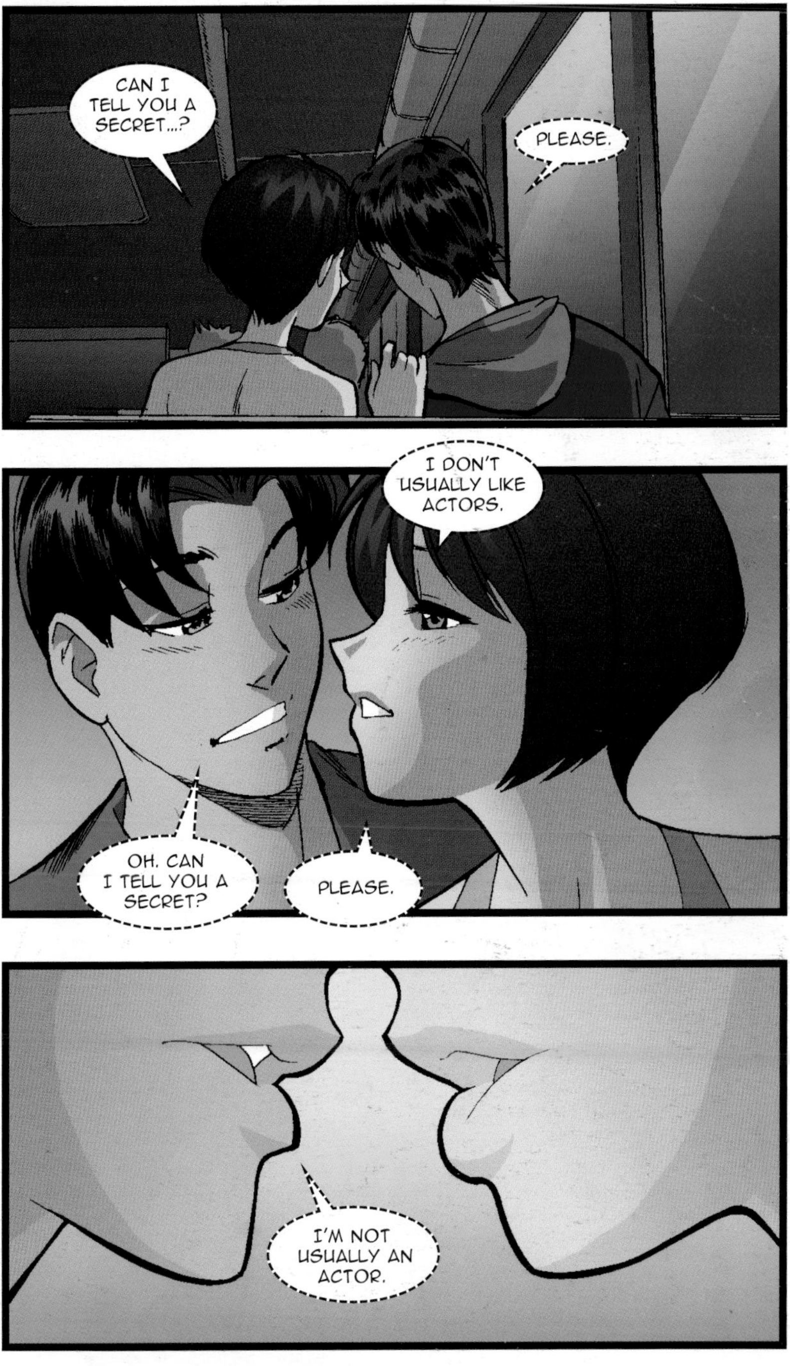

CAN I TELL YOU A SECRET...?
PLEASE.
I DON'T USUALLY LIKE ACTORS.
OH. CAN I TELL YOU A SECRET?
PLEASE.
I'M NOT USUALLY AN ACTOR.

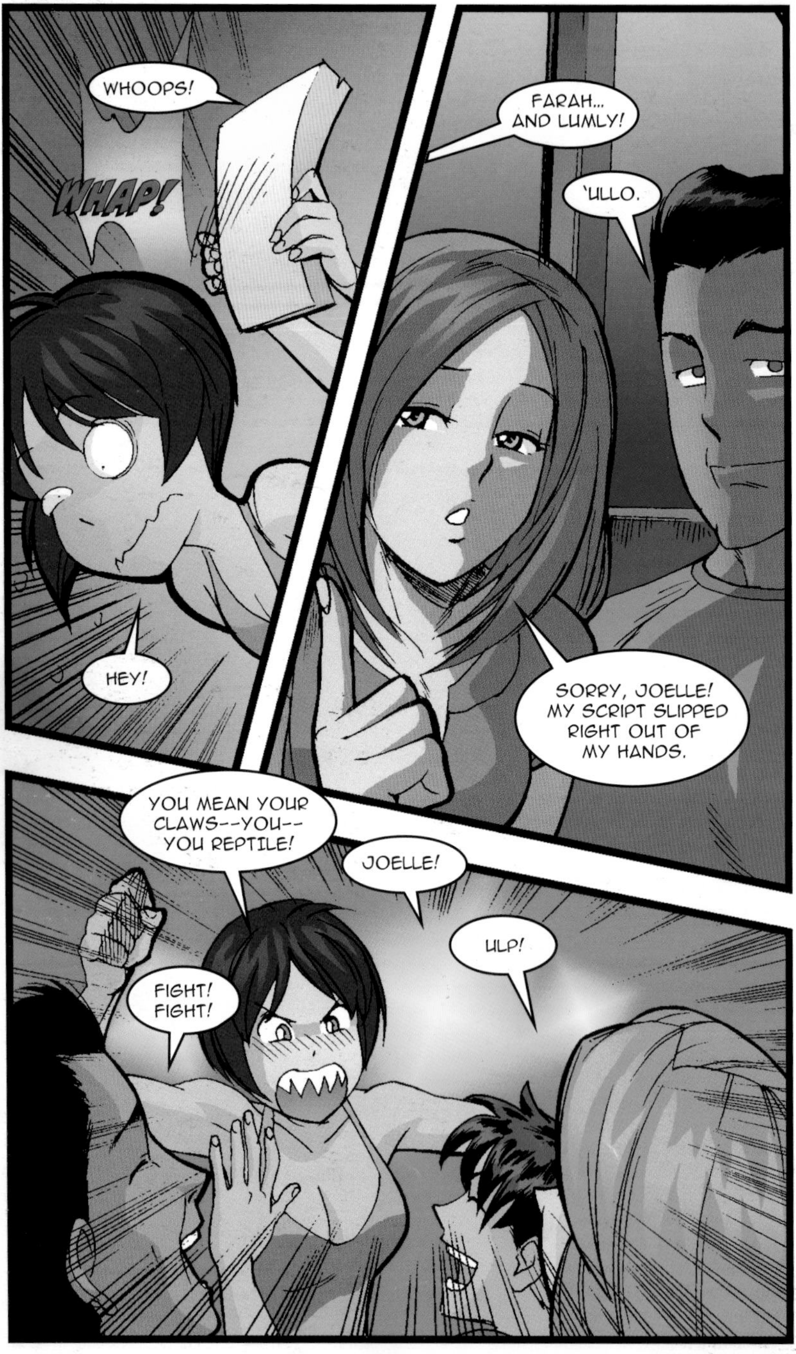
WHOOPS!
WHAP!
HEY!
FARAH... AND LUMLY!
'ULLO.
SORRY, JOELLE! MY SCRIPT SLIPPED RIGHT OUT OF MY HANDS.
YOU MEAN YOUR CLAWS--YOU--YOU REPTILE!
JOELLE!
ULP!
FIGHT! FIGHT!

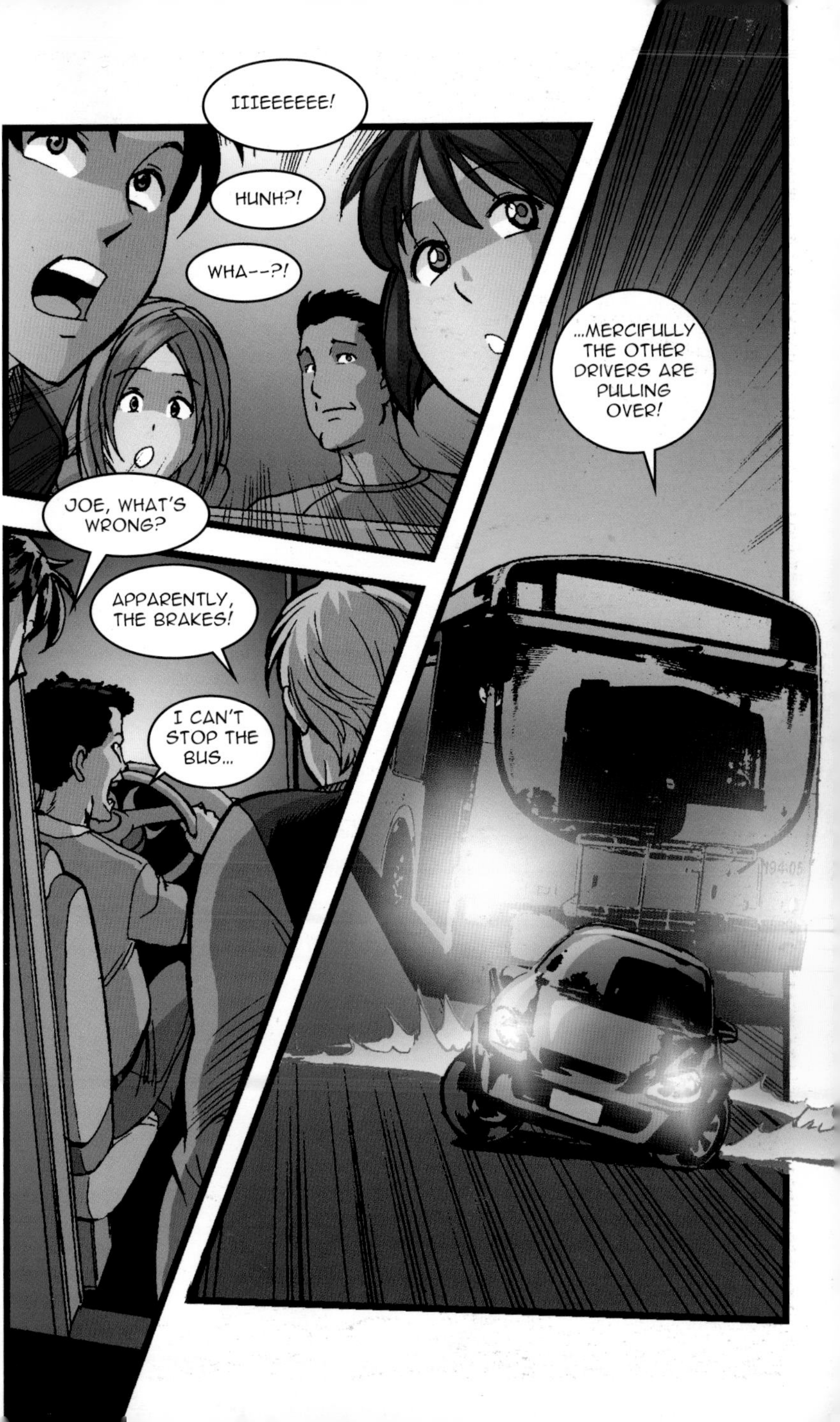
IIIEEEEEE!
HUNH?!
WHA--?!
JOE, WHAT'S WRONG?
APPARENTLY, THE BRAKES!
I CAN'T STOP THE BUS...
...MERCIFULLY THE OTHER DRIVERS ARE PULLING OVER!

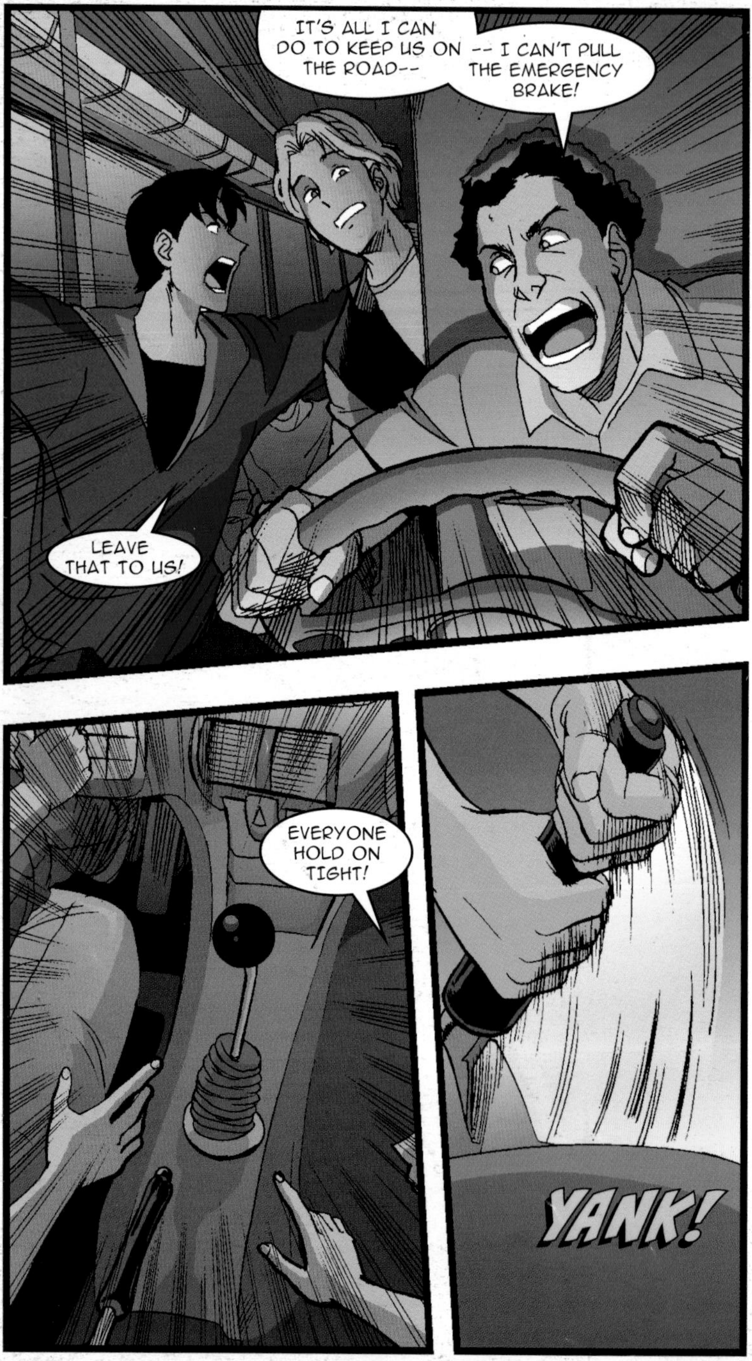
IT'S ALL I CAN DO TO KEEP US ON THE ROAD--
-- I CAN'T PULL THE EMERGENCY BRAKE!
LEAVE THAT TO US!
EVERYONE HOLD ON TIGHT!
YANK!

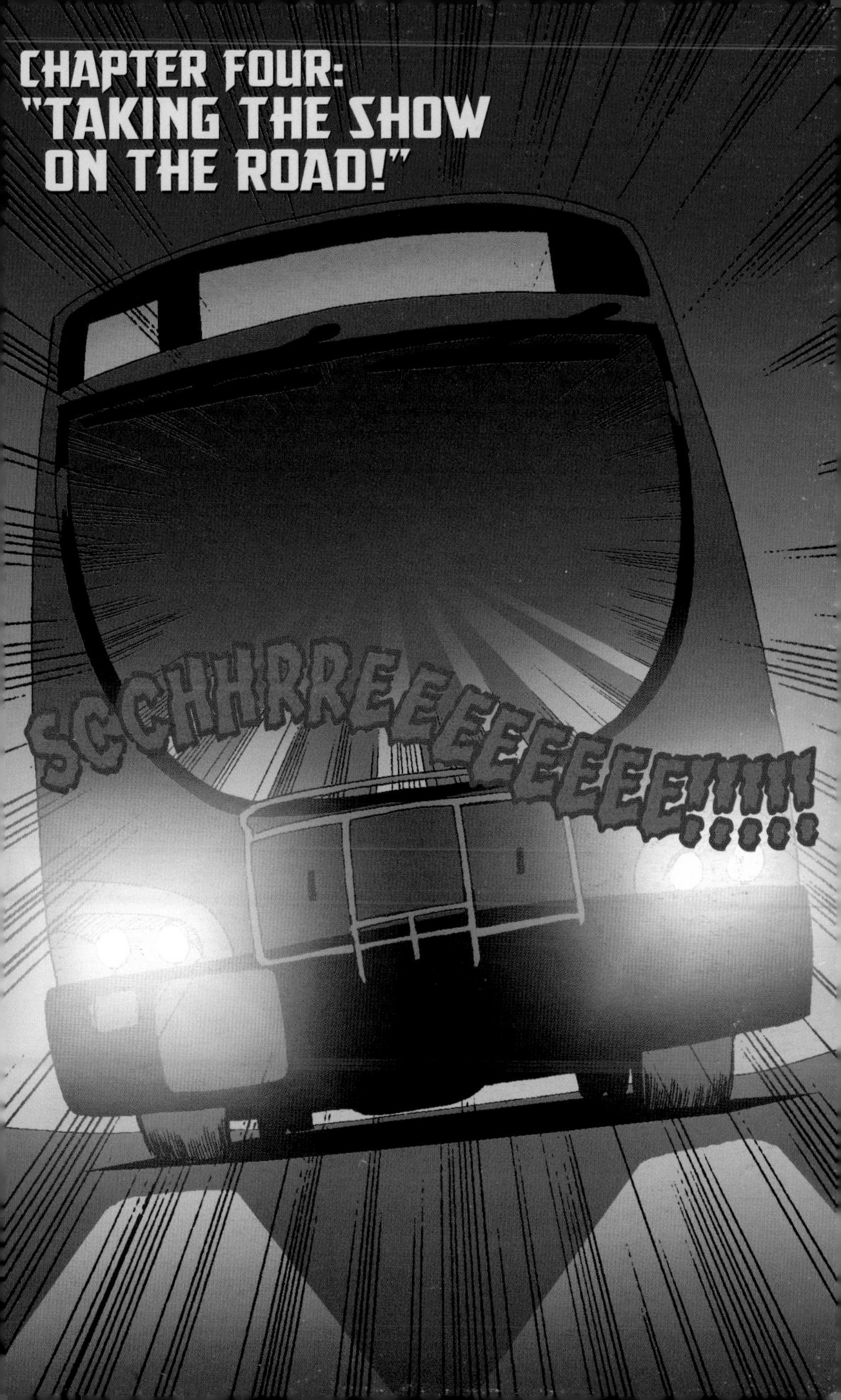
CHAPTER FOUR:
"TAKING THE SHOW
ON THE ROAD!"
SCCHHRREEEEEEEEEEEE!!!!!!

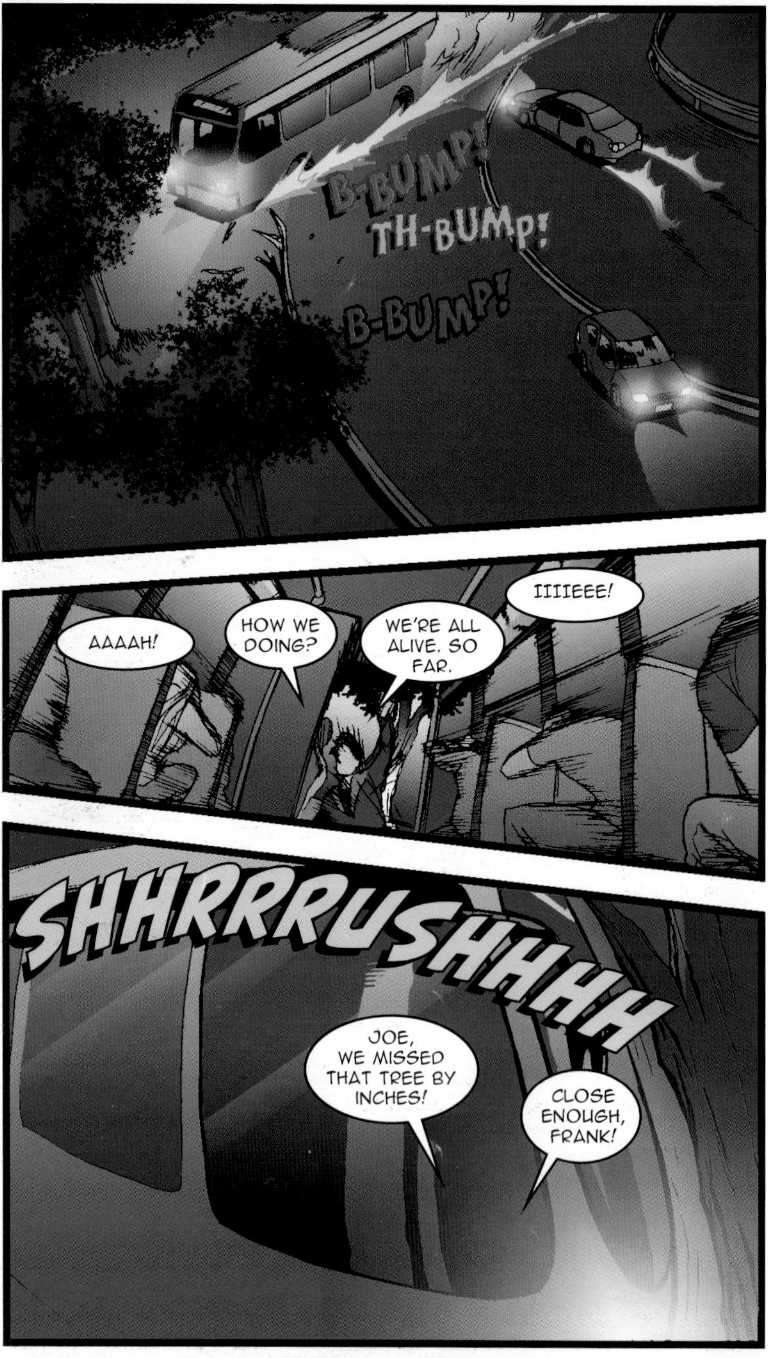

B-BUMP!
TH-BUMP!
B-BUMP!
AAAAH!
HOW WE DOING?
WE'RE ALL ALIVE. SO FAR.
IIIIEEE!
SHHRRRUSHHHH
JOE, WE MISSED THAT TREE BY INCHES!
CLOSE ENOUGH, FRANK!

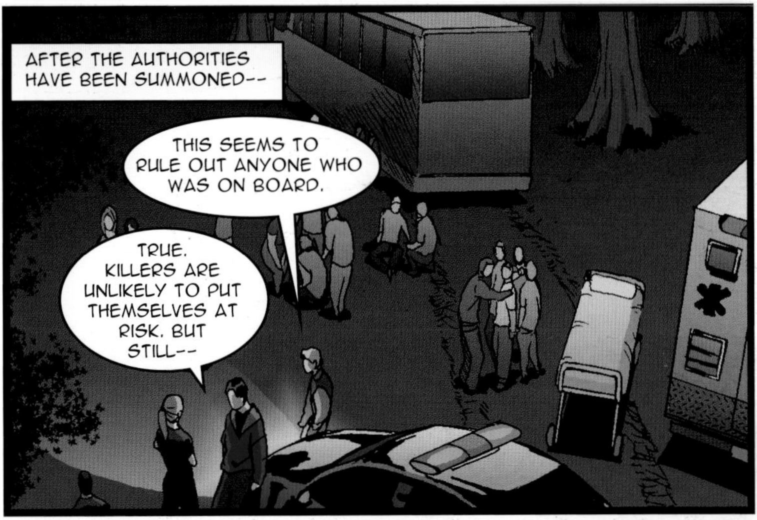
AFTER THE AUTHORITIES HAVE BEEN SUMMONED--
THIS SEEMS TO RULE OUT ANYONE WHO WAS ON BOARD.
TRUE. KILLERS ARE UNLIKELY TO PUT THEMSELVES AT RISK. BUT STILL--

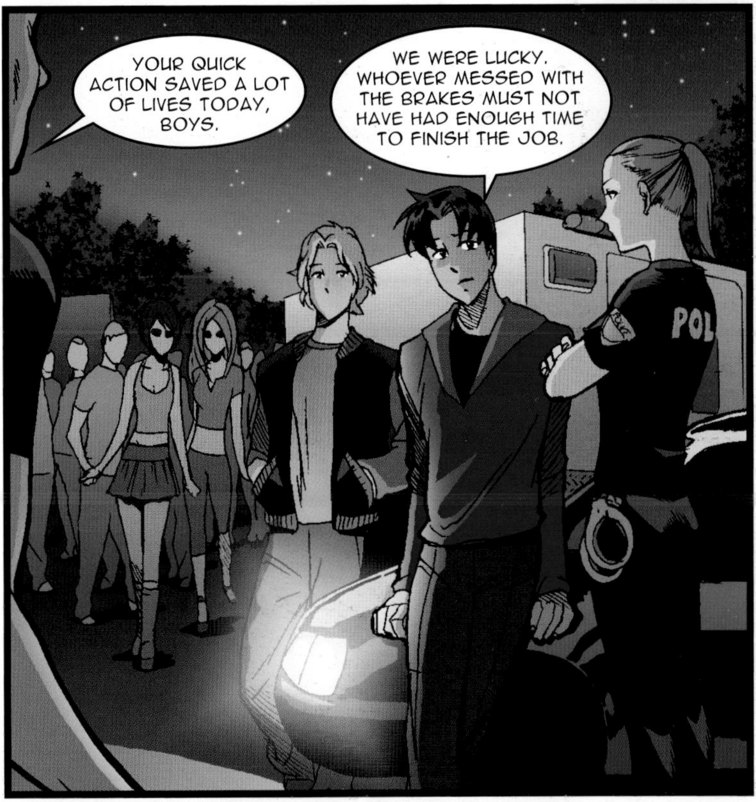
YOUR QUICK ACTION SAVED A LOT OF LIVES TODAY, BOYS.
WE WERE LUCKY. WHOEVER MESSED WITH THE BRAKES MUST NOT HAVE HAD ENOUGH TIME TO FINISH THE JOB.
POL

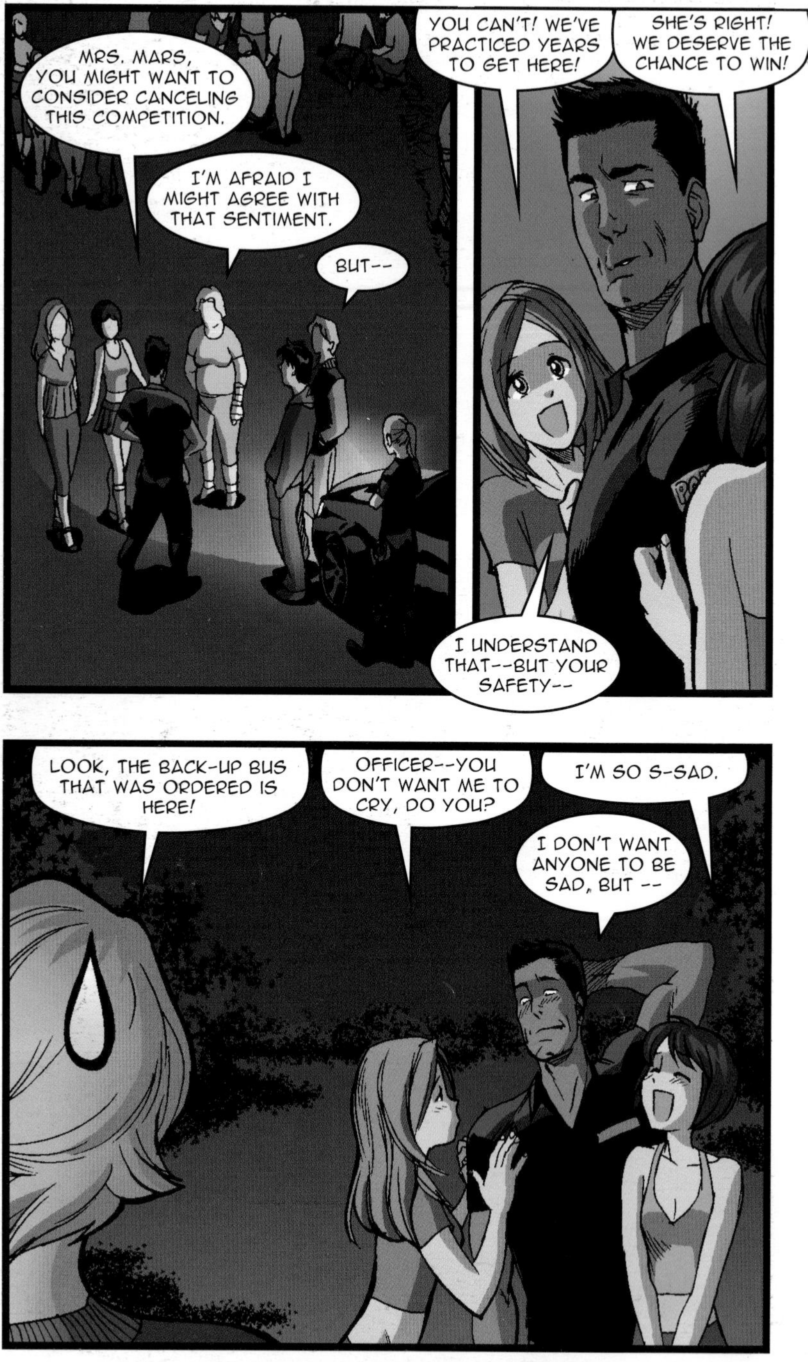
MRS. MARS, YOU MIGHT WANT TO CONSIDER CANCELING THIS COMPETITION.
I'M AFRAID I MIGHT AGREE WITH THAT SENTIMENT.
BUT--
YOU CAN'T! WE'VE PRACTICED YEARS TO GET HERE!
SHE'S RIGHT! WE DESERVE THE CHANCE TO WIN!
I UNDERSTAND THAT--BUT YOUR SAFETY--
LOOK, THE BACK-UP BUS THAT WAS ORDERED IS HERE!
OFFICER--YOU DON'T WANT ME TO CRY, DO YOU?
I'M SO S-SAD.
I DON'T WANT ANYONE TO BE SAD, BUT --

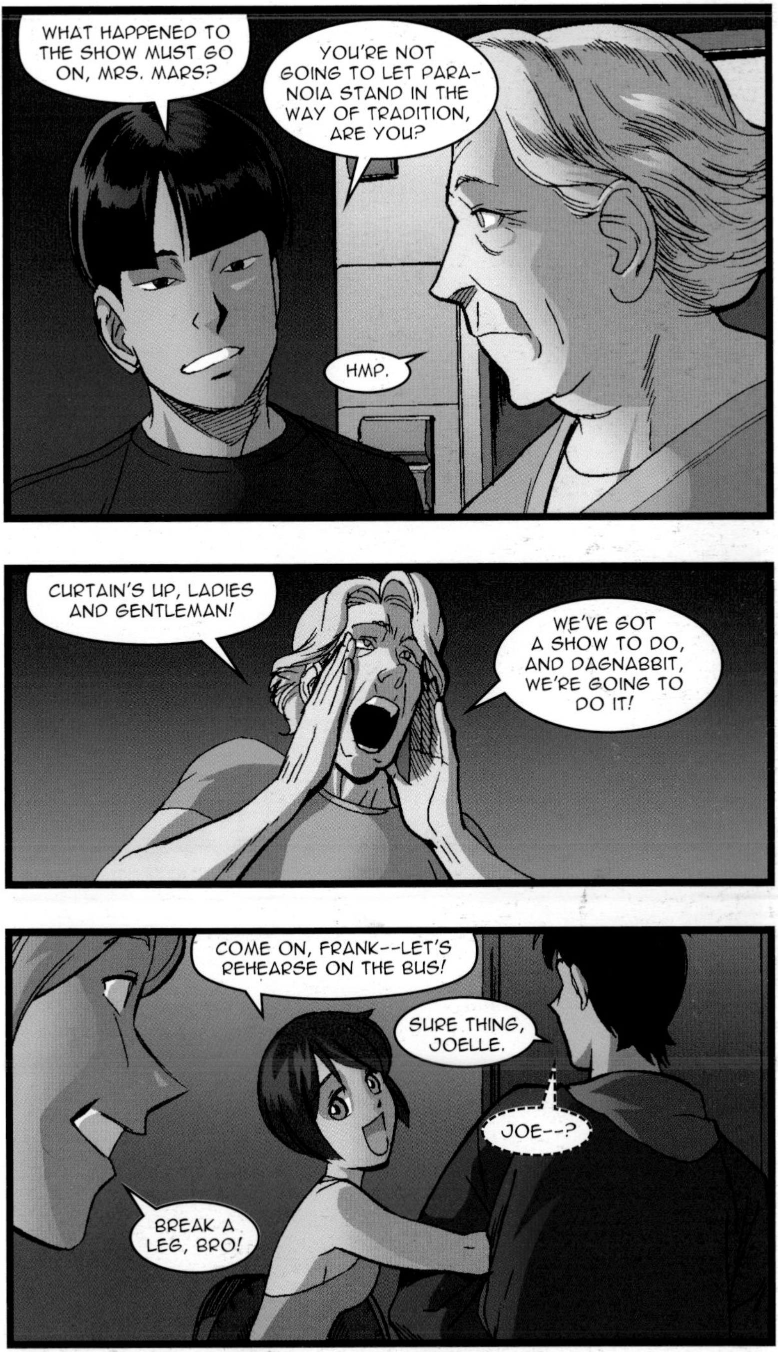
WHAT HAPPENED TO THE SHOW MUST GO ON, MRS. MARS?
YOU'RE NOT GOING TO LET PARA-NOIA STAND IN THE WAY OF TRADITION, ARE YOU?
HMP.
CURTAIN'S UP, LADIES AND GENTLEMAN!
WE'VE GOT A SHOW TO DO, AND DAGNABBIT, WE'RE GOING TO DO IT!
COME ON, FRANK--LET'S REHEARSE ON THE BUS!
SURE THING, JOELLE.
JOE--?
BREAK A LEG, BRO!

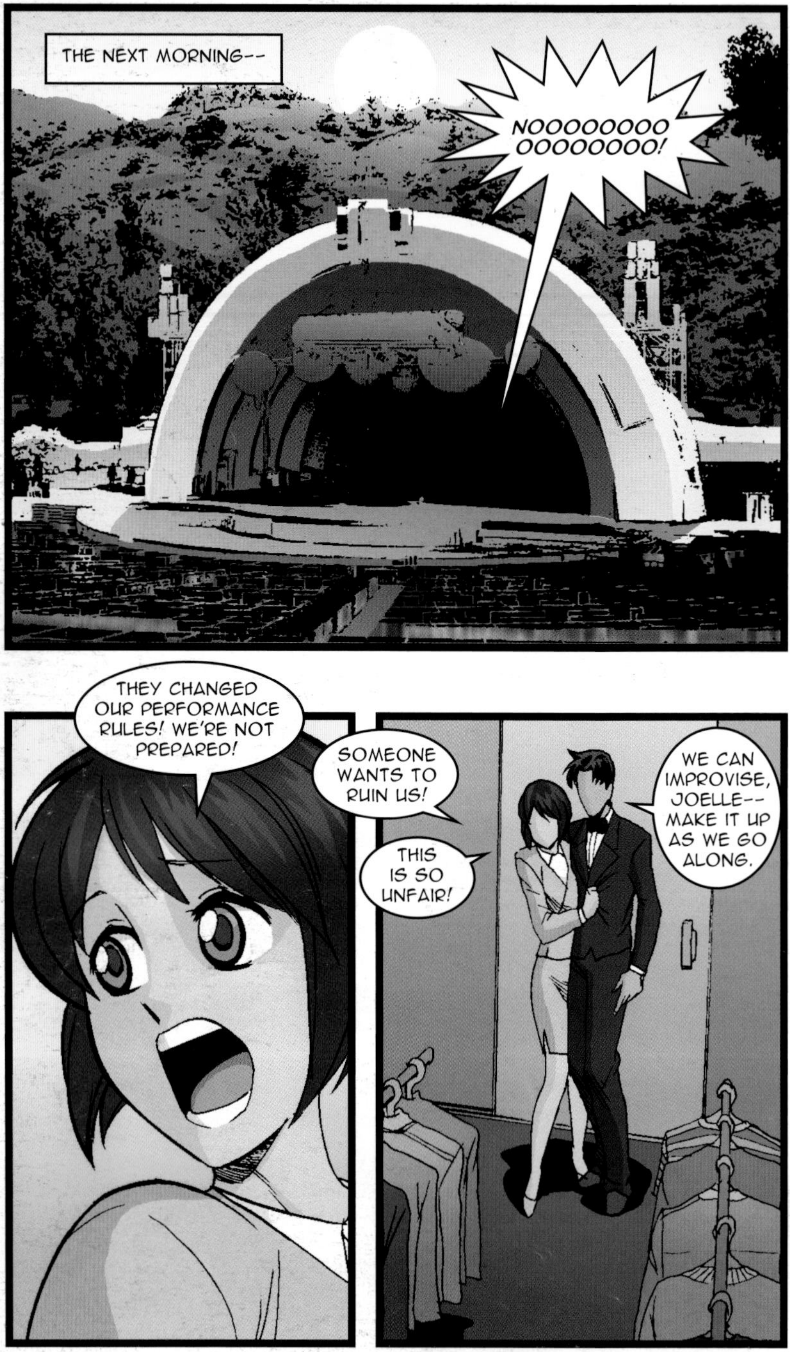
THE NEXT MORNING--
NOOOOOOOO OOOOOOOO!
THEY CHANGED OUR PERFORMANCE RULES! WE'RE NOT PREPARED!
SOMEONE WANTS TO RUIN US!
THIS IS SO UNFAIR!
WE CAN IMPROVISE, JOELLE-- MAKE IT UP AS WE GO ALONG.

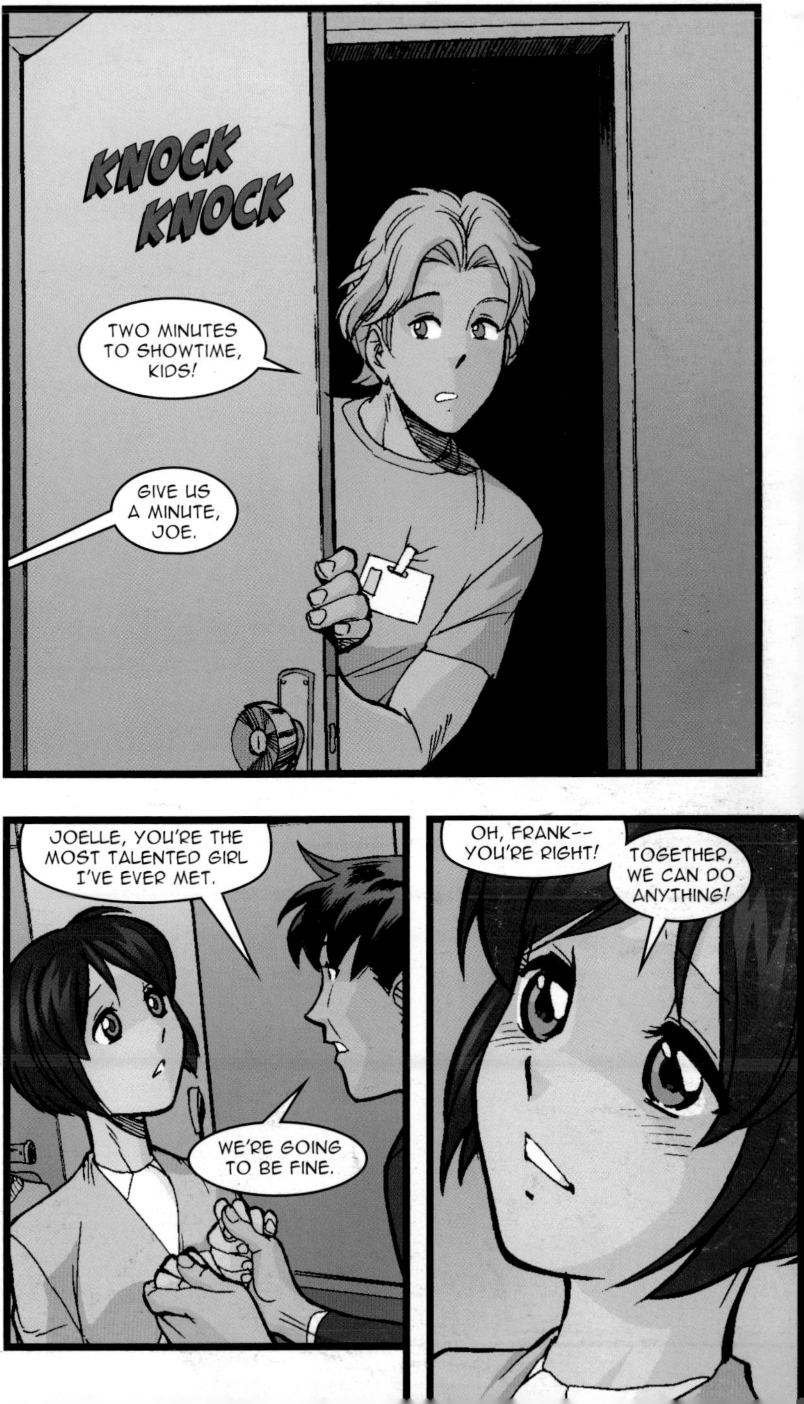
KNOCK KNOCK
TWO MINUTES TO SHOWTIME, KIDS!
GIVE US A MINUTE, JOE.
JOELLE, YOU'RE THE MOST TALENTED GIRL I'VE EVER MET.
WE'RE GOING TO BE FINE.
OH, FRANK-- YOU'RE RIGHT!
TOGETHER, WE CAN DO ANYTHING!

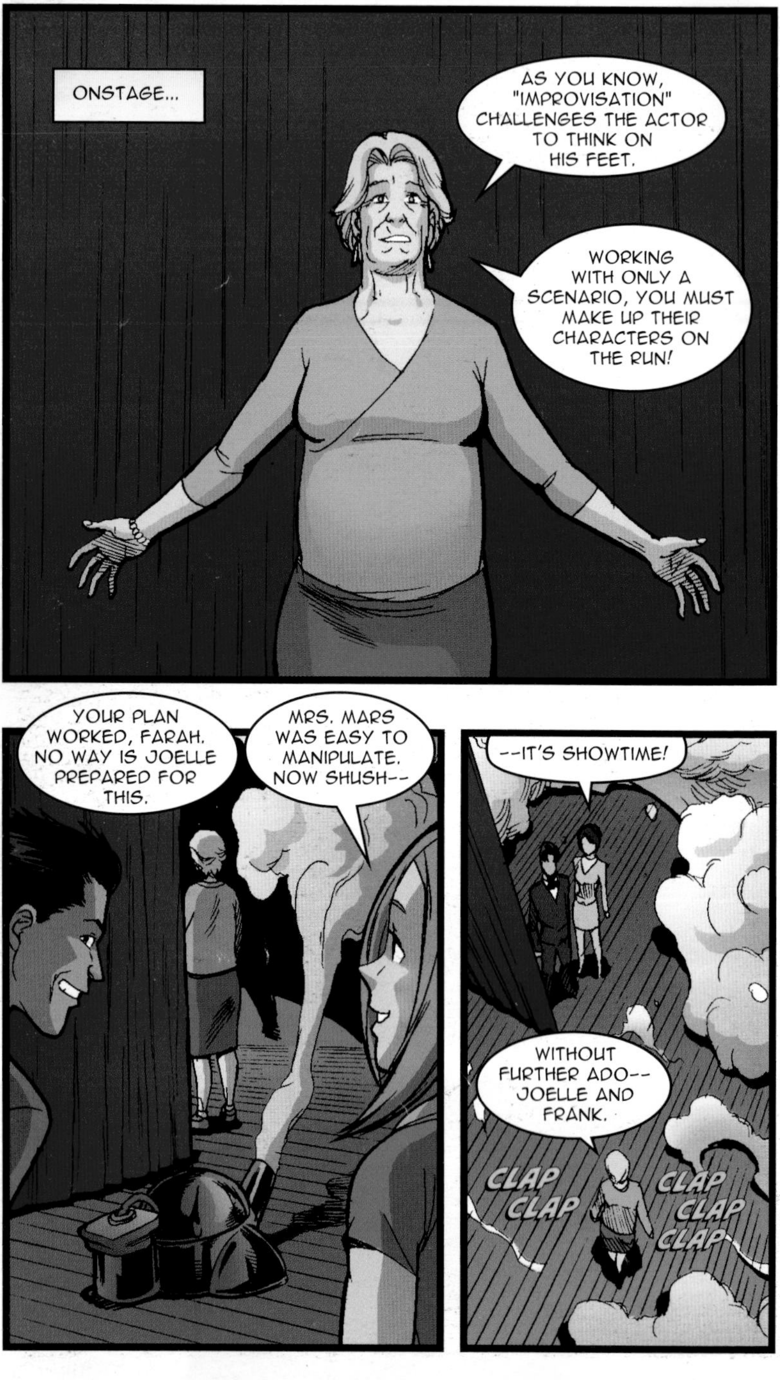
ONSTAGE...
AS YOU KNOW, "IMPROVISATION" CHALLENGES THE ACTOR TO THINK ON HIS FEET.
WORKING WITH ONLY A SCENARIO, YOU MUST MAKE UP THEIR CHARACTERS ON THE RUN!
YOUR PLAN WORKED, FARAH. NO WAY IS JOELLE PREPARED FOR THIS.
MRS. MARS WAS EASY TO MANIPULATE. NOW SHUSH--
--IT'S SHOWTIME!
WITHOUT FURTHER ADO-- JOELLE AND FRANK.
CLAP CLAP
CLAP CLAP CLAP

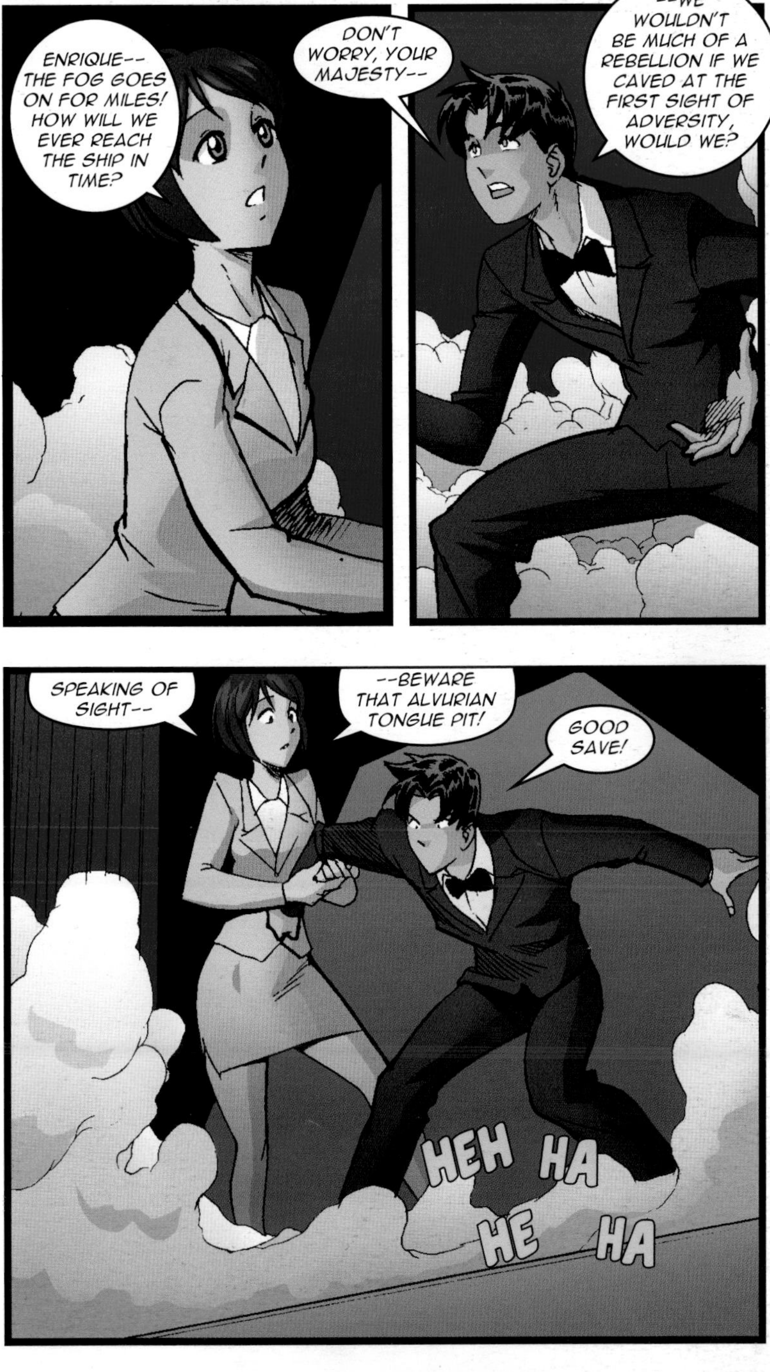
ENRIQUE-- THE FOG GOES ON FOR MILES! HOW WILL WE EVER REACH THE SHIP IN TIME?
DON'T WORRY, YOUR MAJESTY--
--WE WOULDN'T BE MUCH OF A REBELLION IF WE CAVED AT THE FIRST SIGHT OF ADVERSITY, WOULD WE?
SPEAKING OF SIGHT--
--BEWARE THAT ALVURIAN TONGUE PIT!
GOOD SAVE!
HEH HA
HE HA

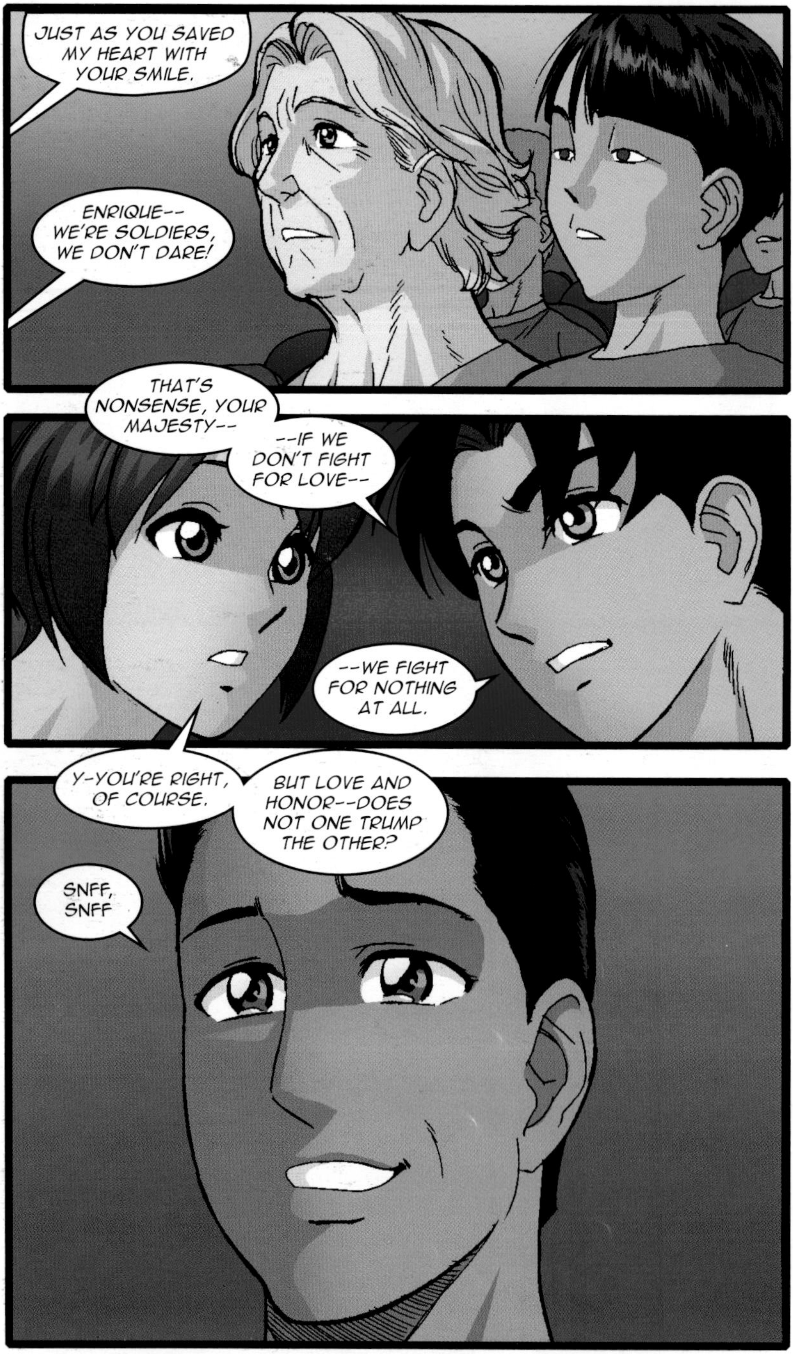
JUST AS YOU SAVED MY HEART WITH YOUR SMILE.
ENRIQUE-- WE'RE SOLDIERS, WE DON'T DARE!
THAT'S NONSENSE, YOUR MAJESTY--
--IF WE DON'T FIGHT FOR LOVE--
--WE FIGHT FOR NOTHING AT ALL.
Y-YOU'RE RIGHT, OF COURSE.
BUT LOVE AND HONOR--DOES NOT ONE TRUMP THE OTHER?
SNFF, SNFF

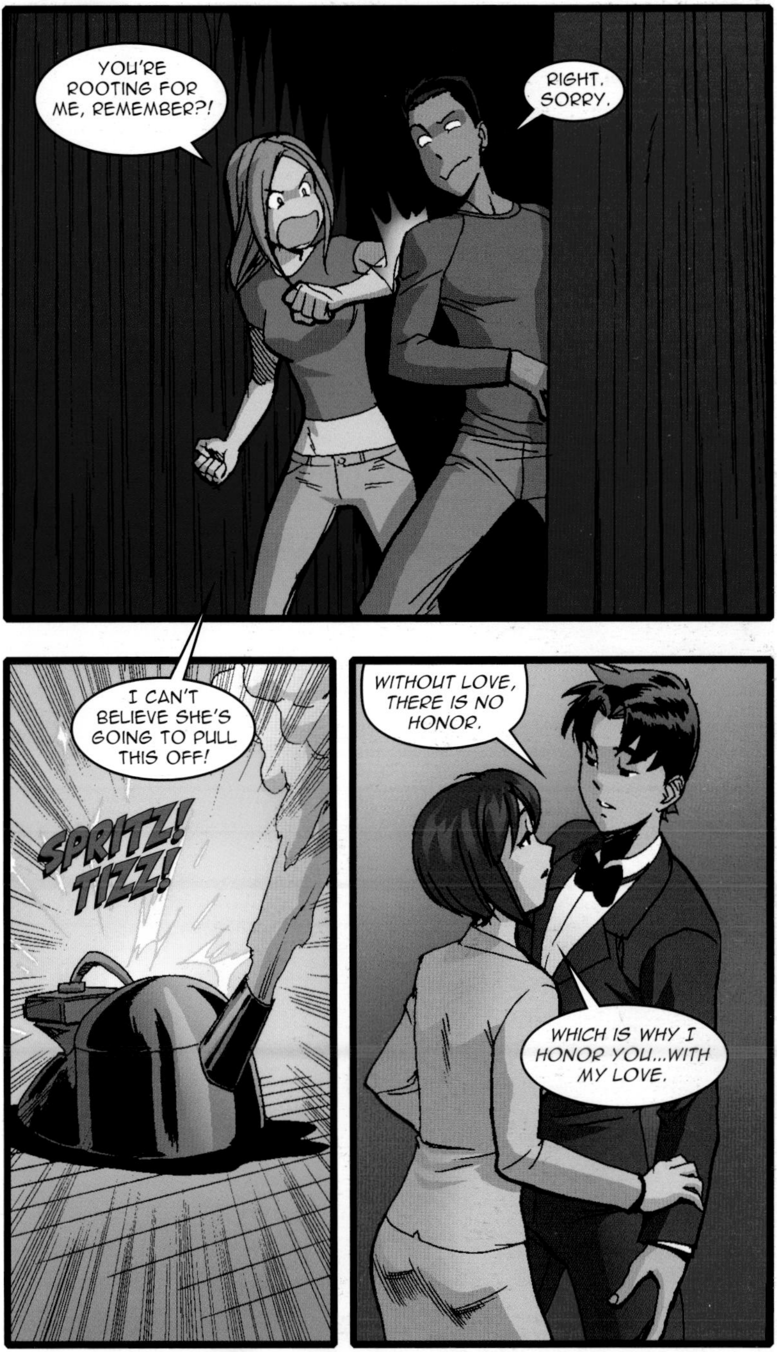
YOU'RE ROOTING FOR ME, REMEMBER?!
RIGHT. SORRY.
I CAN'T BELIEVE SHE'S GOING TO PULL THIS OFF!
SPRITZ! TIZZ!
WITHOUT LOVE, THERE IS NO HONOR.
WHICH IS WHY I HONOR YOU...WITH MY LOVE.

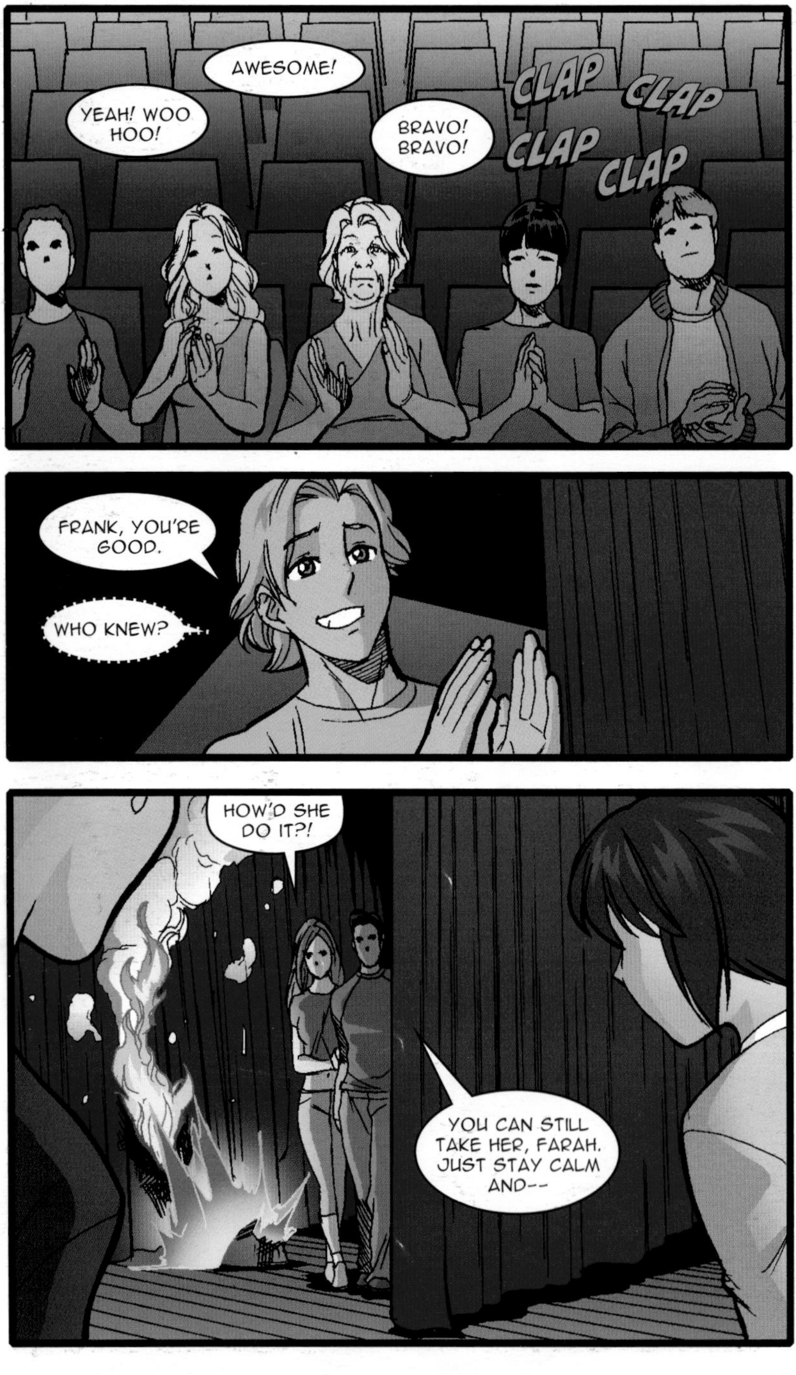

YEAH! WOO HOO!
AWESOME!
BRAVO! BRAVO!
CLAP CLAP CLAP CLAP
FRANK, YOU'RE GOOD.
WHO KNEW?
HOW'D SHE DO IT?!
YOU CAN STILL TAKE HER, FARAH. JUST STAY CALM AND--

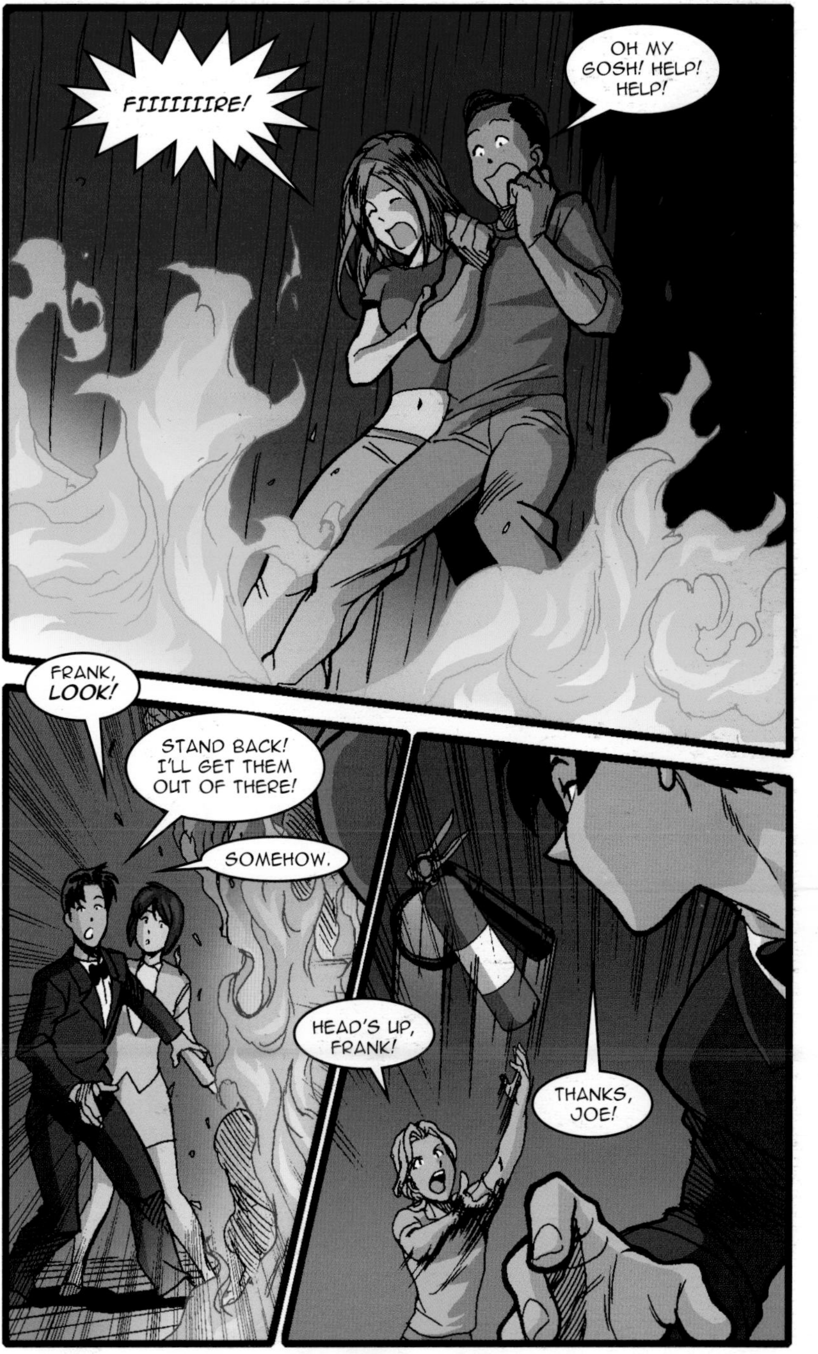
FIIIIIIIRE!
OH MY GOSH! HELP! HELP!
FRANK, LOOK!
STAND BACK! I'LL GET THEM OUT OF THERE!
SOMEHOW.
HEAD'S UP, FRANK!
THANKS, JOE!

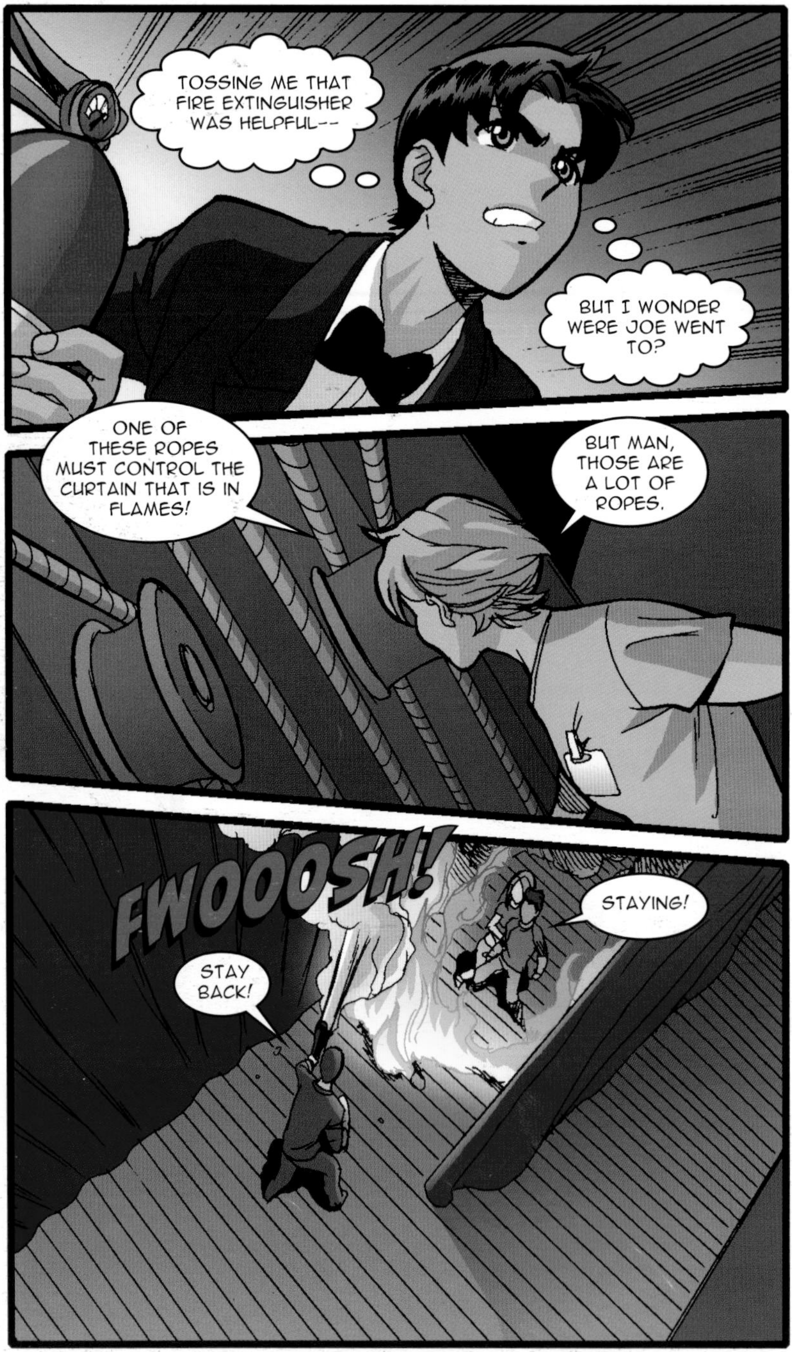
TOSSING ME THAT FIRE EXTINGUISHER WAS HELPFUL--
BUT I WONDER WERE JOE WENT TO?
ONE OF THESE ROPES MUST CONTROL THE CURTAIN THAT IS IN FLAMES!
BUT MAN, THOSE ARE A LOT OF ROPES.
FWOOOSH!
STAYING!
STAY BACK!

CHAPTER FIVE: "IT'S CURTAINS FOR YOU, FRANK HARDY!"

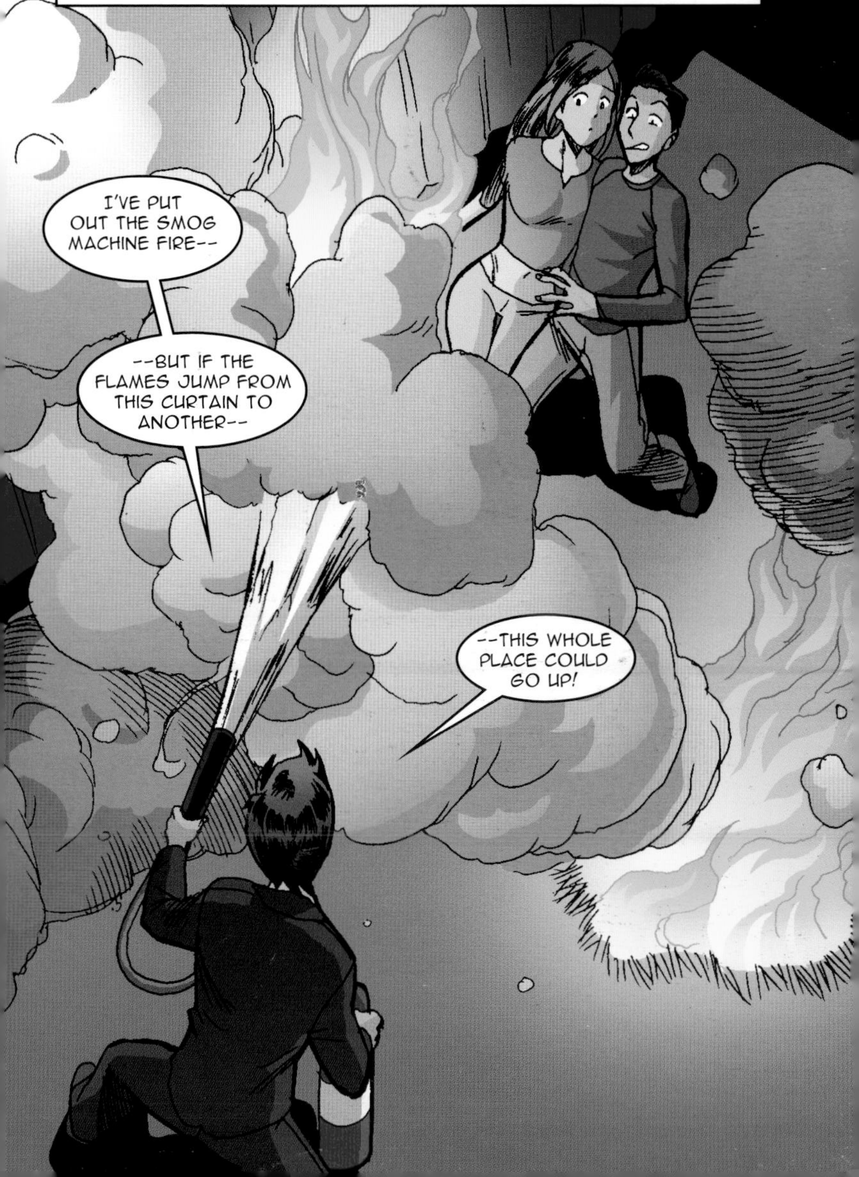
I'VE PUT OUT THE SMOG MACHINE FIRE--
--BUT IF THE FLAMES JUMP FROM THIS CURTAIN TO ANOTHER--
--THIS WHOLE PLACE COULD GO UP!

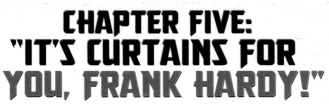

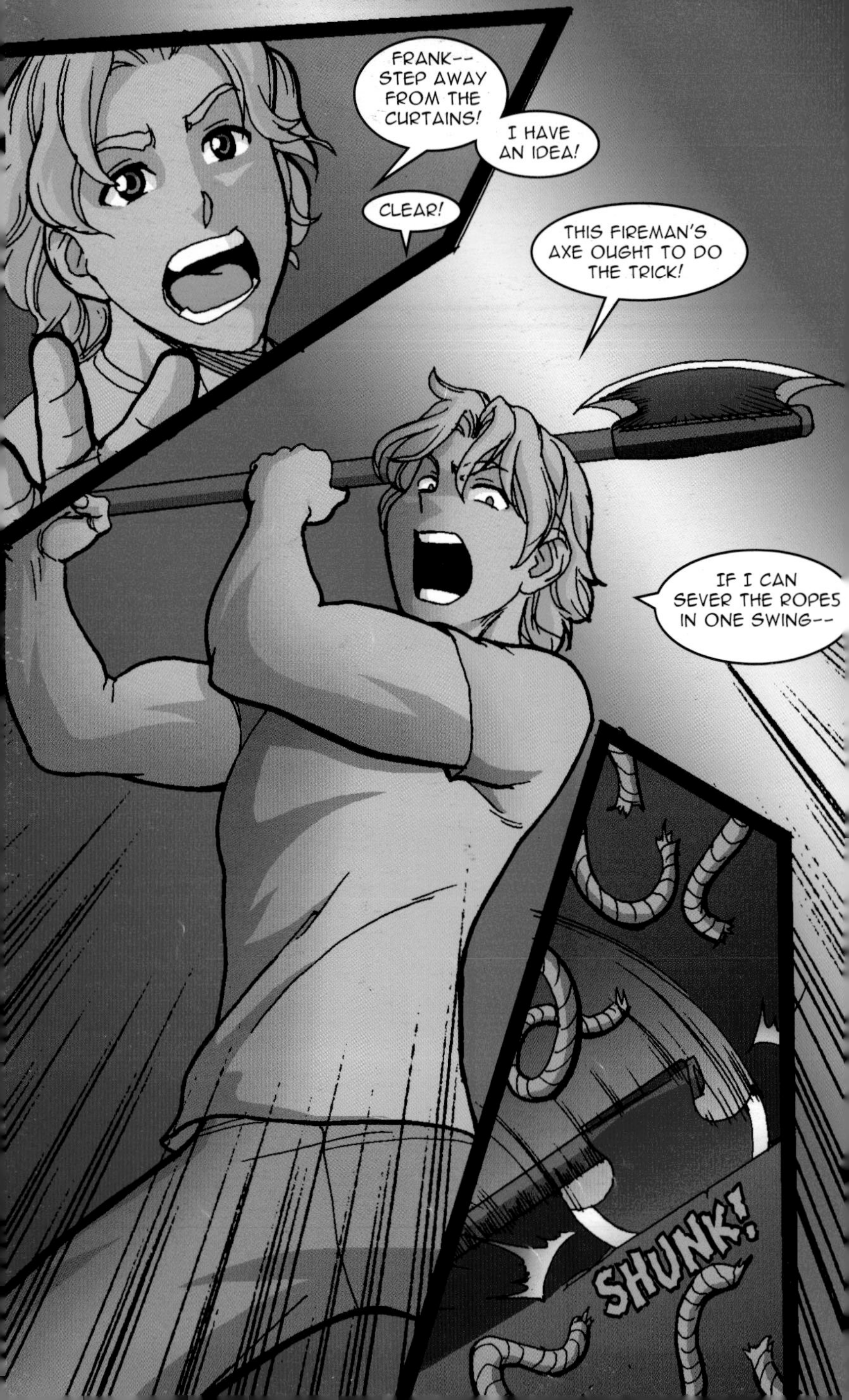
FRANK--
STEP AWAY
FROM THE
CURTAINS!
I HAVE
AN IDEA!
CLEAR!
THIS FIREMAN'S
AXE OUGHT TO DO
THE TRICK!
IF I CAN
SEVER THE ROPES
IN ONE SWING--
SHUNK!

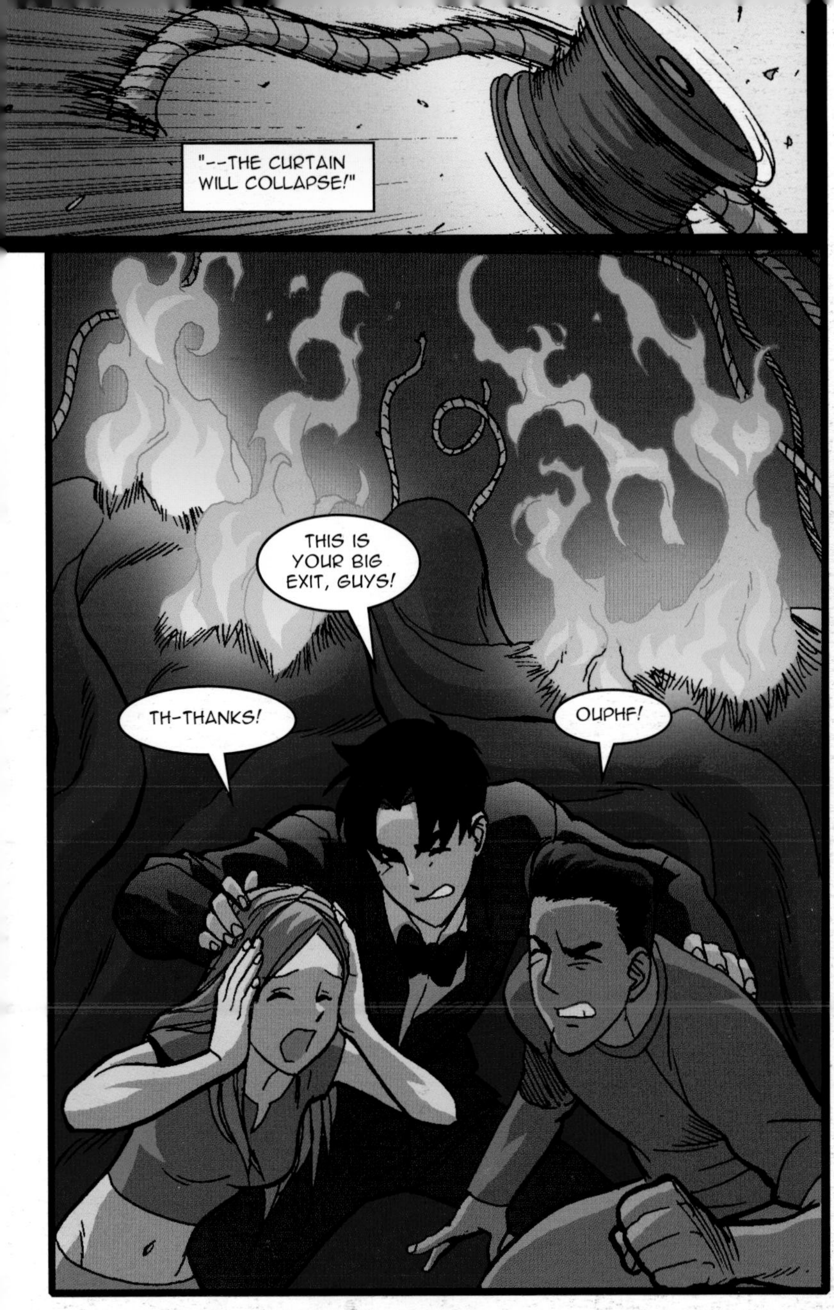
"--THE CURTAIN
WILL COLLAPSE!"
THIS IS
YOUR BIG
EXIT, GUYS!
TH-THANKS!
OUPHF!

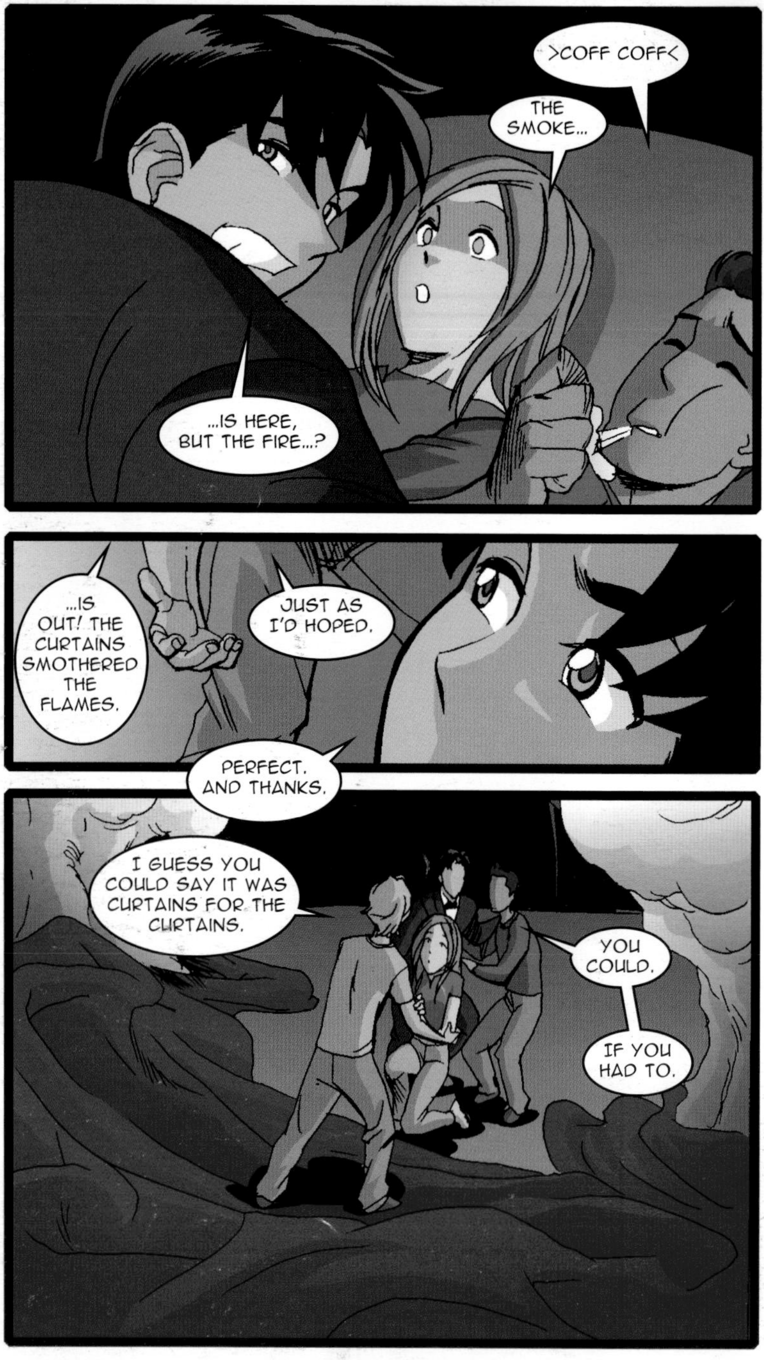

>COFF COFF<
THE SMOKE...
...IS HERE, BUT THE FIRE...?
...IS OUT! THE CURTAINS SMOTHERED THE FLAMES.
JUST AS I'D HOPED.
PERFECT. AND THANKS.
I GUESS YOU COULD SAY IT WAS CURTAINS FOR THE CURTAINS.
YOU COULD.
IF YOU HAD TO.

HMM. I'M AFRAID THE FOG MACHINE ISN'T GOING TO GIVE US ANY CLUES--
--AS TO WHETHER IT WAS DELIBERATELY SABOTAGED OR NOT.
YEAH, SORRY ABOUT THAT.
I GUESS I SMASHED THE EVIDENCE.
YEAH, BUT IT SAVED OUR LIVES SO IT'S--
EEEEEEEEEEEEE!
WHA--?!
IT SOUNDS LIKE FARAH!

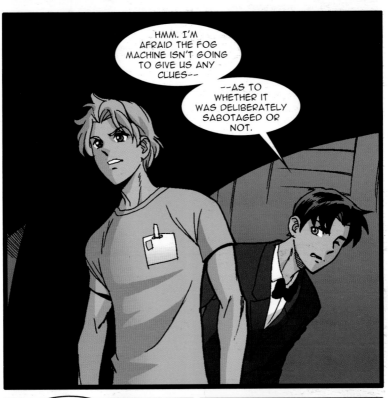

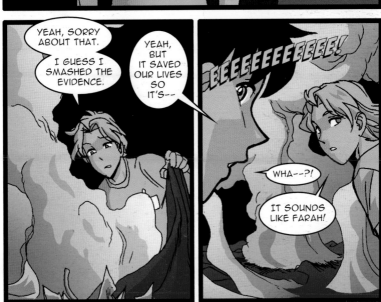

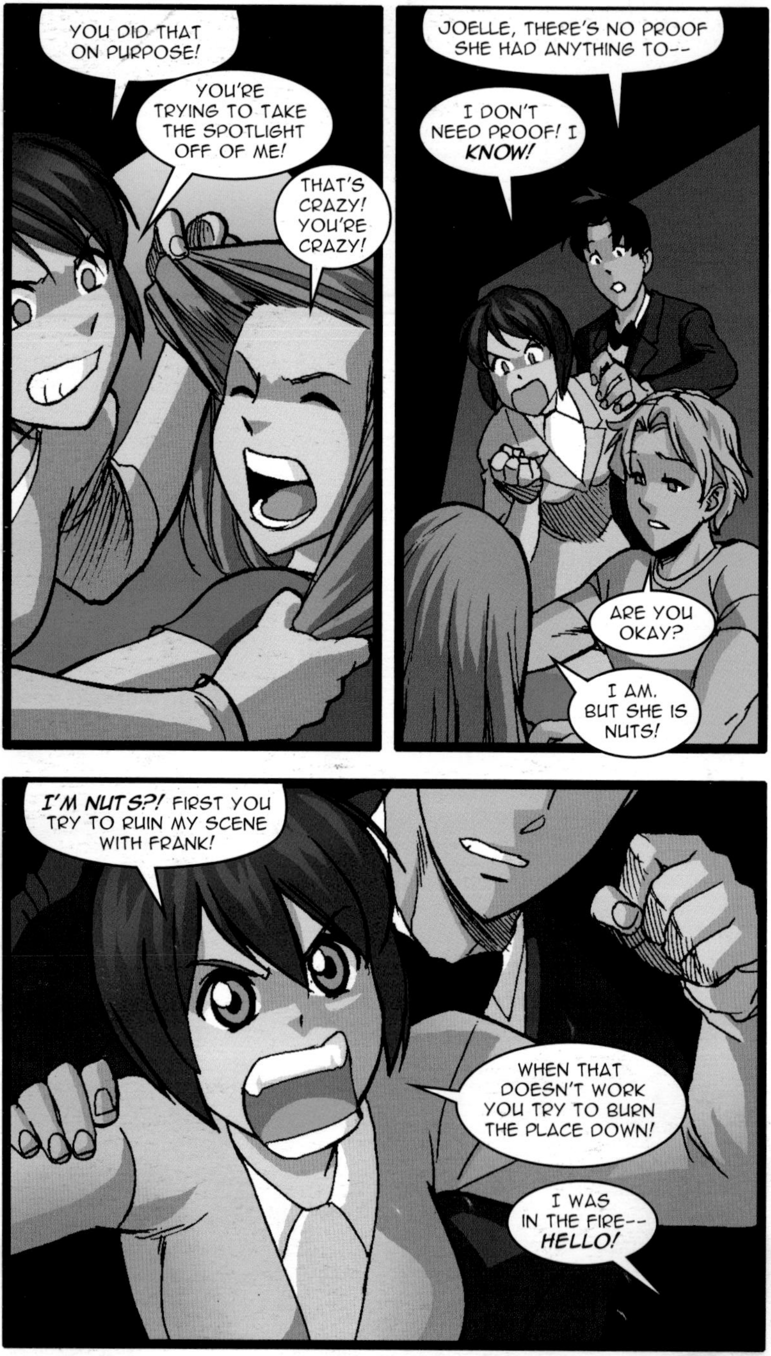
YOU DID THAT ON PURPOSE!
YOU'RE TRYING TO TAKE THE SPOTLIGHT OFF OF ME!
THAT'S CRAZY! YOU'RE CRAZY!
JOELLE, THERE'S NO PROOF SHE HAD ANYTHING TO--
I DON'T NEED PROOF! I *KNOW!*
ARE YOU OKAY?
I AM. BUT SHE IS NUTS!
I'M NUTS?! FIRST YOU TRY TO RUIN MY SCENE WITH FRANK!
WHEN THAT DOESN'T WORK YOU TRY TO BURN THE PLACE DOWN!
I WAS IN THE FIRE-- *HELLO!*

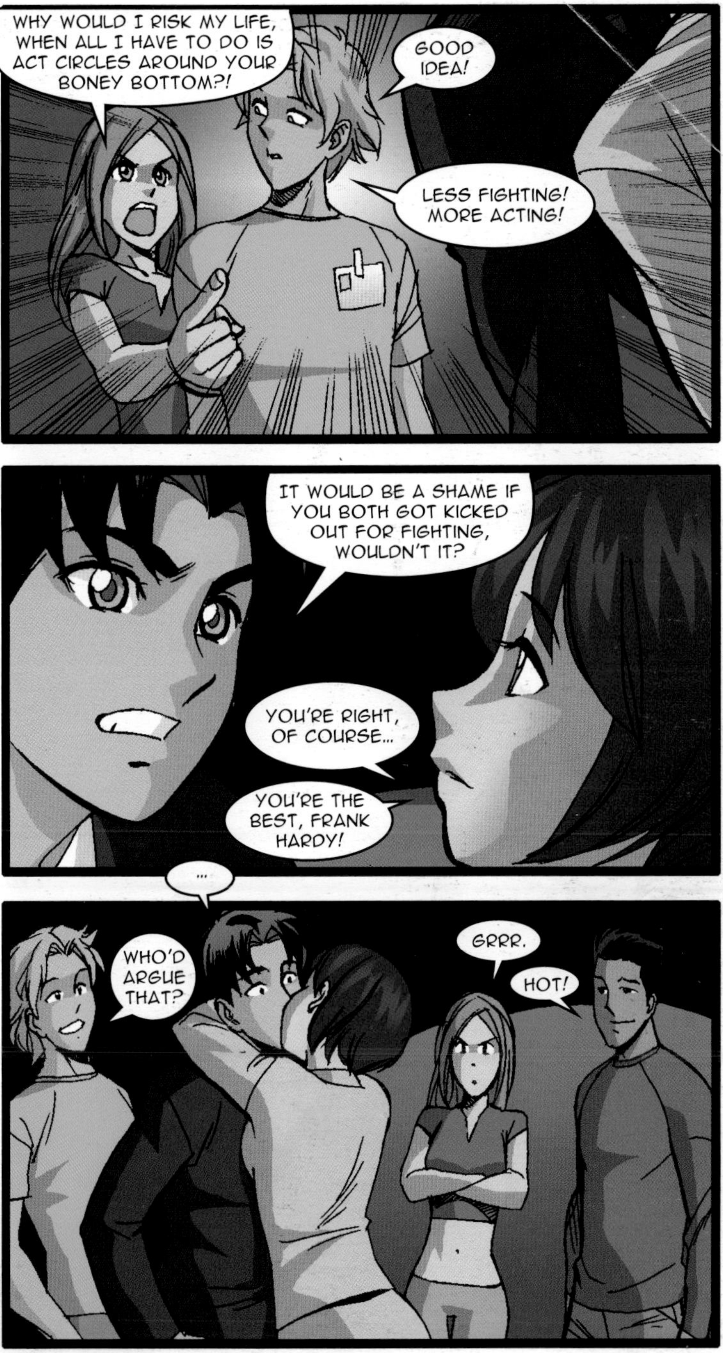
WHY WOULD I RISK MY LIFE, WHEN ALL I HAVE TO DO IS ACT CIRCLES AROUND YOUR BONEY BOTTOM?!
GOOD IDEA!
LESS FIGHTING! MORE ACTING!
IT WOULD BE A SHAME IF YOU BOTH GOT KICKED OUT FOR FIGHTING, WOULDN'T IT?
YOU'RE RIGHT, OF COURSE...
YOU'RE THE BEST, FRANK HARDY!
...
WHO'D ARGUE THAT?
GRRR.
HOT!

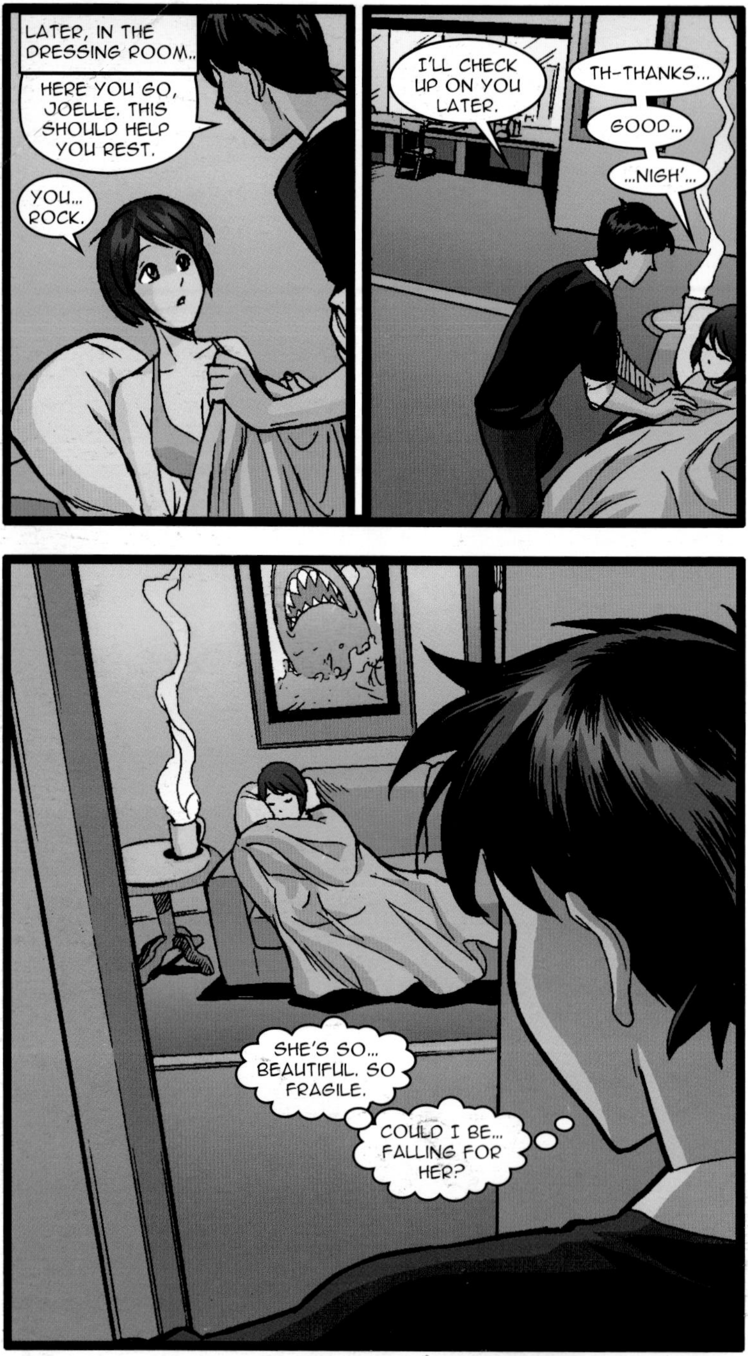
LATER, IN THE DRESSING ROOM...
HERE YOU GO, JOELLE. THIS SHOULD HELP YOU REST.
YOU... ROCK.
I'LL CHECK UP ON YOU LATER.
TH-THANKS...
GOOD...
...NIGH'...
SHE'S SO... BEAUTIFUL. SO FRAGILE.
COULD I BE... FALLING FOR HER?

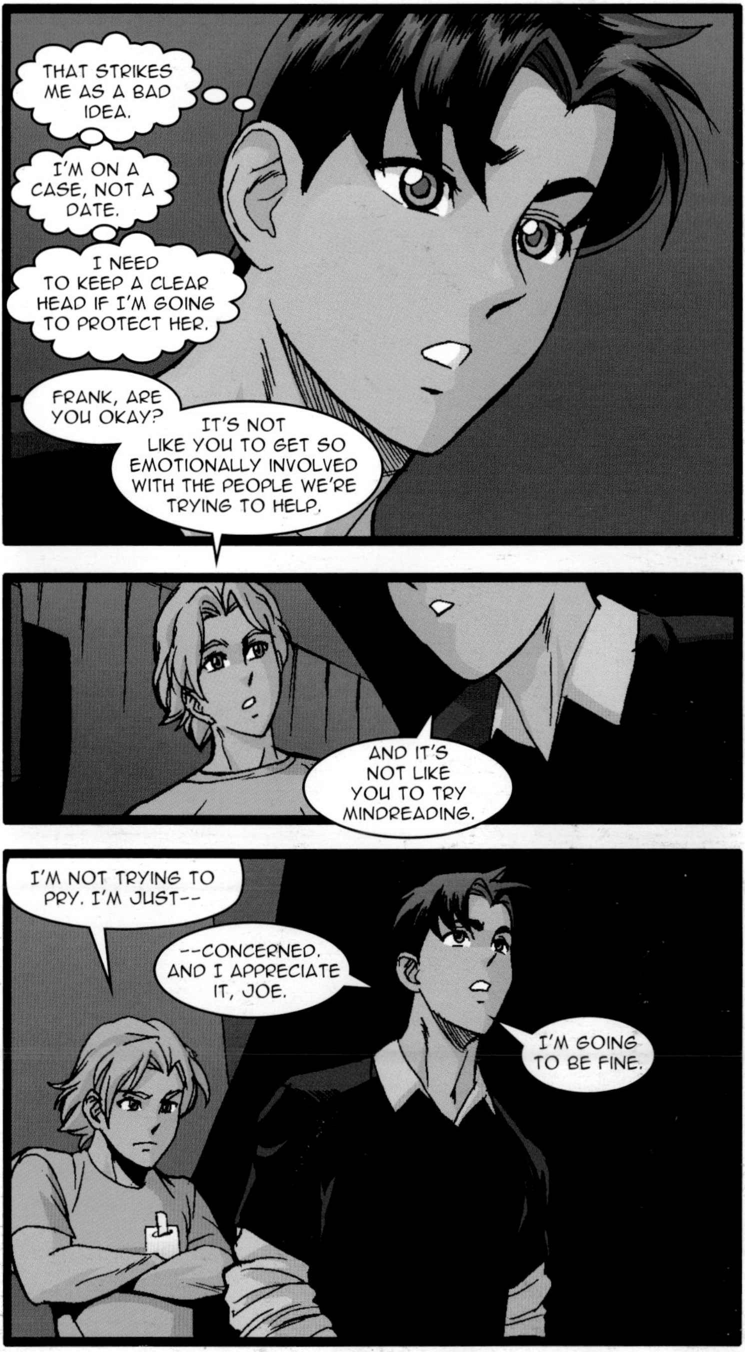
THAT STRIKES ME AS A BAD IDEA.
I'M ON A CASE, NOT A DATE.
I NEED TO KEEP A CLEAR HEAD IF I'M GOING TO PROTECT HER.
FRANK, ARE YOU OKAY?
IT'S NOT LIKE YOU TO GET SO EMOTIONALLY INVOLVED WITH THE PEOPLE WE'RE TRYING TO HELP.
AND IT'S NOT LIKE YOU TO TRY MINDREADING.
I'M NOT TRYING TO PRY. I'M JUST--
--CONCERNED. AND I APPRECIATE IT, JOE.
I'M GOING TO BE FINE.

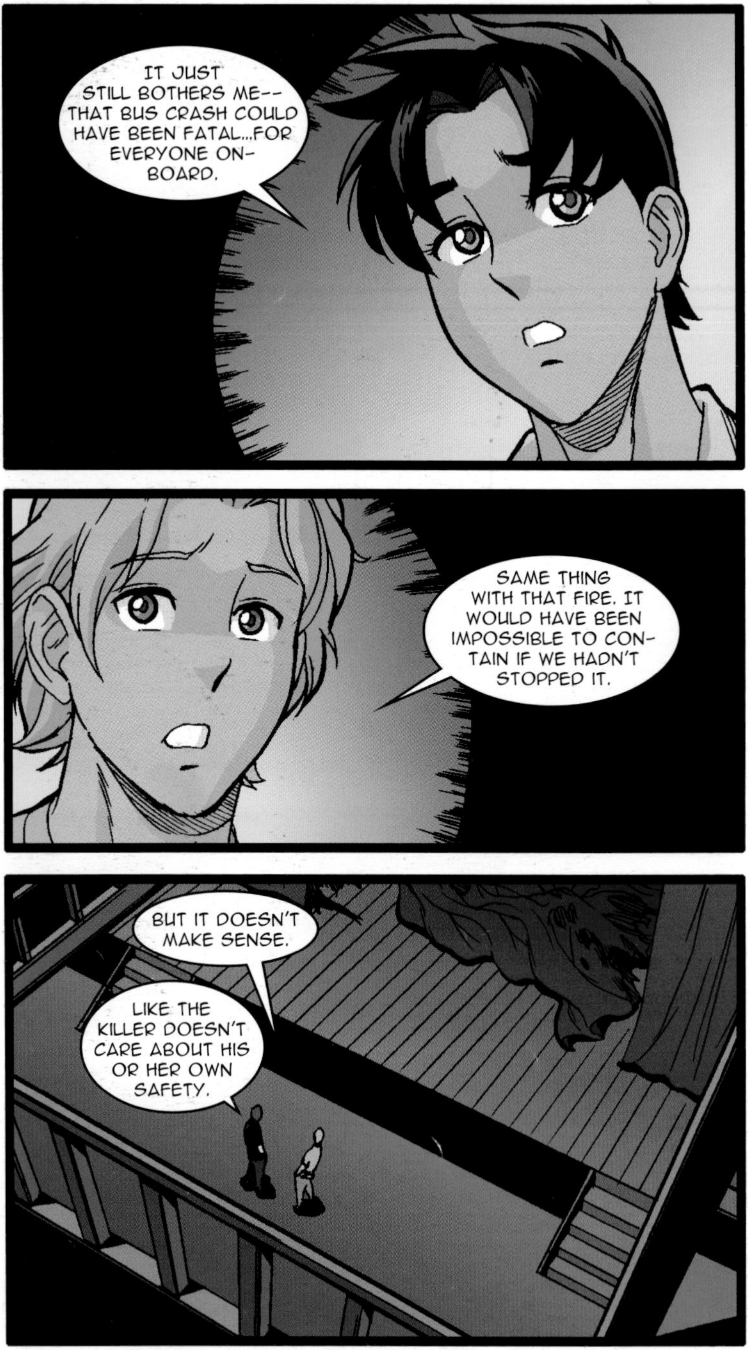
IT JUST STILL BOTHERS ME-- THAT BUS CRASH COULD HAVE BEEN FATAL...FOR EVERYONE ON-BOARD.
SAME THING WITH THAT FIRE. IT WOULD HAVE BEEN IMPOSSIBLE TO CON-TAIN IF WE HADN'T STOPPED IT.
BUT IT DOESN'T MAKE SENSE.
LIKE THE KILLER DOESN'T CARE ABOUT HIS OR HER OWN SAFETY.

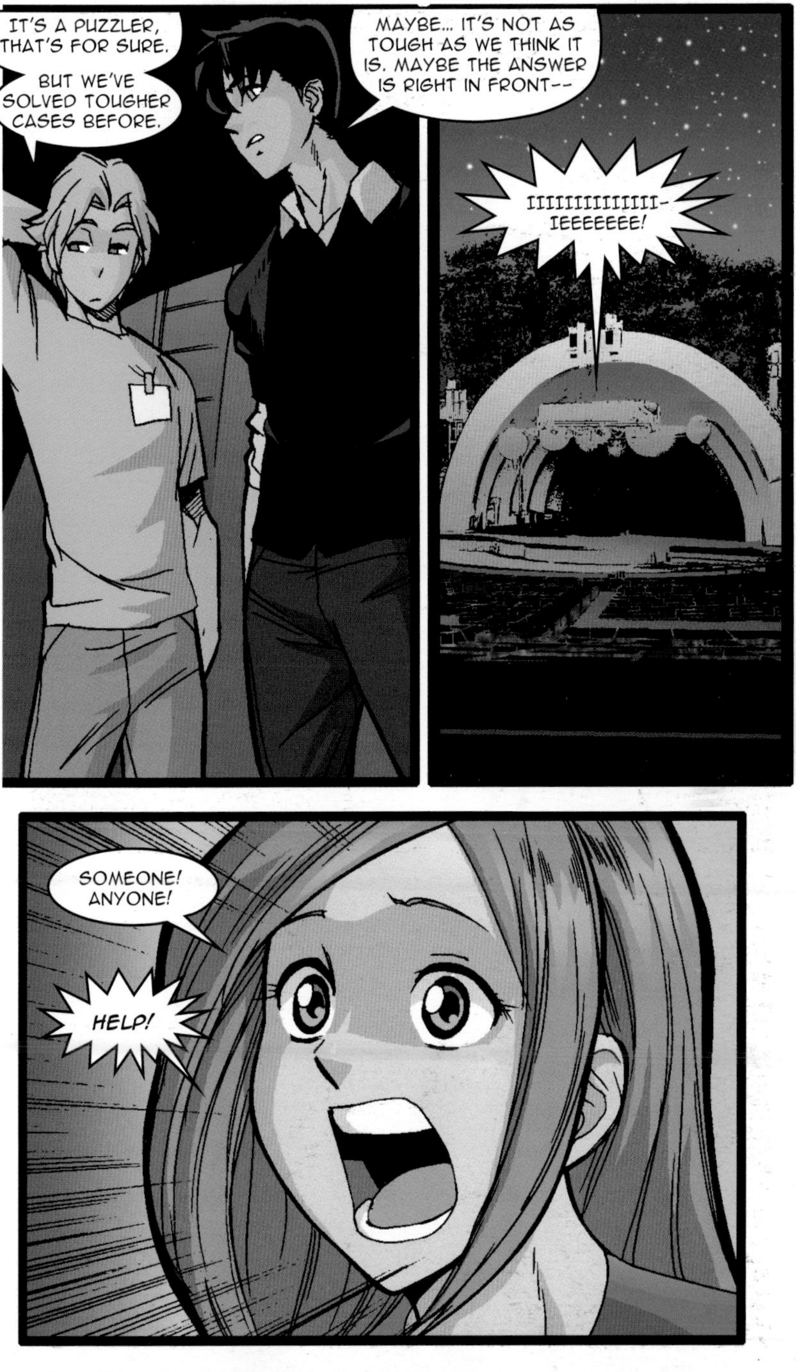
IT'S A PUZZLER, THAT'S FOR SURE.
BUT WE'VE SOLVED TOUGHER CASES BEFORE.
MAYBE... IT'S NOT AS TOUGH AS WE THINK IT IS. MAYBE THE ANSWER IS RIGHT IN FRONT--
IIIIIIIIIIIII-IEEEEEEE!
SOMEONE! ANYONE!
HELP!

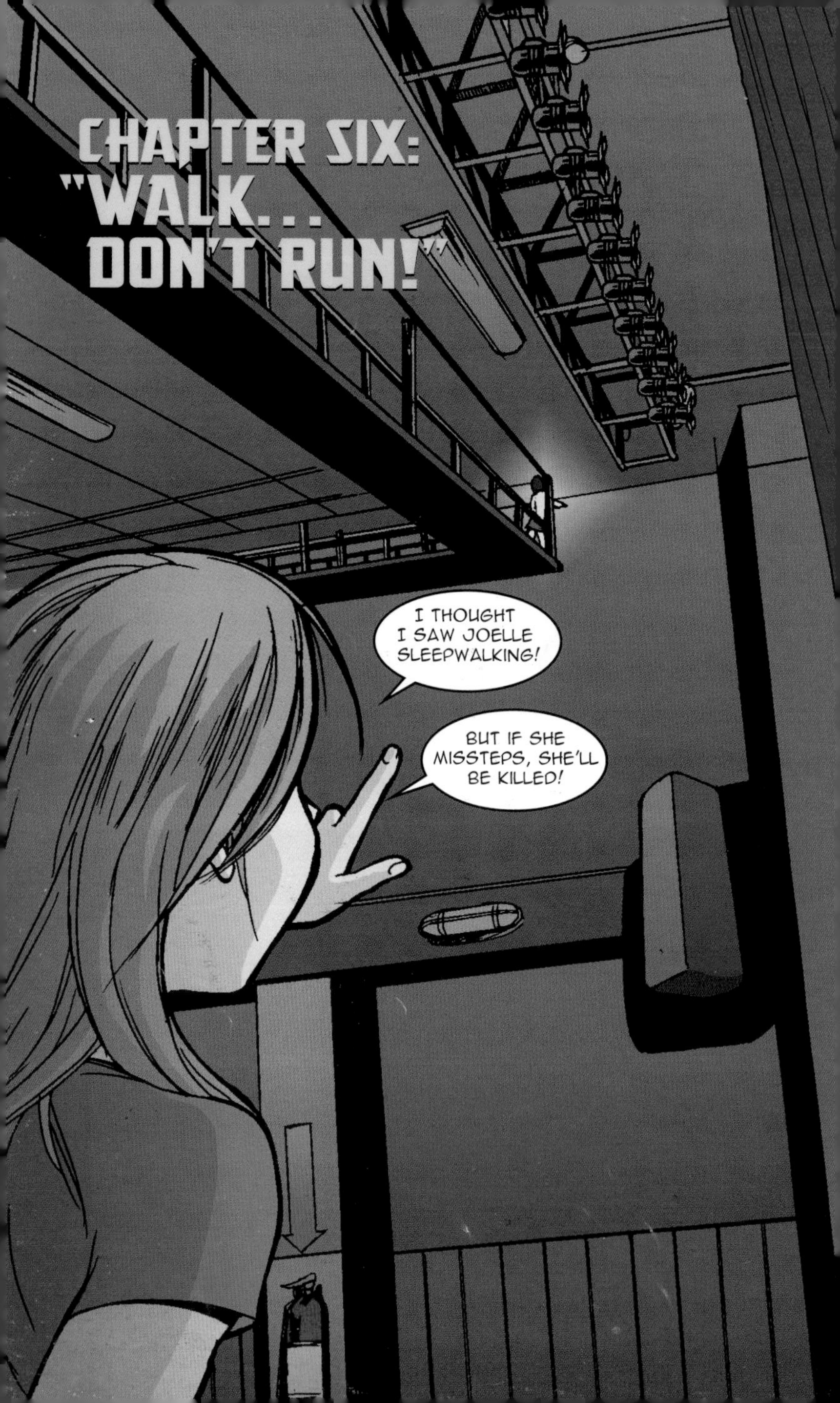
CHAPTER SIX:
"WALK... DON'T RUN!"
I THOUGHT I SAW JOELLE SLEEPWALKING!
BUT IF SHE MISSTEPS, SHE'LL BE KILLED!

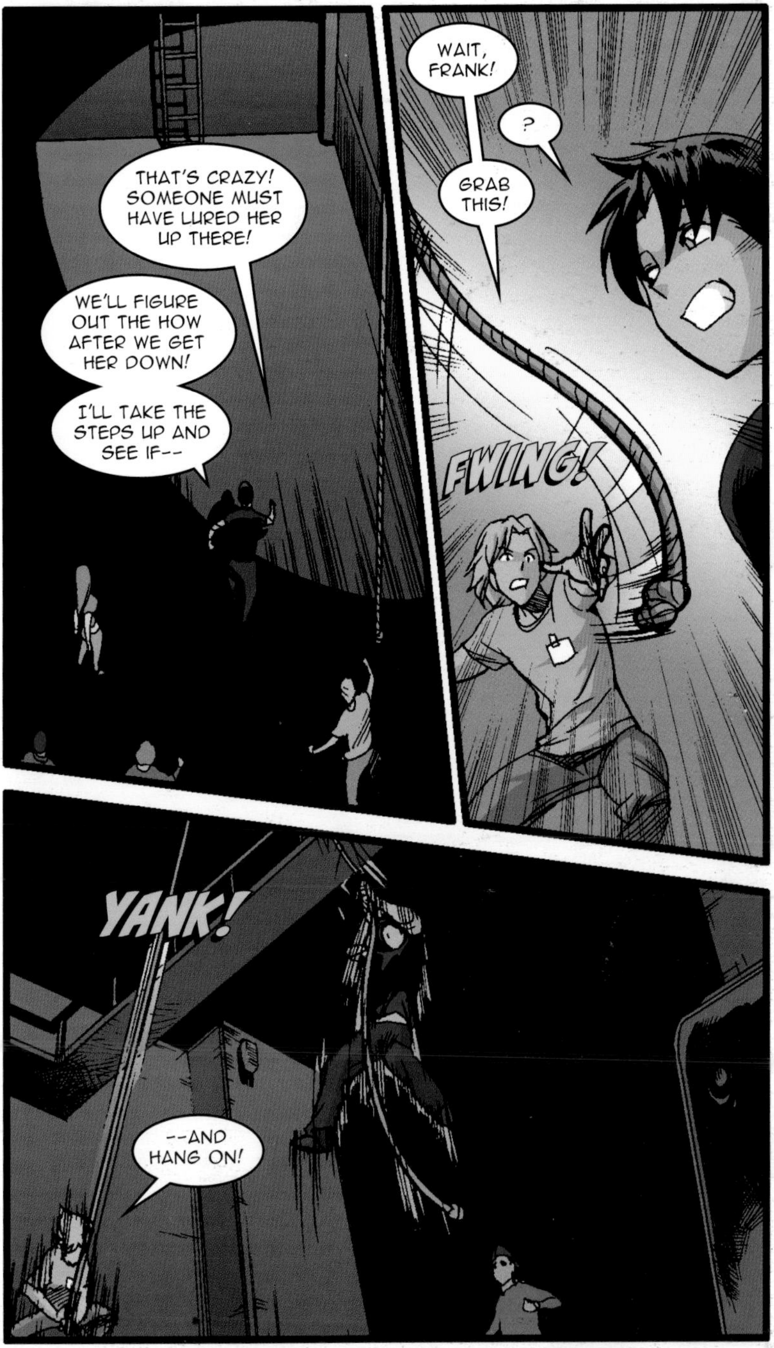
THAT'S CRAZY! SOMEONE MUST HAVE LURED HER UP THERE!
WE'LL FIGURE OUT THE HOW AFTER WE GET HER DOWN!
I'LL TAKE THE STEPS UP AND SEE IF--
WAIT, FRANK!
?
GRAB THIS!
FWING!
YANK!
--AND HANG ON!

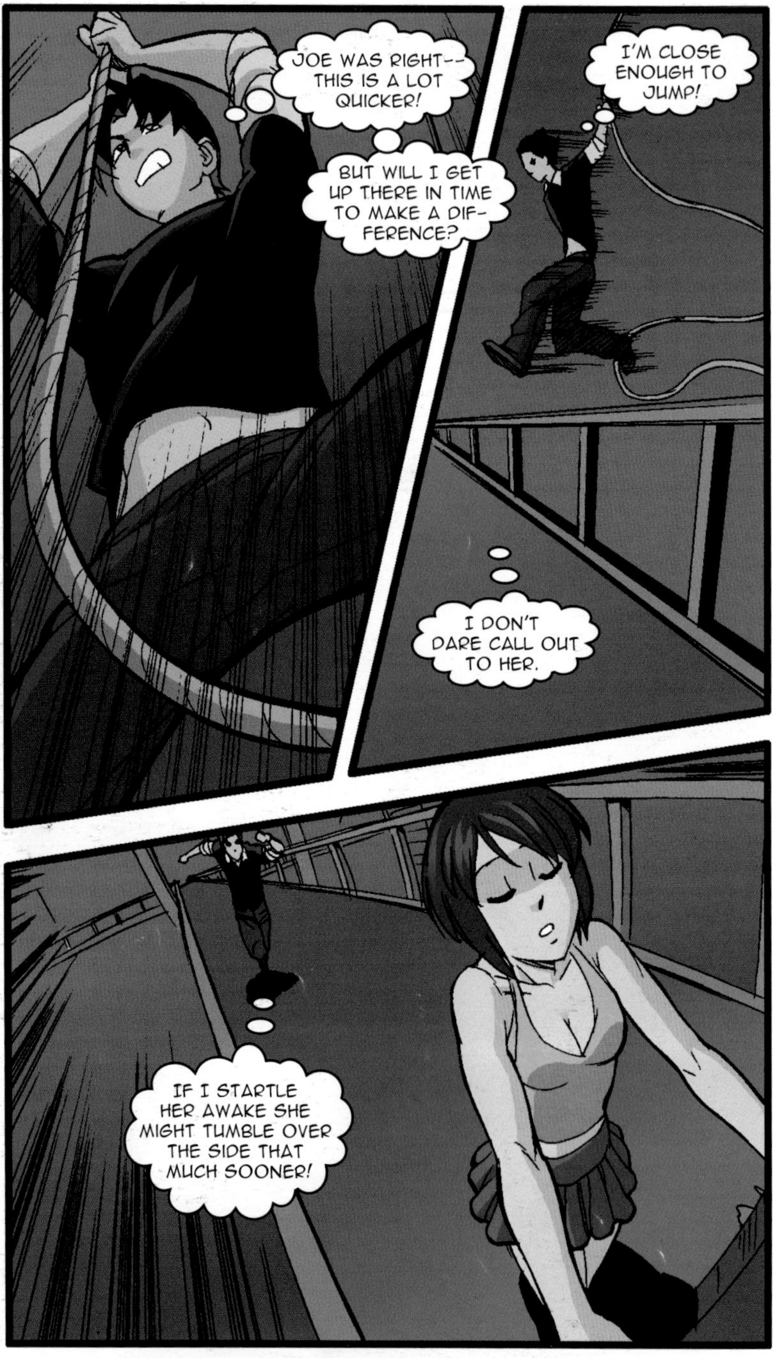
JOE WAS RIGHT--
THIS IS A LOT
QUICKER!
BUT WILL I GET
UP THERE IN TIME
TO MAKE A DIF-
FERENCE?
I'M CLOSE
ENOUGH TO
JUMP!
I DON'T
DARE CALL OUT
TO HER.
IF I STARTLE
HER AWAKE SHE
MIGHT TUMBLE OVER
THE SIDE THAT
MUCH SOONER!

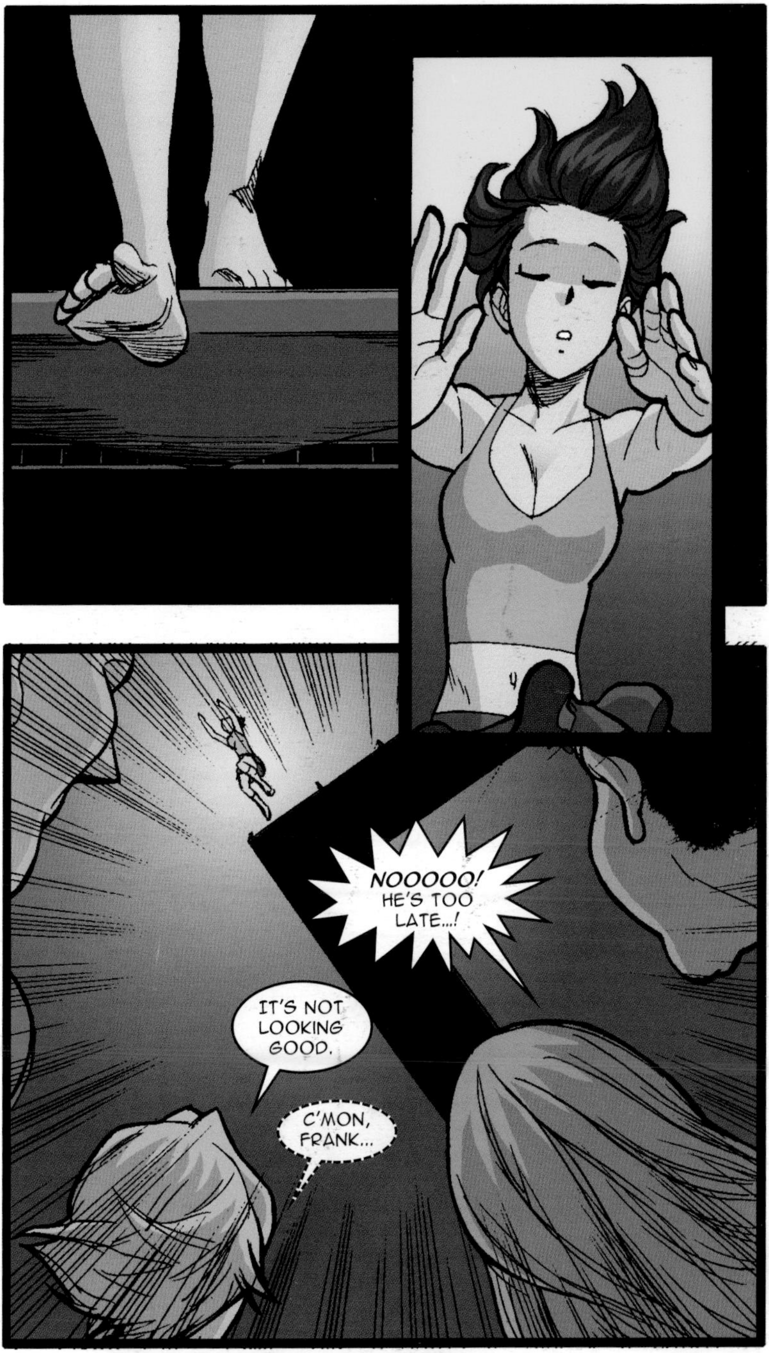
NOOOOO!
HE'S TOO
LATE...!
IT'S NOT
LOOKING
GOOD.
C'MON,
FRANK...

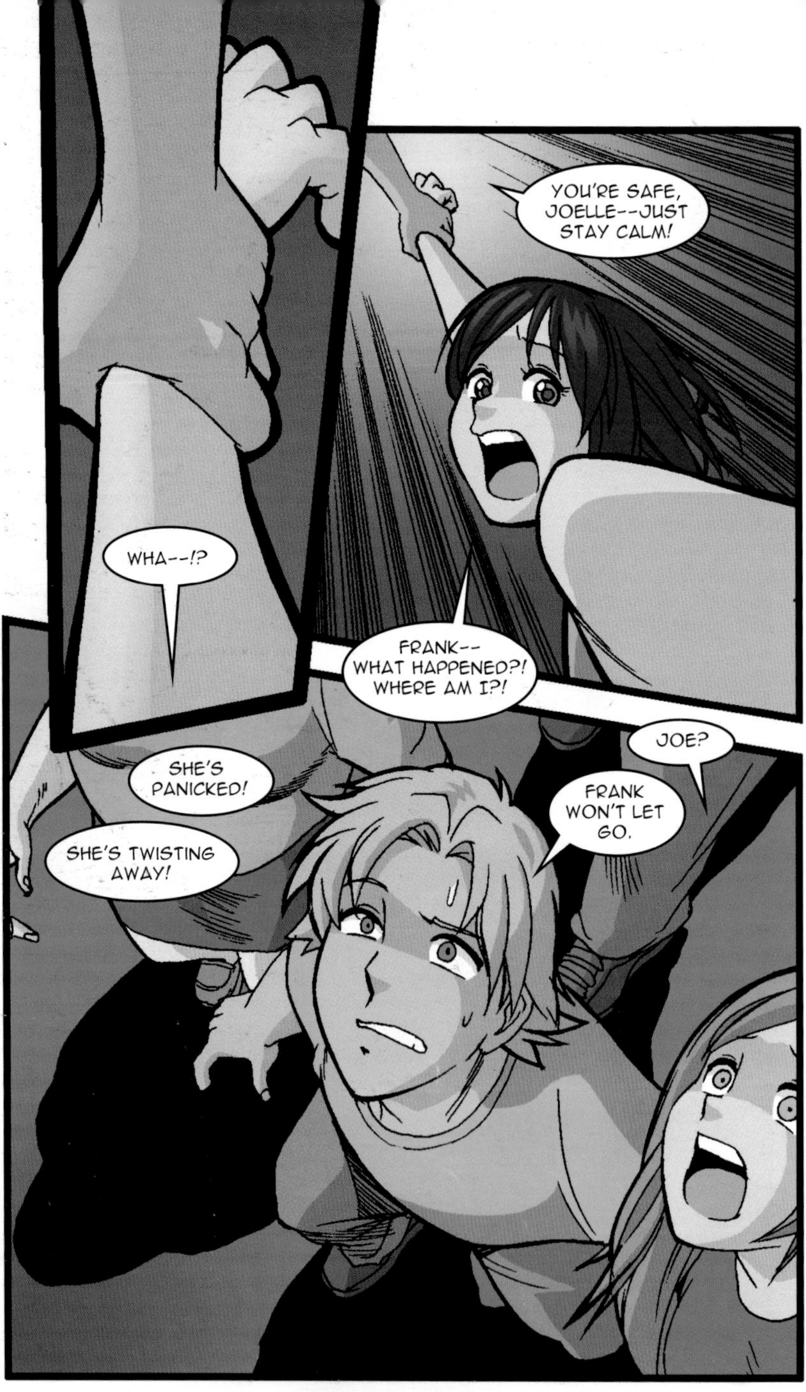

YOU'RE SAFE, JOELLE--JUST STAY CALM!
WHA--!?
FRANK-- WHAT HAPPENED?! WHERE AM I?!
JOE?
SHE'S PANICKED!
FRANK WON'T LET GO.
SHE'S TWISTING AWAY!

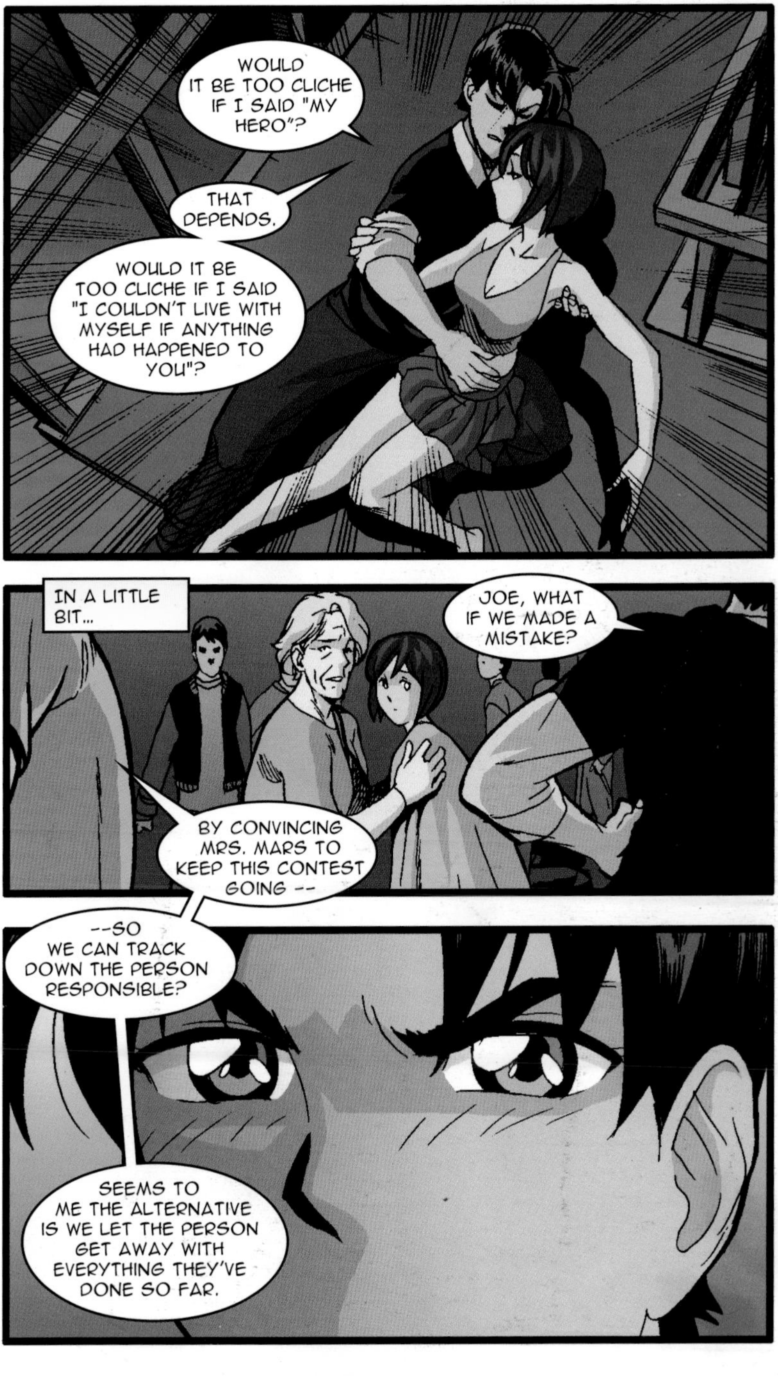
WOULD IT BE TOO CLICHE IF I SAID "MY HERO"?
THAT DEPENDS.
WOULD IT BE TOO CLICHE IF I SAID "I COULDN'T LIVE WITH MYSELF IF ANYTHING HAD HAPPENED TO YOU"?
IN A LITTLE BIT...
JOE, WHAT IF WE MADE A MISTAKE?
BY CONVINCING MRS. MARS TO KEEP THIS CONTEST GOING --
--SO WE CAN TRACK DOWN THE PERSON RESPONSIBLE?
SEEMS TO ME THE ALTERNATIVE IS WE LET THE PERSON GET AWAY WITH EVERYTHING THEY'VE DONE SO FAR.

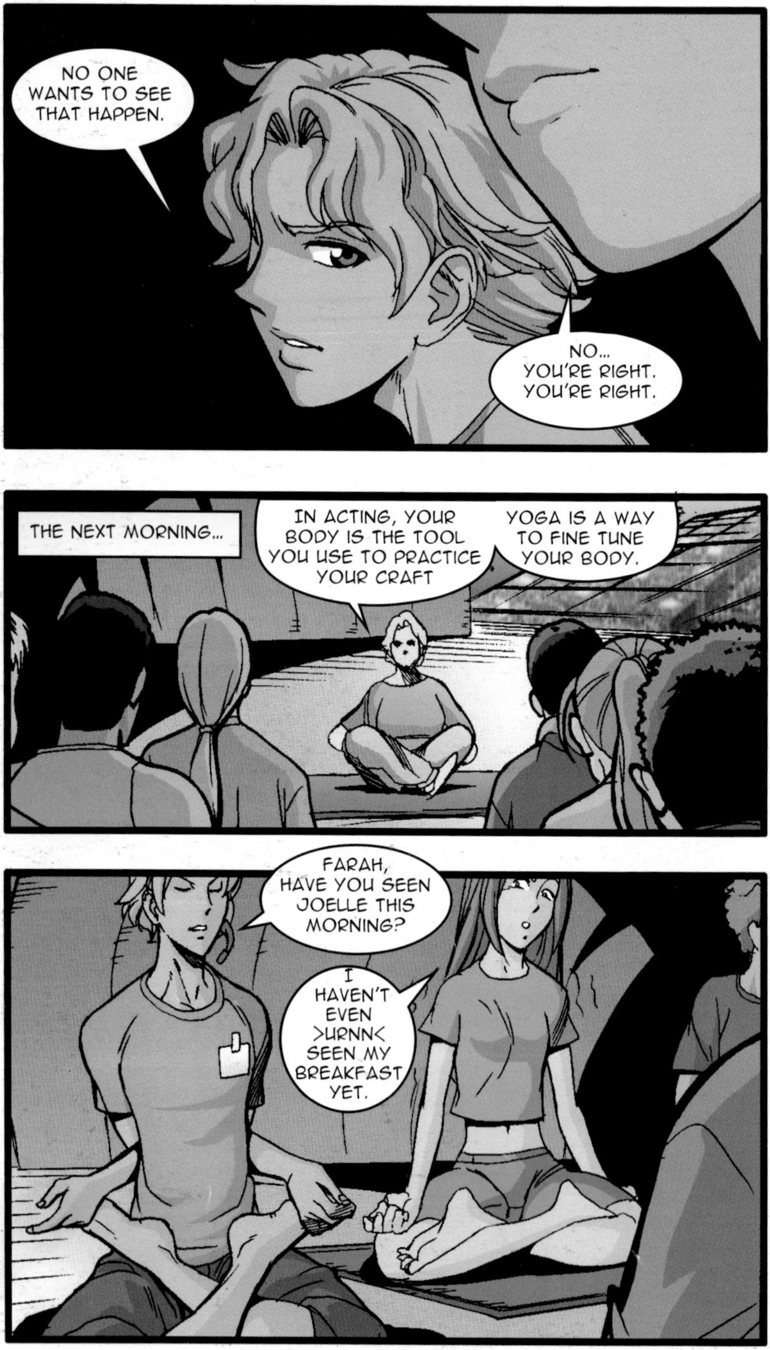

NO ONE WANTS TO SEE THAT HAPPEN.
NO... YOU'RE RIGHT. YOU'RE RIGHT.
THE NEXT MORNING...
IN ACTING, YOUR BODY IS THE TOOL YOU USE TO PRACTICE YOUR CRAFT
YOGA IS A WAY TO FINE TUNE YOUR BODY.
FARAH, HAVE YOU SEEN JOELLE THIS MORNING?
I HAVEN'T EVEN >URNN< SEEN MY BREAKFAST YET.

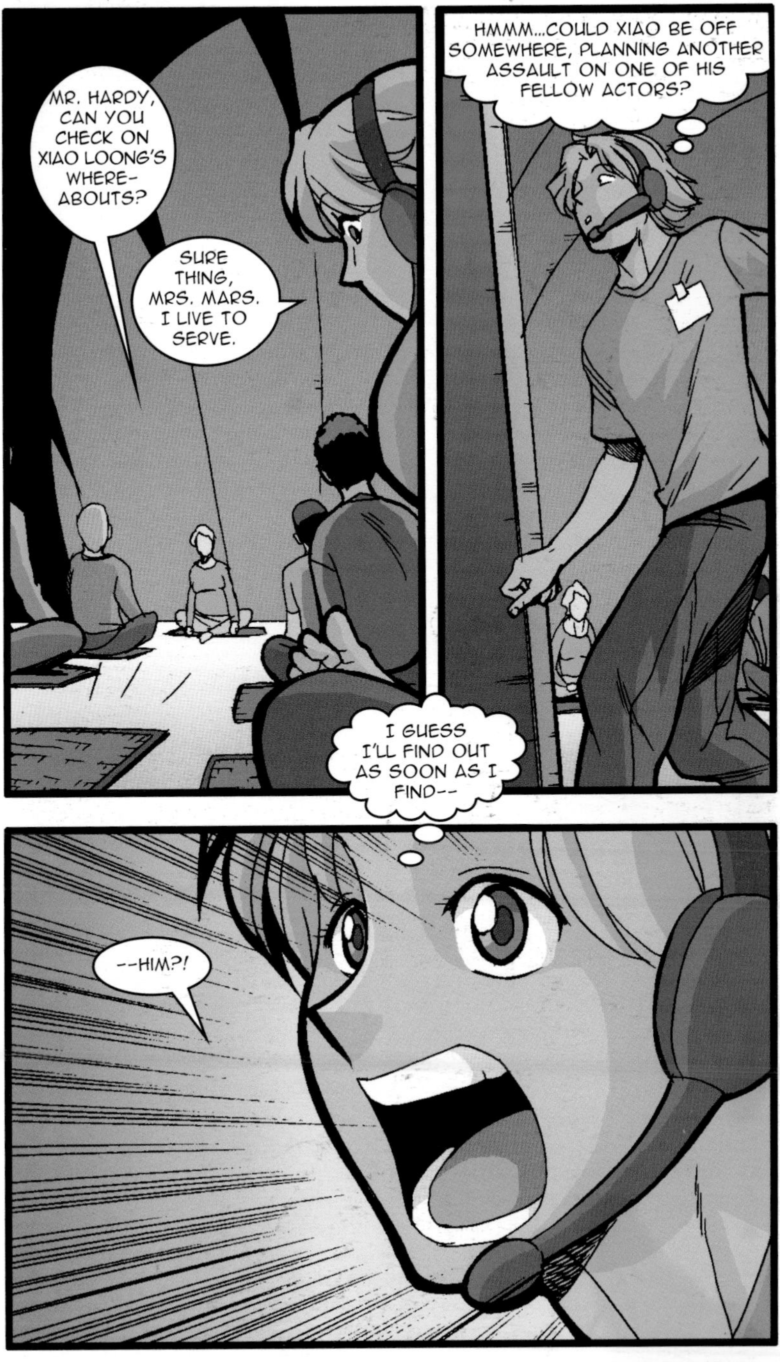
MR. HARDY, CAN YOU CHECK ON XIAO LOONG'S WHERE-ABOUTS?
SURE THING, MRS. MARS. I LIVE TO SERVE.
HMMM...COULD XIAO BE OFF SOMEWHERE, PLANNING ANOTHER ASSAULT ON ONE OF HIS FELLOW ACTORS?
I GUESS I'LL FIND OUT AS SOON AS I FIND--
--HIM?!

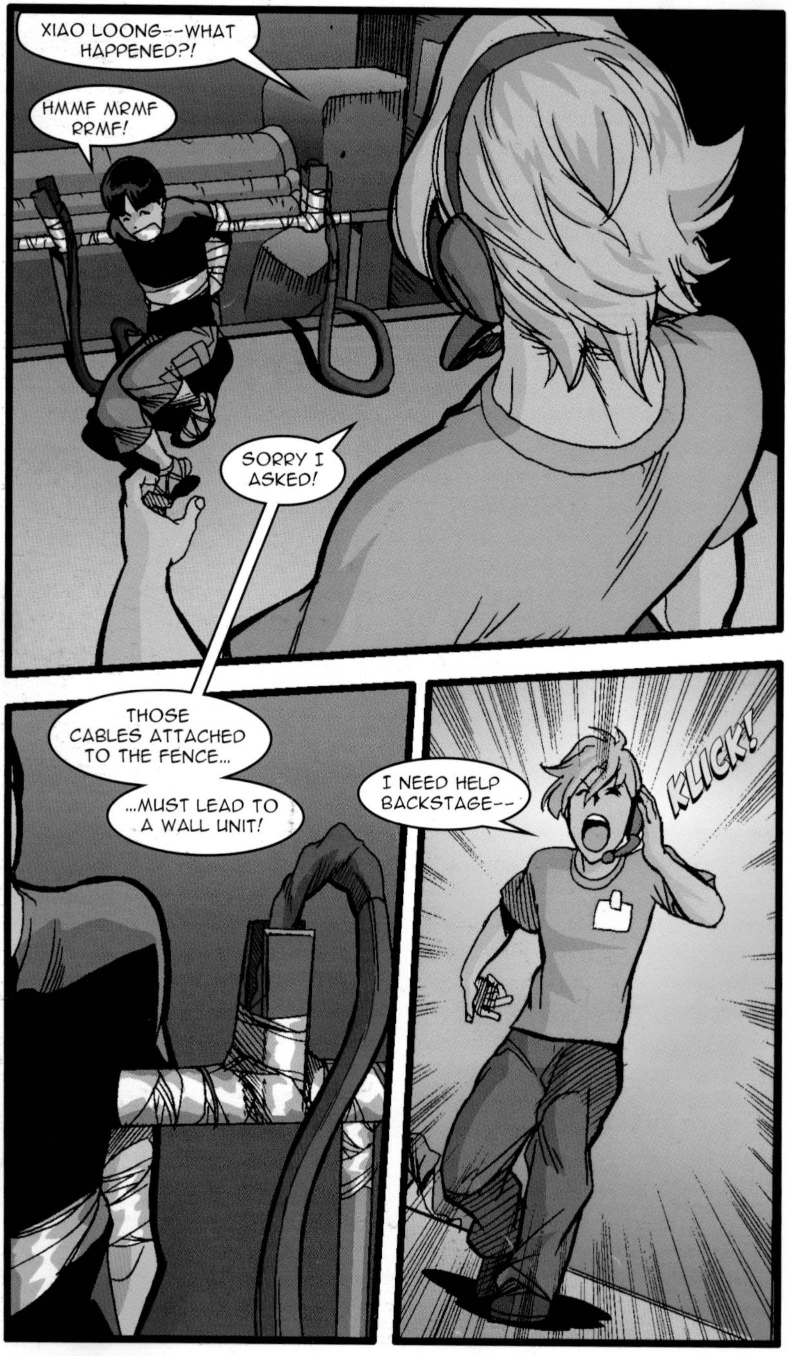
XIAO LOONG--WHAT HAPPENED?!
HMMF MRMF RRMF!
SORRY I ASKED!
THOSE CABLES ATTACHED TO THE FENCE...
...MUST LEAD TO A WALL UNIT!
I NEED HELP BACKSTAGE--
KLICK!

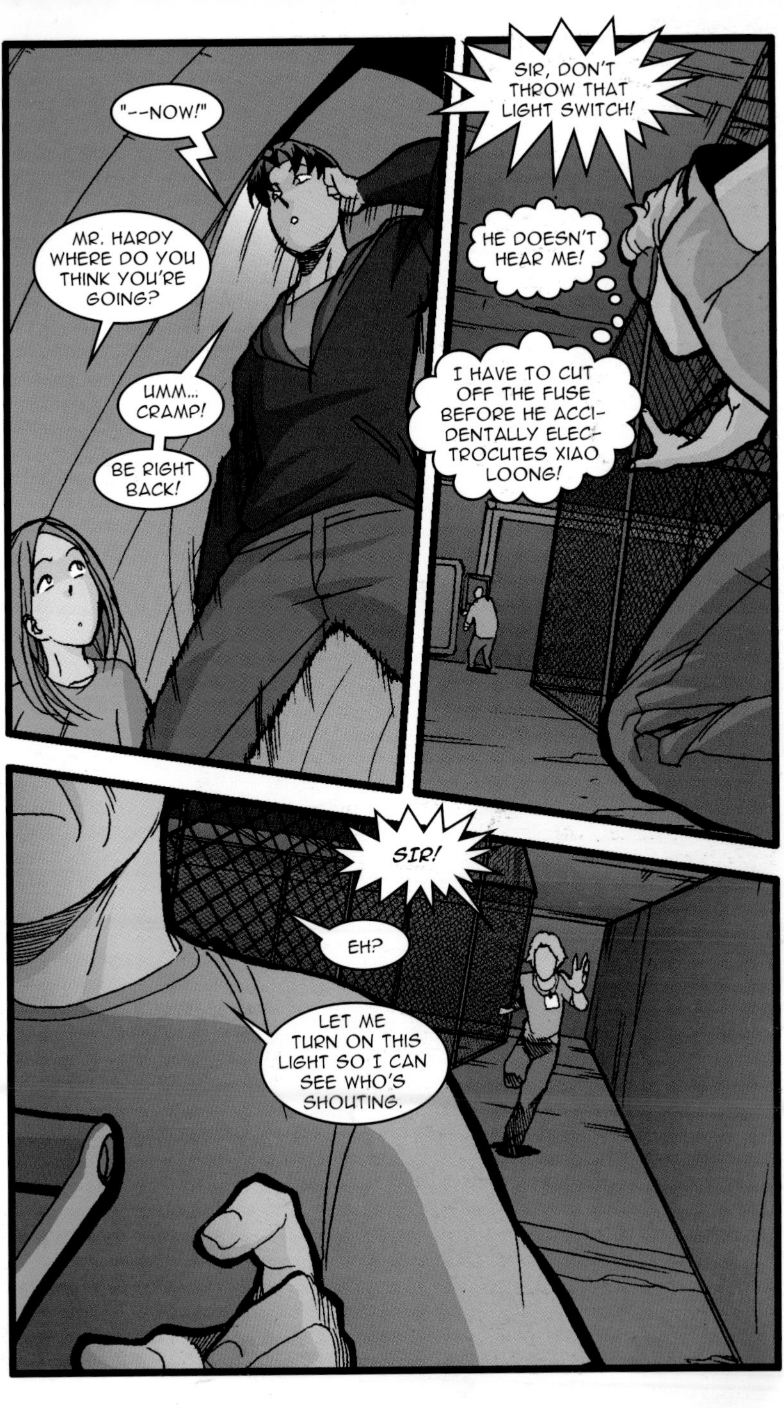
"--NOW!"
MR. HARDY WHERE DO YOU THINK YOU'RE GOING?
UMM... CRAMP!
BE RIGHT BACK!
SIR, DON'T THROW THAT LIGHT SWITCH!
HE DOESN'T HEAR ME!
I HAVE TO CUT OFF THE FUSE BEFORE HE ACCI-DENTALLY ELEC-TROCUTES XIAO LOONG!
SIR!
EH?
LET ME TURN ON THIS LIGHT SO I CAN SEE WHO'S SHOUTING.

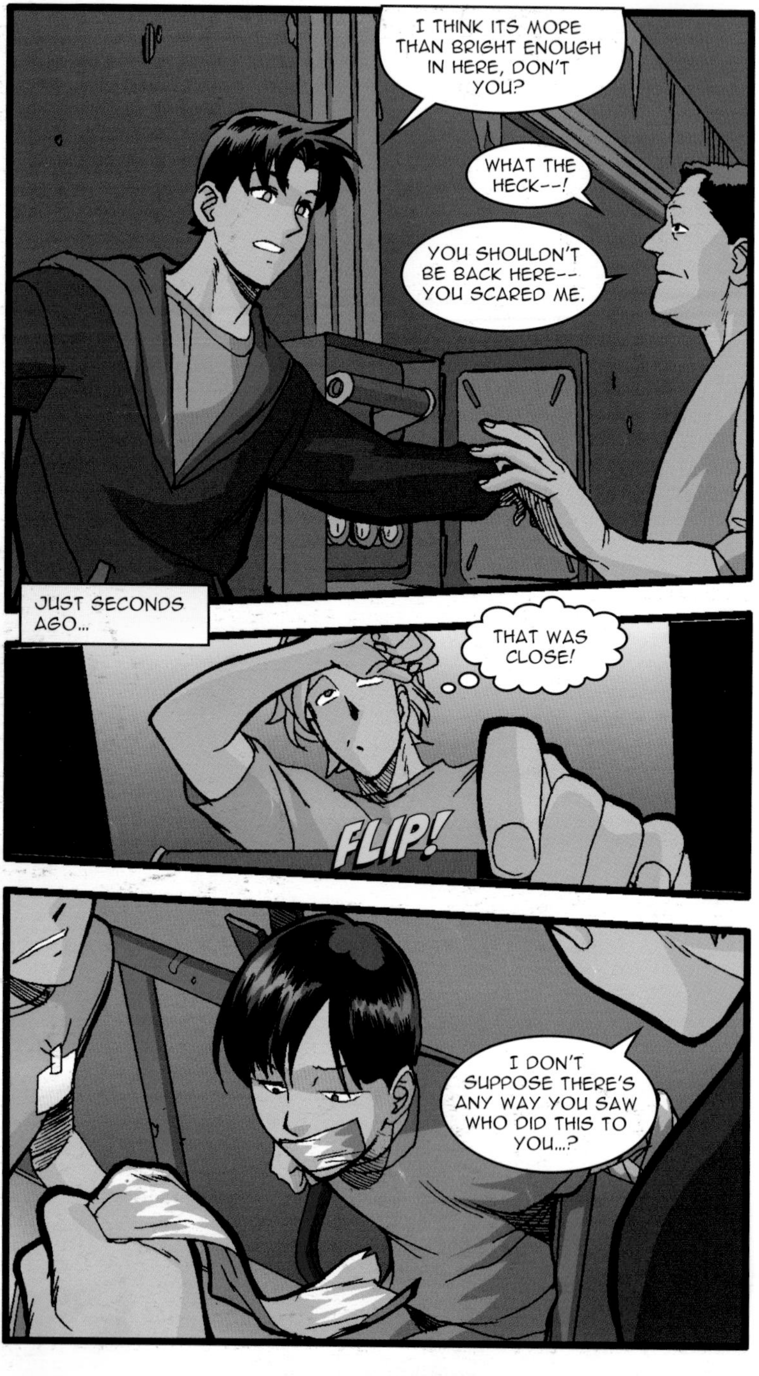
I THINK ITS MORE THAN BRIGHT ENOUGH IN HERE, DON'T YOU?
WHAT THE HECK--!
YOU SHOULDN'T BE BACK HERE-- YOU SCARED ME.
JUST SECONDS AGO...
THAT WAS CLOSE!
FLIP!
I DON'T SUPPOSE THERE'S ANY WAY YOU SAW WHO DID THIS TO YOU...?

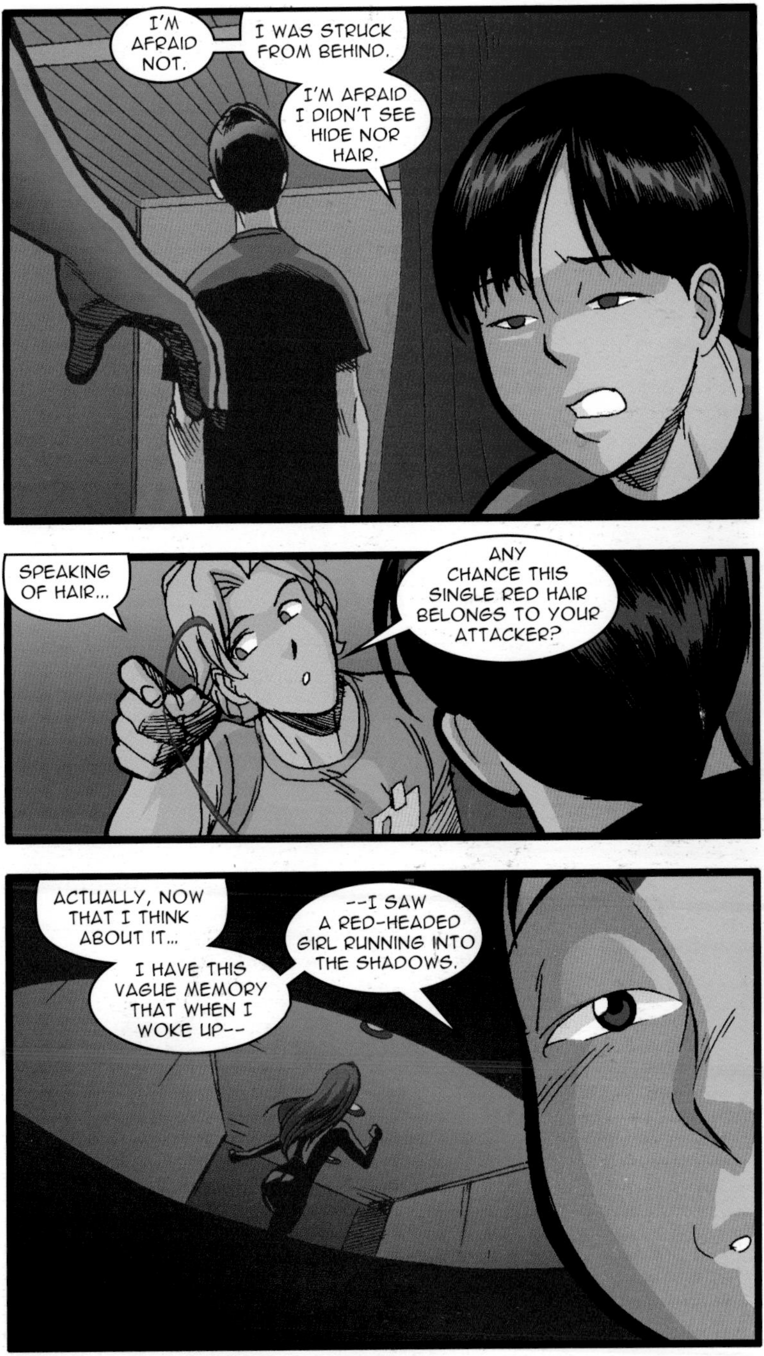
I'M AFRAID NOT.
I WAS STRUCK FROM BEHIND.
I'M AFRAID I DIDN'T SEE HIDE NOR HAIR.
SPEAKING OF HAIR...
ANY CHANCE THIS SINGLE RED HAIR BELONGS TO YOUR ATTACKER?
ACTUALLY, NOW THAT I THINK ABOUT IT...
I HAVE THIS VAGUE MEMORY THAT WHEN I WOKE UP--
--I SAW A RED-HEADED GIRL RUNNING INTO THE SHADOWS.

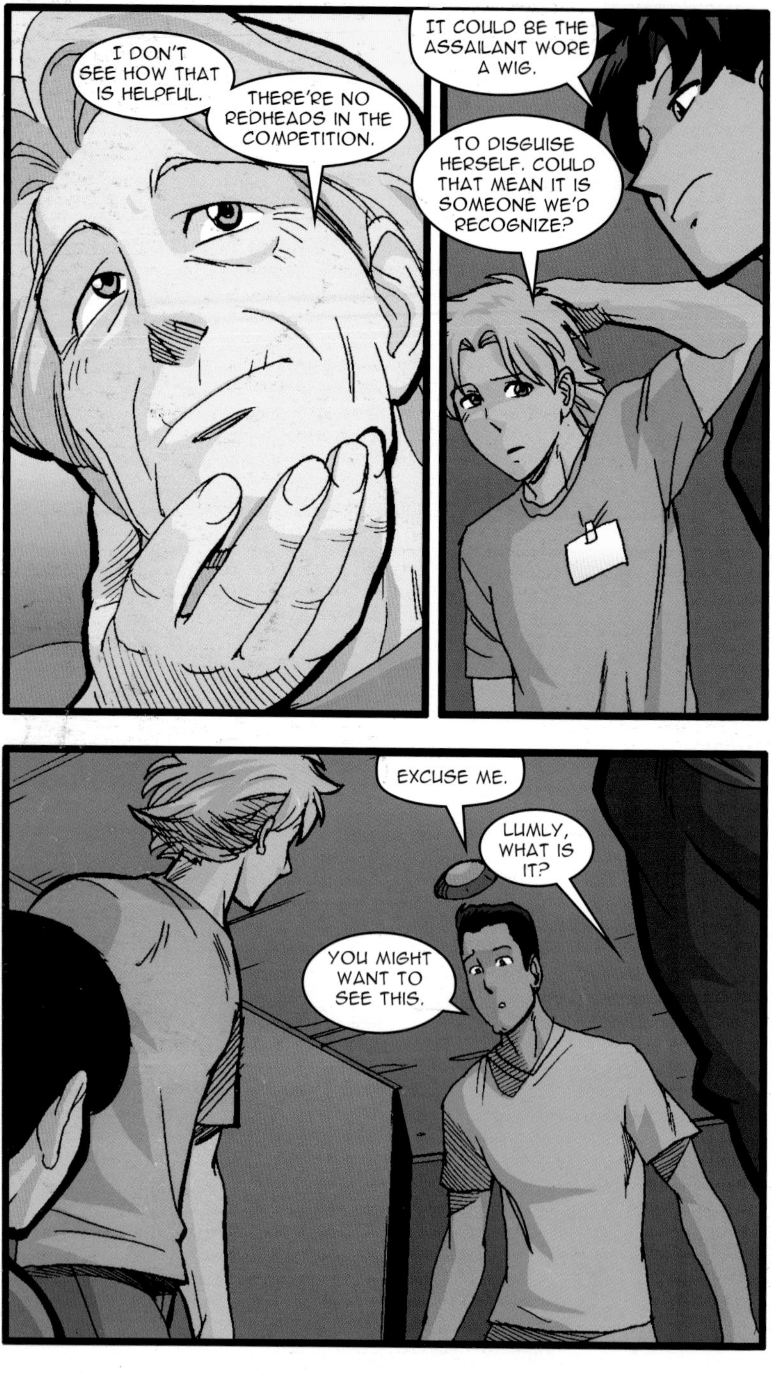
I DON'T SEE HOW THAT IS HELPFUL.
THERE'RE NO REDHEADS IN THE COMPETITION.
IT COULD BE THE ASSAILANT WORE A WIG.
TO DISGUISE HERSELF. COULD THAT MEAN IT IS SOMEONE WE'D RECOGNIZE?
EXCUSE ME.
LUMLY, WHAT IS IT?
YOU MIGHT WANT TO SEE THIS.

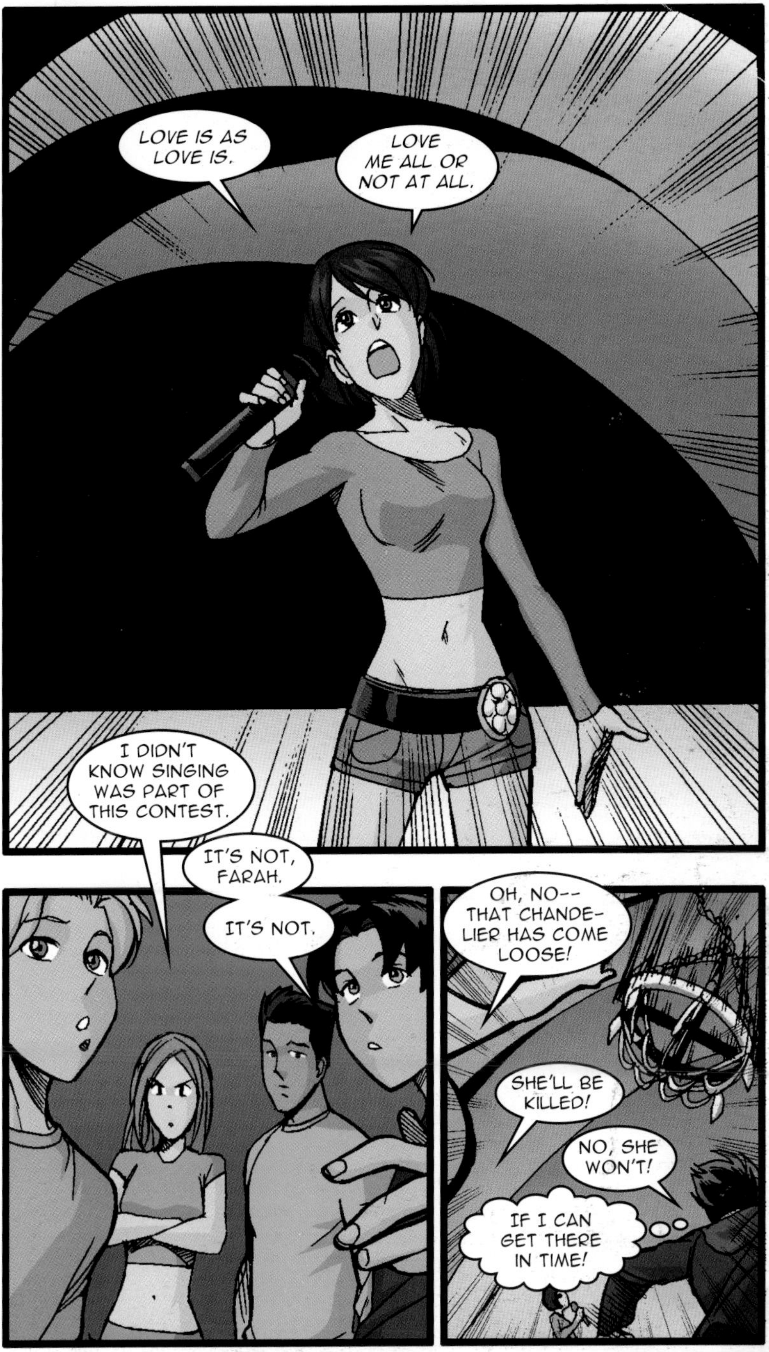
LOVE IS AS LOVE IS.
LOVE ME ALL OR NOT AT ALL.
I DIDN'T KNOW SINGING WAS PART OF THIS CONTEST.
IT'S NOT, FARAH.
IT'S NOT.
OH, NO-- THAT CHANDE-LIER HAS COME LOOSE!
SHE'LL BE KILLED!
NO, SHE WON'T!
IF I CAN GET THERE IN TIME!

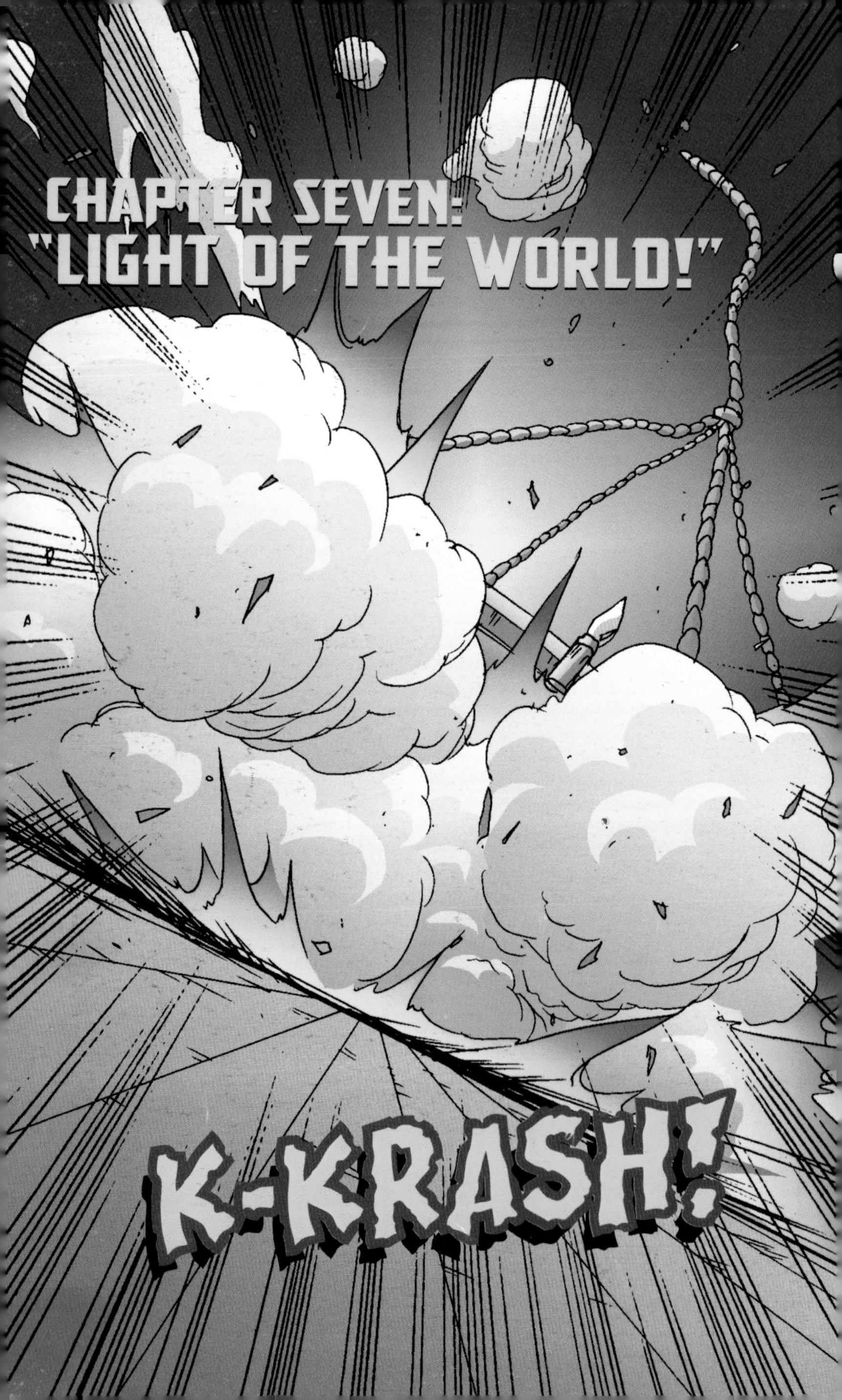
CHAPTER SEVEN:
"LIGHT OF THE WORLD!"
K-KRASH!

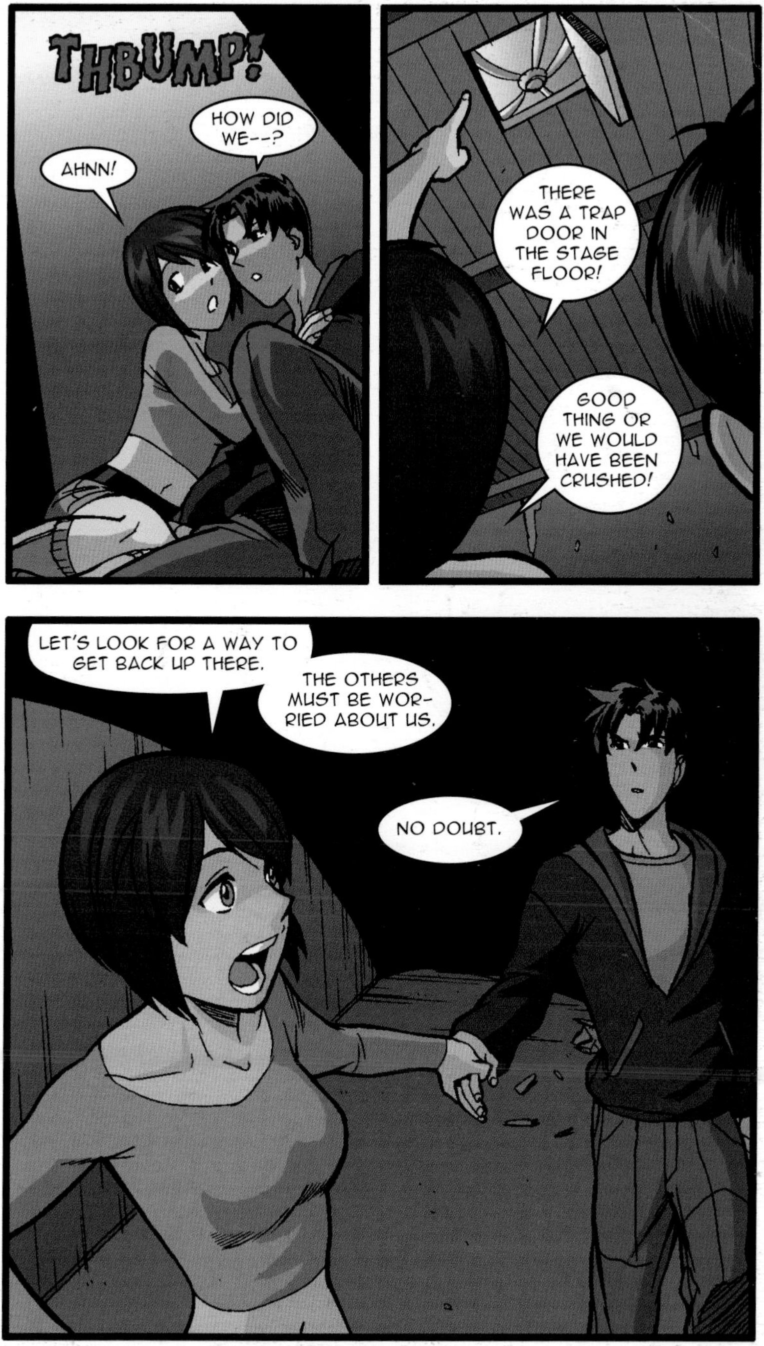
THBUMP!
HOW DID WE--?
AHNN!
THERE WAS A TRAP DOOR IN THE STAGE FLOOR!
GOOD THING OR WE WOULD HAVE BEEN CRUSHED!
LET'S LOOK FOR A WAY TO GET BACK UP THERE.
THE OTHERS MUST BE WOR-RIED ABOUT US.
NO DOUBT.

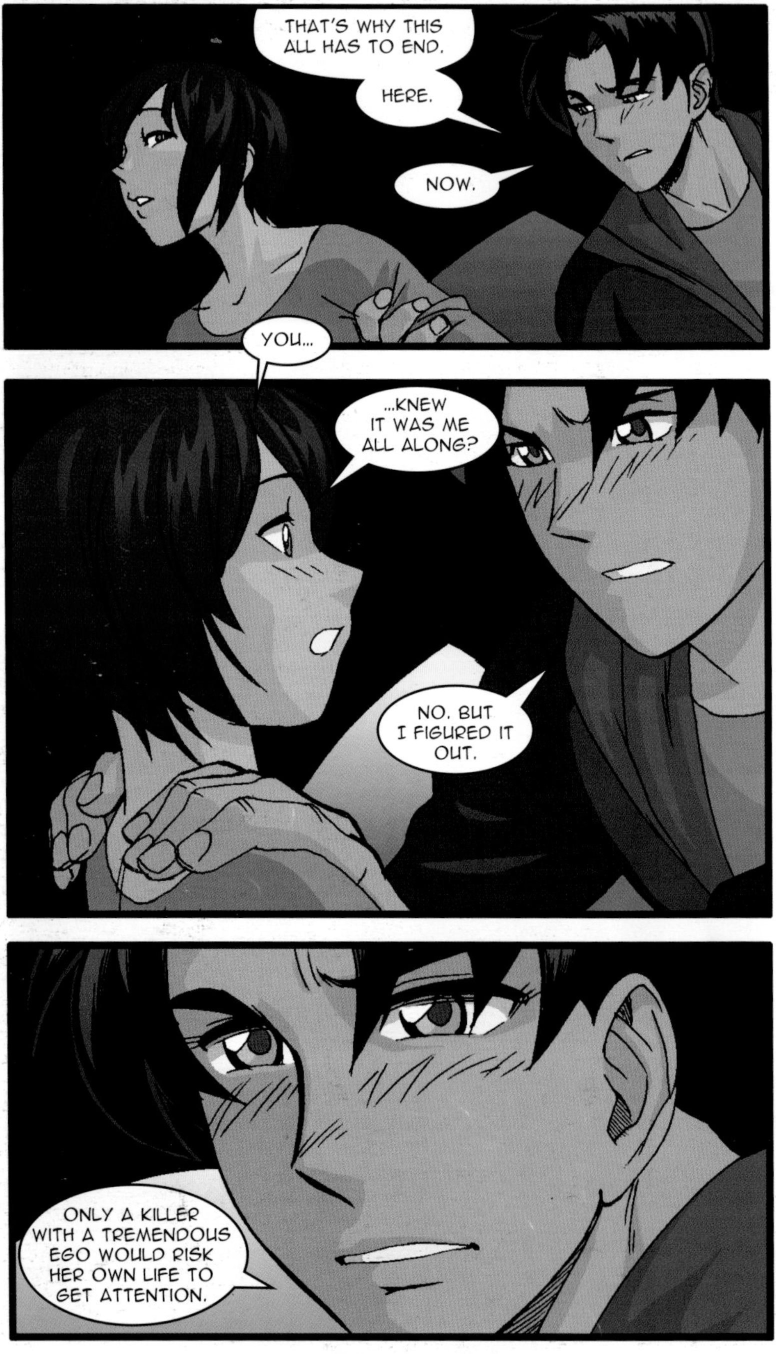
THAT'S WHY THIS ALL HAS TO END.
HERE.
NOW.
YOU...
...KNEW IT WAS ME ALL ALONG?
NO. BUT I FIGURED IT OUT.
ONLY A KILLER WITH A TREMENDOUS EGO WOULD RISK HER OWN LIFE TO GET ATTENTION.

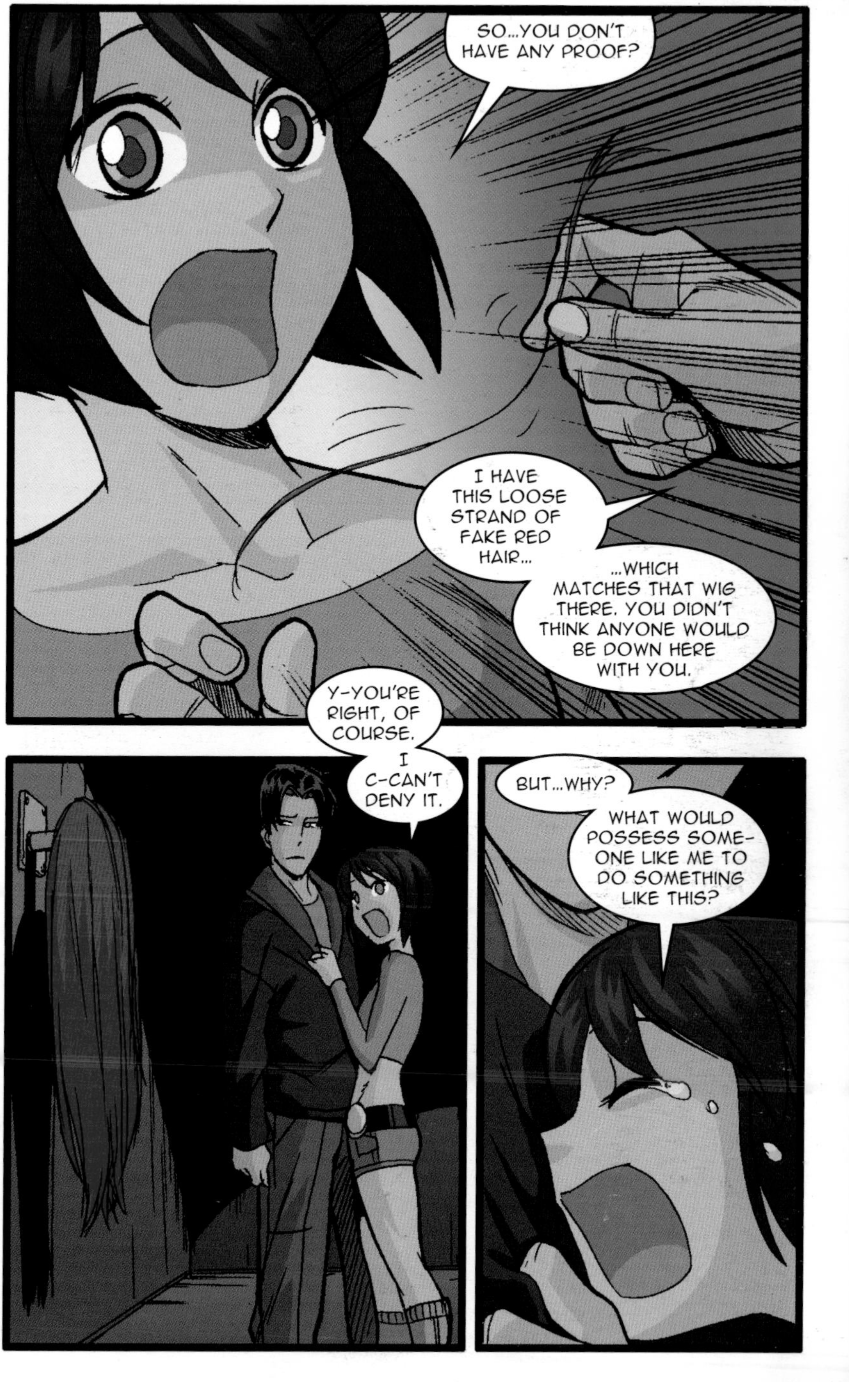
SO...YOU DON'T HAVE ANY PROOF?
I HAVE THIS LOOSE STRAND OF FAKE RED HAIR...
...WHICH MATCHES THAT WIG THERE. YOU DIDN'T THINK ANYONE WOULD BE DOWN HERE WITH YOU.
Y-YOU'RE RIGHT, OF COURSE.
I C-CAN'T DENY IT.
BUT...WHY?
WHAT WOULD POSSESS SOME-ONE LIKE ME TO DO SOMETHING LIKE THIS?

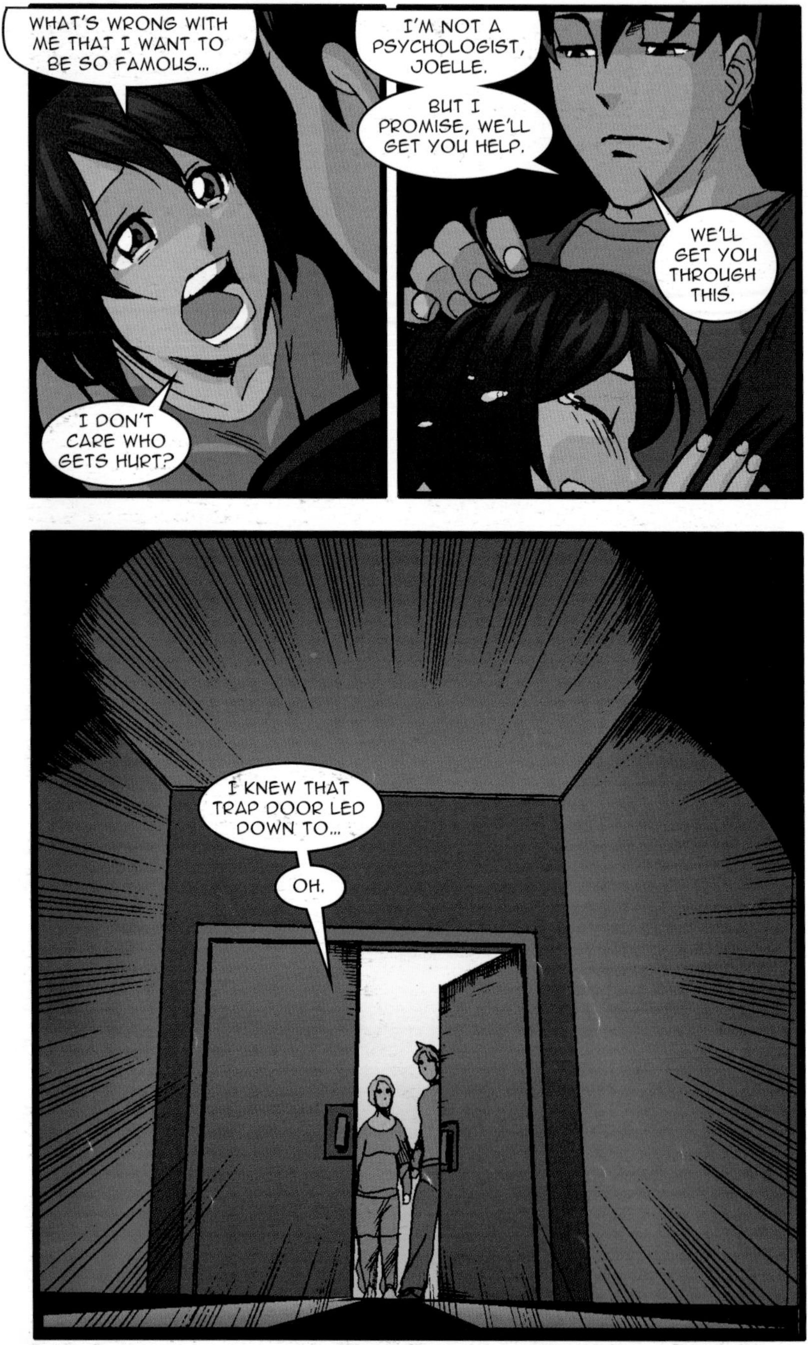
WHAT'S WRONG WITH ME THAT I WANT TO BE SO FAMOUS...
I DON'T CARE WHO GETS HURT?
I'M NOT A PSYCHOLOGIST, JOELLE.
BUT I PROMISE, WE'LL GET YOU HELP.
WE'LL GET YOU THROUGH THIS.
I KNEW THAT TRAP DOOR LED DOWN TO...
OH.

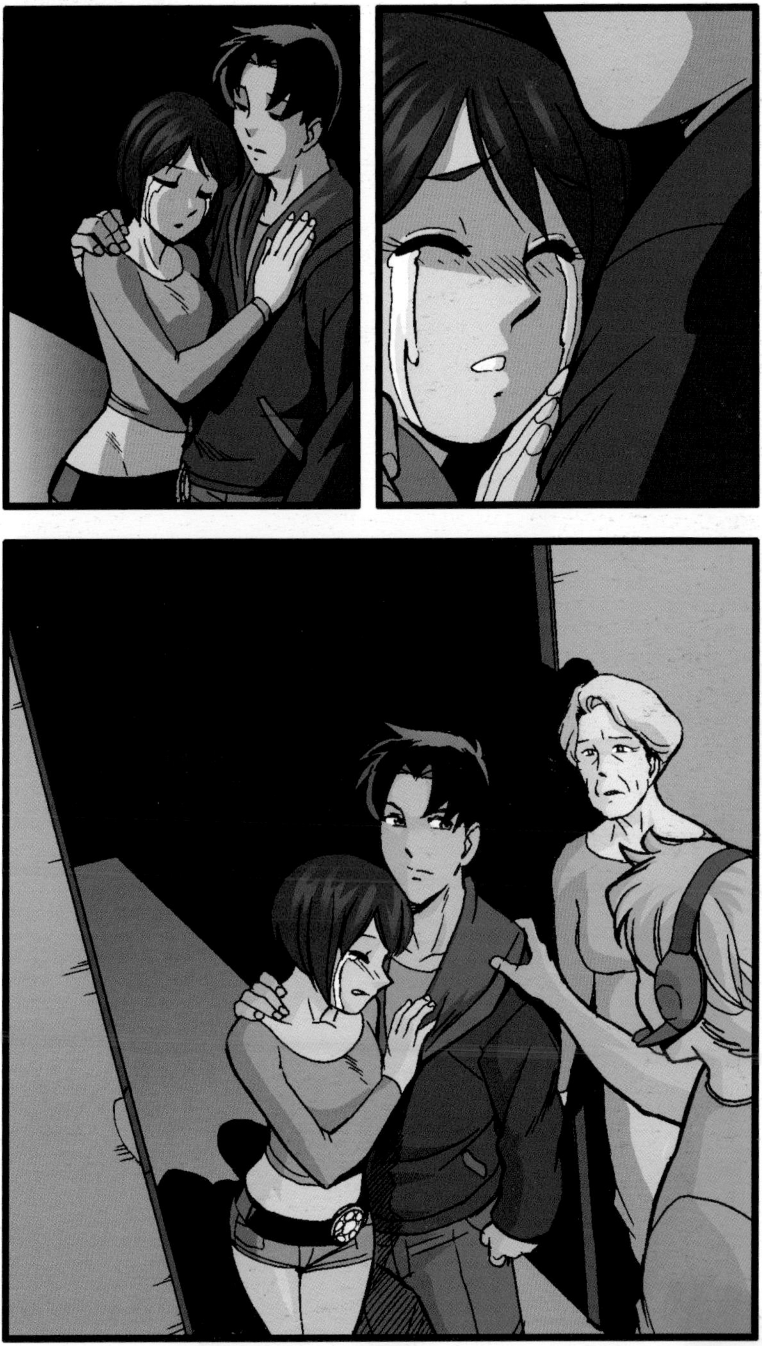

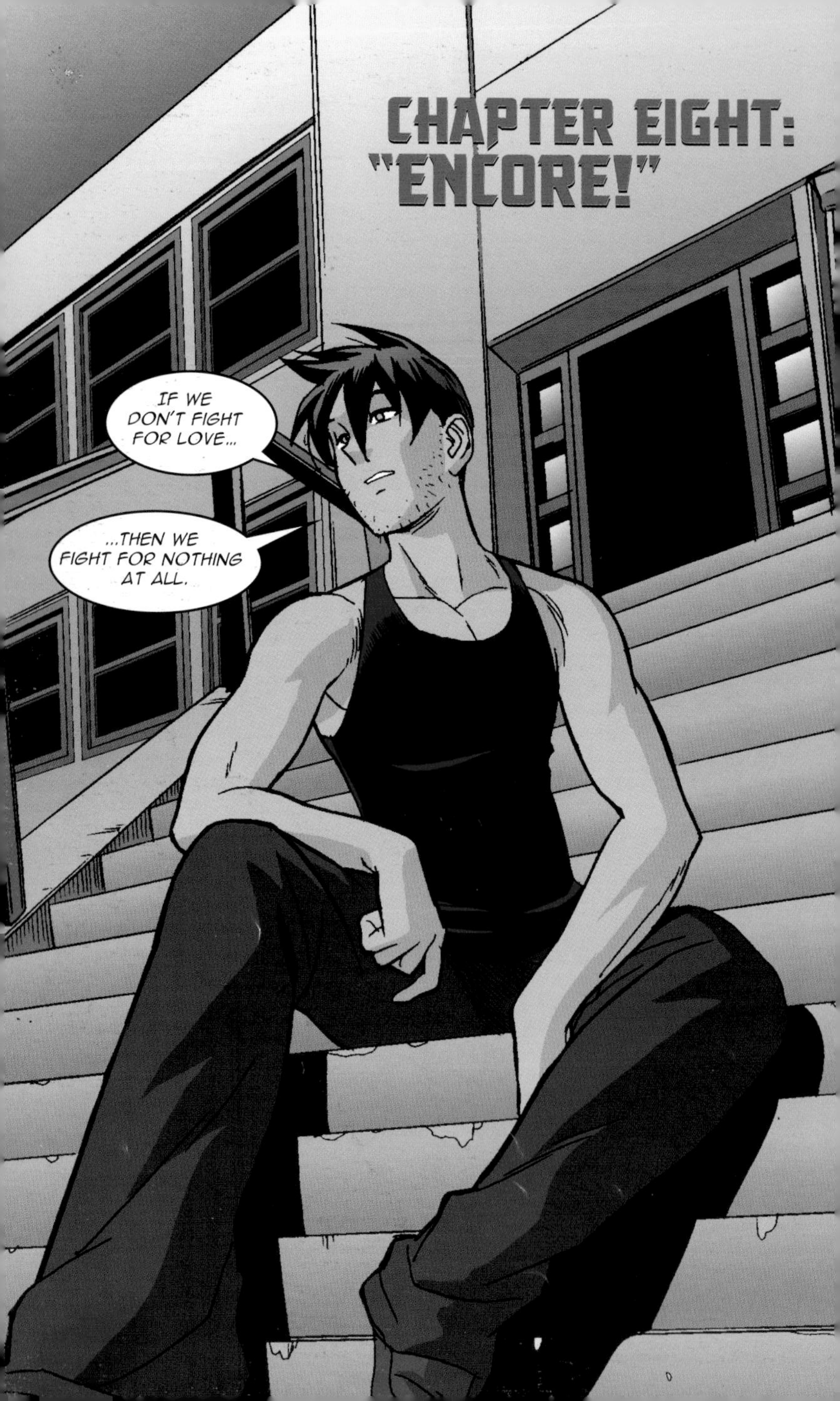
CHAPTER EIGHT:
"ENCORE!"
IF WE DON'T FIGHT FOR LOVE...
...THEN WE FIGHT FOR NOTHING AT ALL.

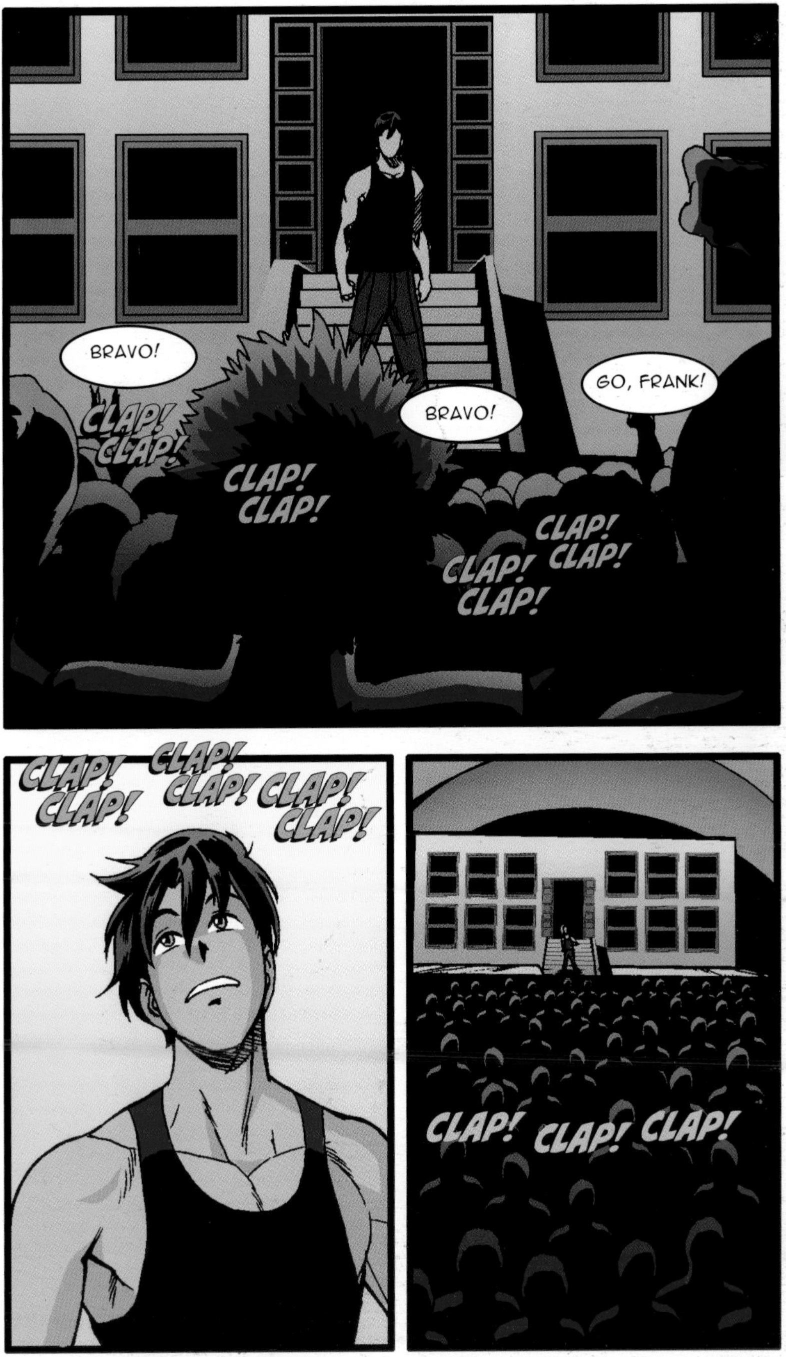
BRAVO!
CLAP! CLAP!
CLAP! CLAP!
BRAVO!
GO, FRANK!
CLAP! CLAP!
CLAP! CLAP!
CLAP! CLAP!
CLAP! CLAP!
CLAP! CLAP!
CLAP! CLAP! CLAP!

EVERYTHING IS GOING TO BE OKAY.

THOSE A.T.A.C. PSYCHOLOGISTS ARE GOING TO HELP HER.

I KNOW.

THANKS.

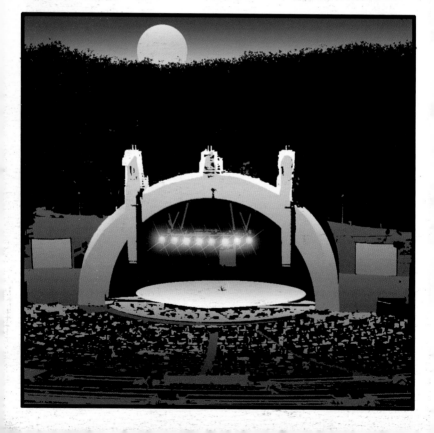

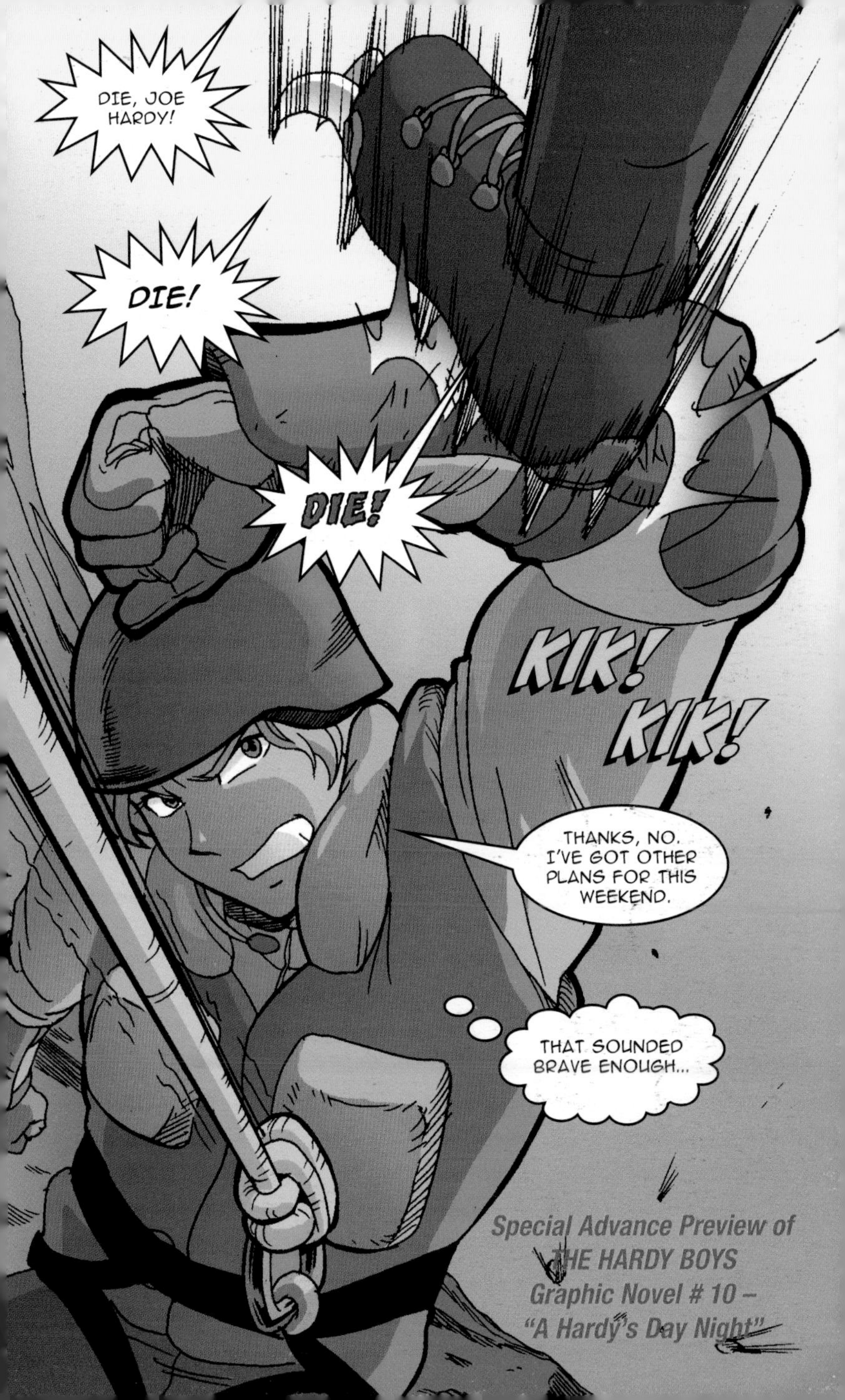
DIE, JOE HARDY!
DIE!
DIE!
KIK! KIK!
THANKS, NO. I'VE GOT OTHER PLANS FOR THIS WEEKEND.
THAT SOUNDED BRAVE ENOUGH...

Special Advance Preview of THE HARDY BOYS Graphic Novel # 10 – "A Hardy's Day Night"

CHAPTER ONE: "THE HIGHER THEY ARE... THE FARTHER THEY FALL!"

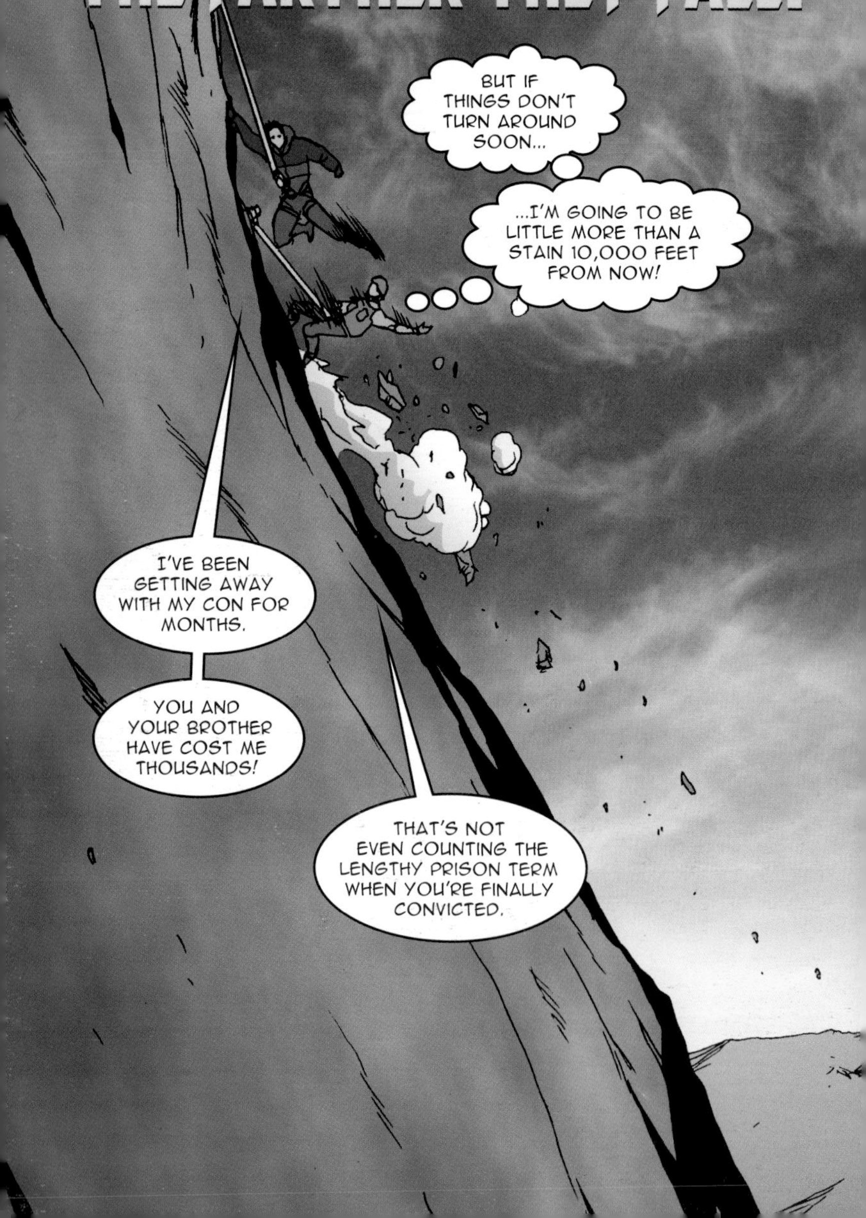
BUT IF THINGS DON'T TURN AROUND SOON...
...I'M GOING TO BE LITTLE MORE THAN A STAIN 10,000 FEET FROM NOW!
I'VE BEEN GETTING AWAY WITH MY CON FOR MONTHS.
YOU AND YOUR BROTHER HAVE COST ME THOUSANDS!
THAT'S NOT EVEN COUNTING THE LENGTHY PRISON TERM WHEN YOU'RE FINALLY CONVICTED.

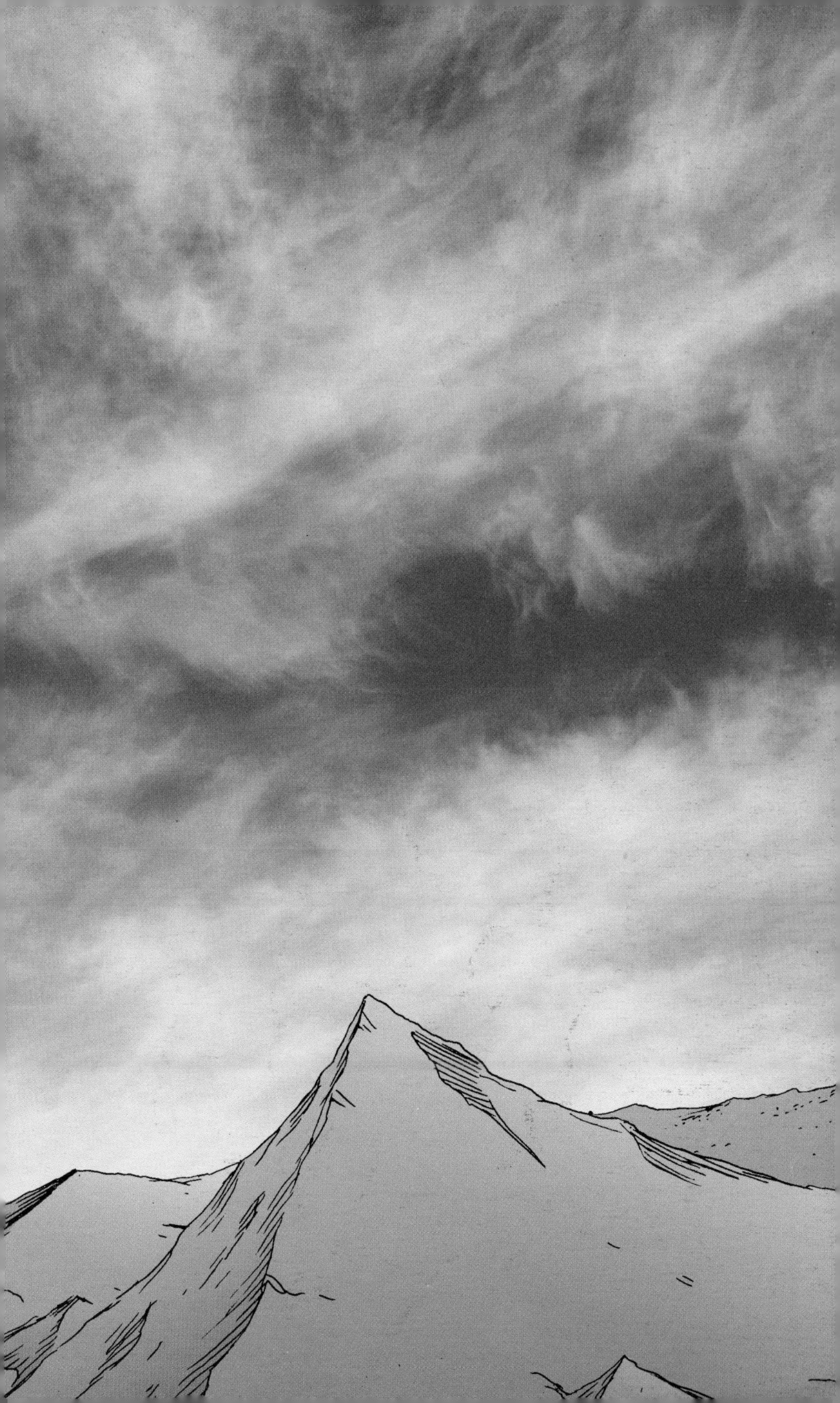

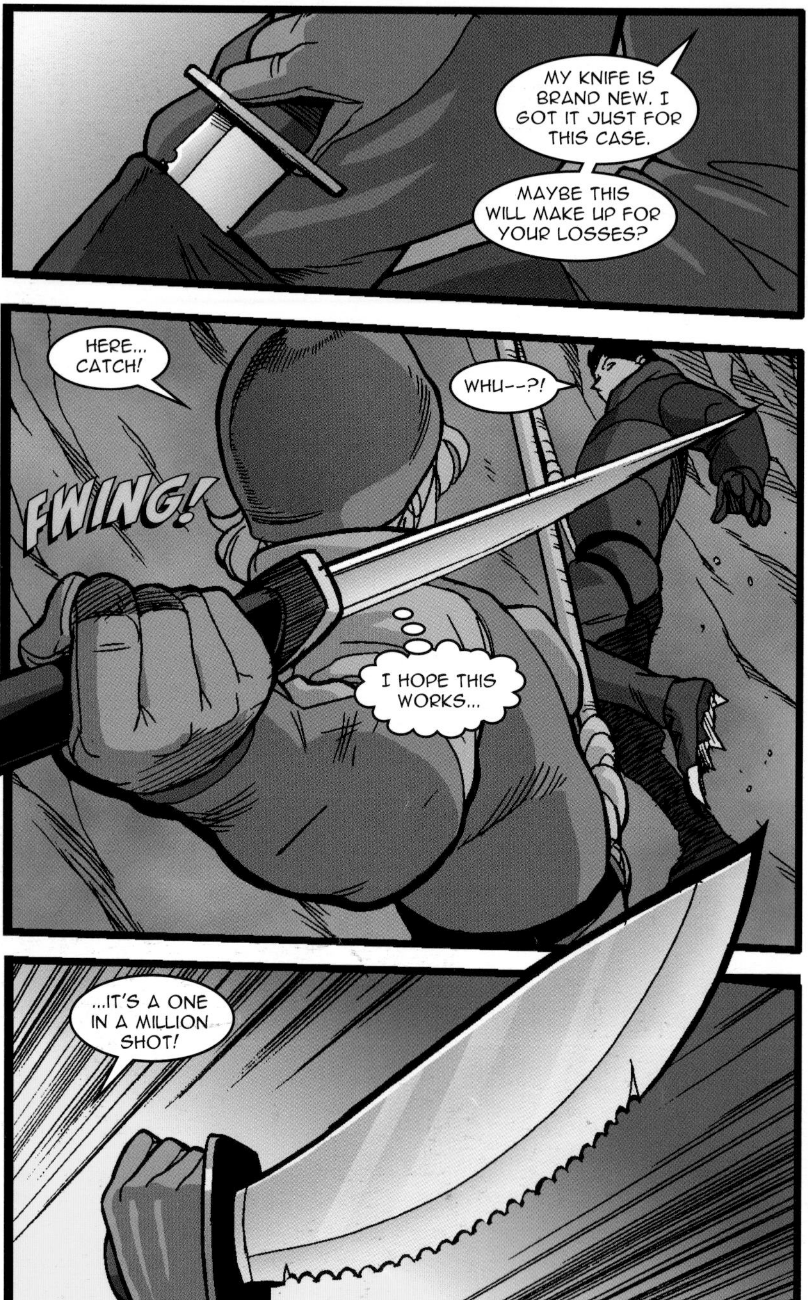
MY KNIFE IS BRAND NEW. I GOT IT JUST FOR THIS CASE.
MAYBE THIS WILL MAKE UP FOR YOUR LOSSES?
HERE... CATCH!
WHU--?!
FWING!
I HOPE THIS WORKS...
...IT'S A ONE IN A MILLION SHOT!

Don't miss THE HARDY BOYS Graphic Novel # 10 – "A Hardy's Day Night"

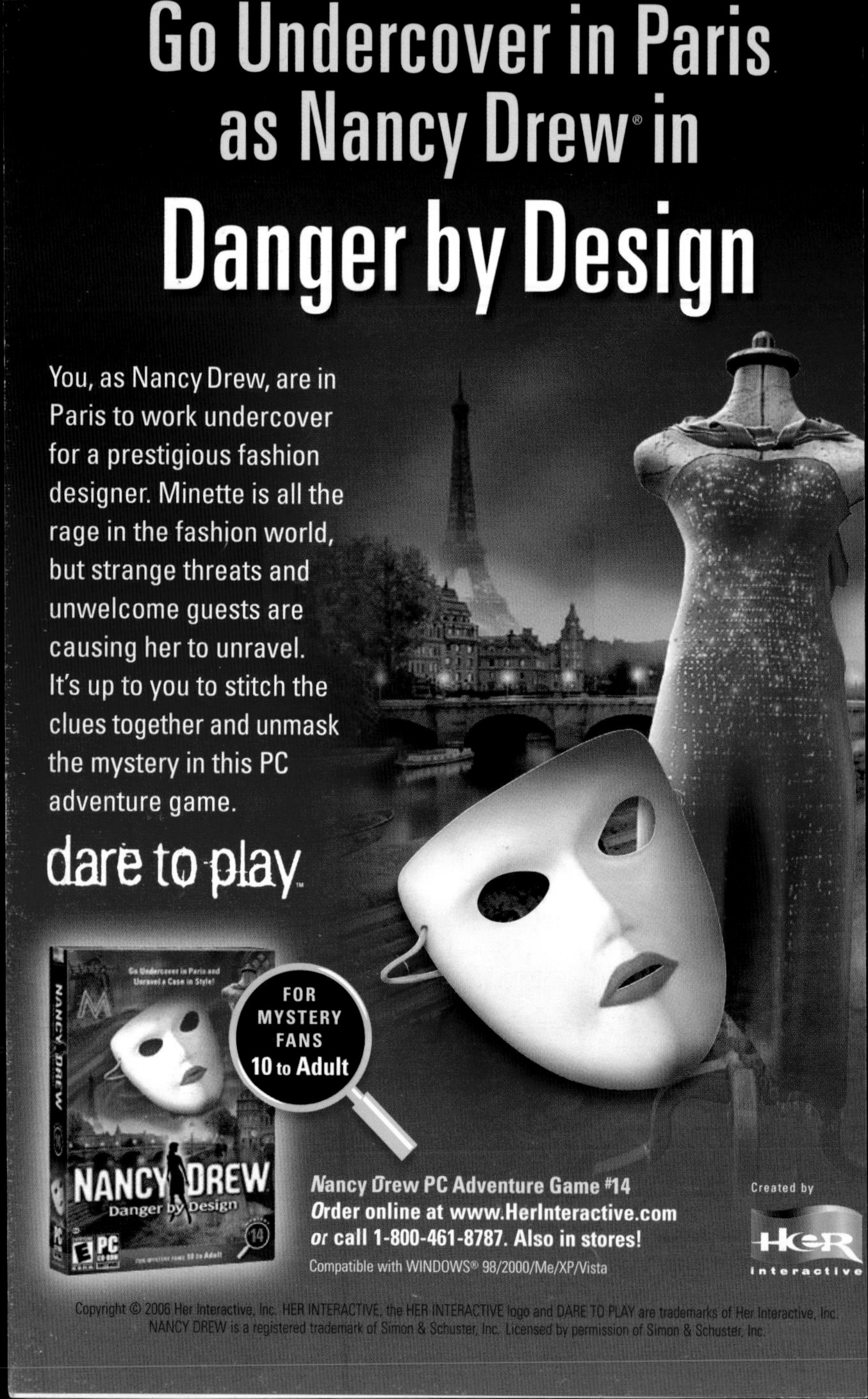
Go Undercover in Paris
as Nancy Drew® in
Danger by Design
You, as Nancy Drew, are in Paris to work undercover for a prestigious fashion designer. Minette is all the rage in the fashion world, but strange threats and unwelcome guests are causing her to unravel. It's up to you to stitch the clues together and unmask the mystery in this PC adventure game.
dare to play™
FOR MYSTERY FANS 10 to Adult
NANCY DREW
Danger by Design
Nancy Drew PC Adventure Game #14
Order online at www.HerInteractive.com
or call 1-800-461-8787. Also in stores!
Compatible with WINDOWS® 98/2000/Me/XP/Vista
Created by
HER interactive
Copyright © 2006 Her Interactive, Inc. HER INTERACTIVE, the HER INTERACTIVE logo and DARE TO PLAY are trademarks of Her Interactive, Inc. NANCY DREW is a registered trademark of Simon & Schuster, Inc. Licensed by permission of Simon & Schuster, Inc.

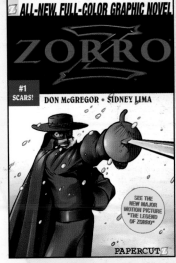

THE HARDY BOYS

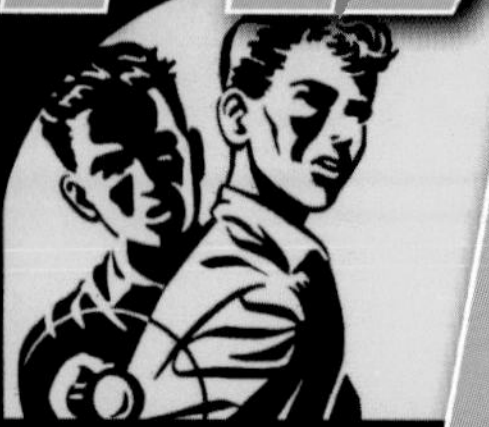

UNDERCOVER BROTHERS

ATAC BRIEFING FOR AGENTS FRANK AND JOE HARDY

ALL NEW ALL NEW ALL NEW #13
THE HARDY BOYS
UNDERCOVER BROTHERS
The Mummy's Curse

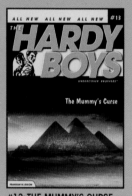

#13: THE MUMMY'S CURSE
Available December 2006

MISSION:

A man has been murdered, possibly over a map to a precious golden mummy. Are there other treasure-hunters trying to find the location of the tomb? Could there be a curse surrounding the ancient mummy and his treasure?

LOCATION:

Cairo, Egypt, and the surrounding area.

SUSPECTS:

Several people on an expedition are suspects. you have to find them before they find the mummy . . . and his treasure

THIS MISSION REQUIRES YOUR IMMEDIATE ATTENTION PICK UP A COPY OF *THE MUMMY'S CURSE* AND GET ON THE CASE!

Have you read Frank and Joe's latest stories of crime, danger, mystery, and death-defying stunts?

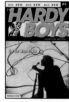

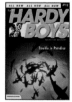

THE HARDY BOYS

TOP TEN WAYS TO DIE

THE HARDY BOYS
Martial Law

MARTIAL LAW

THE HARDY BOYS
Blown Away

BLOWN AWAY

THE HARDY BOYS
Hurricane Joe

HURRICANE JOE

THE HARDY BOYS
Trouble in Paradise

TROUBLE IN PARADISE

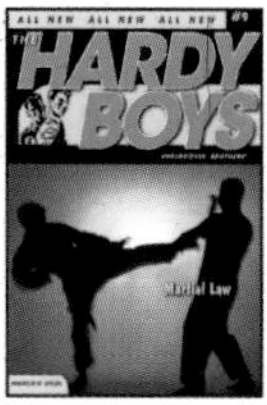

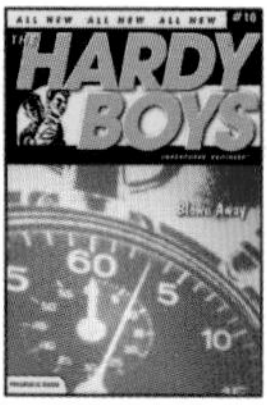

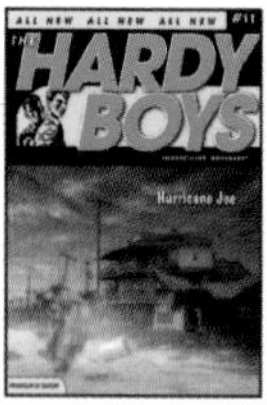

Visit www.SimonSaysSleuth.com for more Hardy Boys adventures.

ALADDIN PAPERBACKS • SIMON & SCHUSTER CHILDREN'S PUBLISHING

WATCH OUT FOR PAPERCUTZ™

Papercutz Editor-in-Chief Jim Salicrup here with something really important to say to you before we kick off this edition of the Papercutz back-pages: **Thank you!**

Thank you for picking up this Papercutz book. Whether this is your very first Papercutz graphic novel or your second, third, fourth, or sixteenth—we greatly appreciate it. We work around the clock to make each and every one of our books the very best we possibly can, so that you can get the absolute maximum amount of enjoyment from each and every page. But it's all for nothing without you!

And thanks to you, Papercutz has become quite a success story. We suspect that's because instead of offering more of the same types of comics that were already being published, Papercutz is devoted to bringing our own brand of fun and excitement to the world of graphic novels.

Thanks to you also for telling us what you like and don't like about Papercutz. That's been a huge help to us in choosing our new, upcoming Papercutz titles. By revealing how much you enjoy the humor in our mystery and adventure titles, such as The Hardy Boys, Nancy Drew, and Totally Spies, we knew our new titles had to be just as much fun. We'll soon be adding a horror anthology to our line-up. And it'll have that Papercutz sense of humor. The new title is revealed on the next few pages, but there's a mighty big clue on this page!

But before you get to the big announcement, on behalf of all the Papercutz writers and artists, allow me to thank you one more time for giving us the opportunity to do what we love— create the very best graphic novels we can for you!

Thanks,

Jim

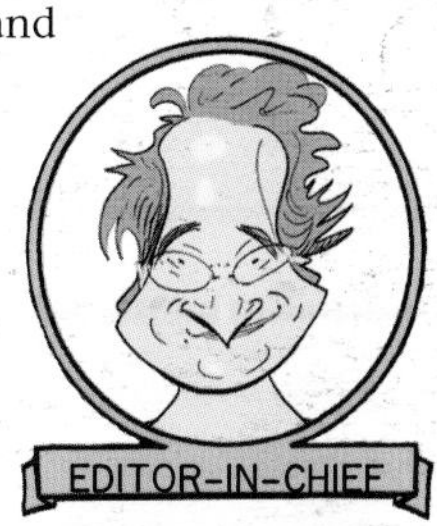
EDITOR-IN-CHIEF

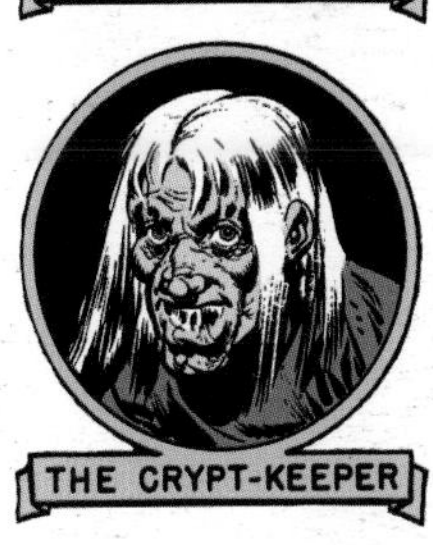
THE CRYPT-KEEPER

Caricature of Jim drawn by Steve Brodner at the MoCCA Art Fest. The Crypt-Keeper is © 2007 William M. Gaines, Agent, Inc.

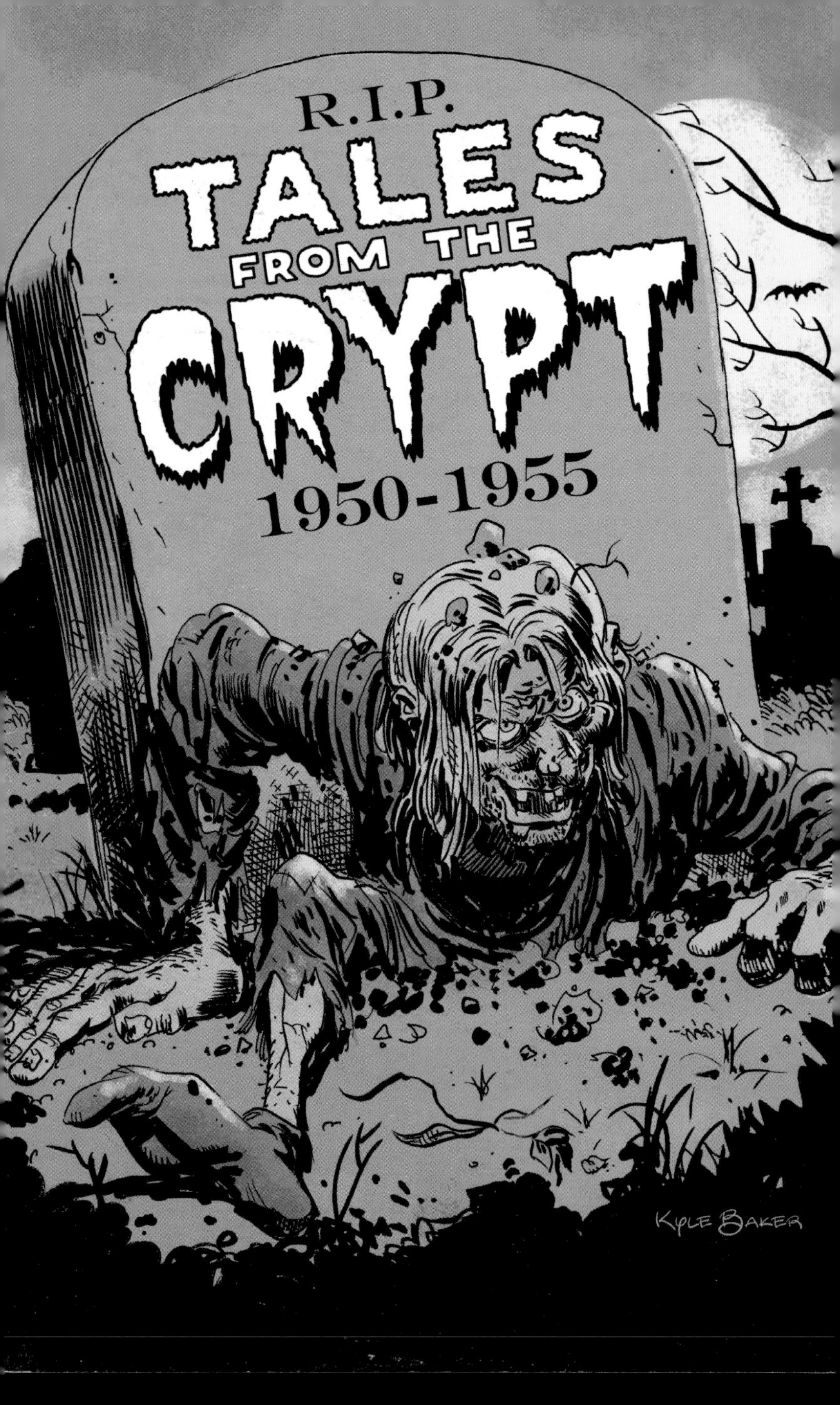
R.I.P.
TALES FROM THE CRYPT
1950-1955
KYLE BAKER

PAPERCUT**Z**™

presents:
The Return of

TALES
FROM THE
CRYPT®

It's one of the biggest surprises in the world of comics and graphic novel publishing! Shortly before the 2007 New York Comic Con, we announced that Papercutz would be publishing all-new TALES FROM THE CRYPT comics. After more than 50 years, EC Comics' legendary flagship title returns with all-new TALES FROM THE CRYPT, narrated by the original Crypt-Keeper, Old Witch, and Vault Keeper. Each issue will feature two 20-page tales of terror in the EC tradition!

Reactions ranged from excitement— from fans thrilled to see the most famous horror comicbook ever return after over fifty years, to shock—that it was to be coming from a publisher primarily known for its graphic novels such as Nancy Drew and The Hardy Boys which contain material suitable for all-ages, as the HBO series certainly contained a fair amount of adult content.

"People forget that the original TALES FROM THE CRYPT comicbook, published by the legendary EC Comics back in the 50s, was also intended for all-ages, and its primary readership was young boys," Papercutz Editor-in-Chief Jim Salicrup is quick to point out. But that may be exactly what fans find so controversial. The original TALES FROM THE CRYPT comics, featuring stories dreamed up by EC publisher William M. Gaines and his editor Al Feldstein, and drawn by Feldstein, as well as Graham Ingles, Jack Davis, Jack Kamen, Joe Orlando, Wally Wood, Harvey Kurtzman, Bill Elder, Reed Crandall, Johnny Craig, Al Williamson, George Evans, and colored by Marie Severin, started a horror comics craze that soon drew the attention of psychiatrist Dr. Frederick Wertham.

Wertham reacted to the popularity of horror comics with children by writing a book called "Seduction of the Innocent," which maintained that comics led to juvenile delinquency and even worse behavior. Parents were understandably alarmed, and soon the Senate Subcommittee to Investigate Juvenile Delinquency was taking a hard look at comicbooks. EC Comics publisher Bill Gaines spoke before the Subcommittee, but was unable to convince them that his comics were entertaining stories told in good taste. Ultimately, comicbook publishers adversely affected by the negative publicity created the Comics Magazine Association of America which would review comics and award a seal of approval to assure parents that the comic's contents were safe, wholesome entertainment.

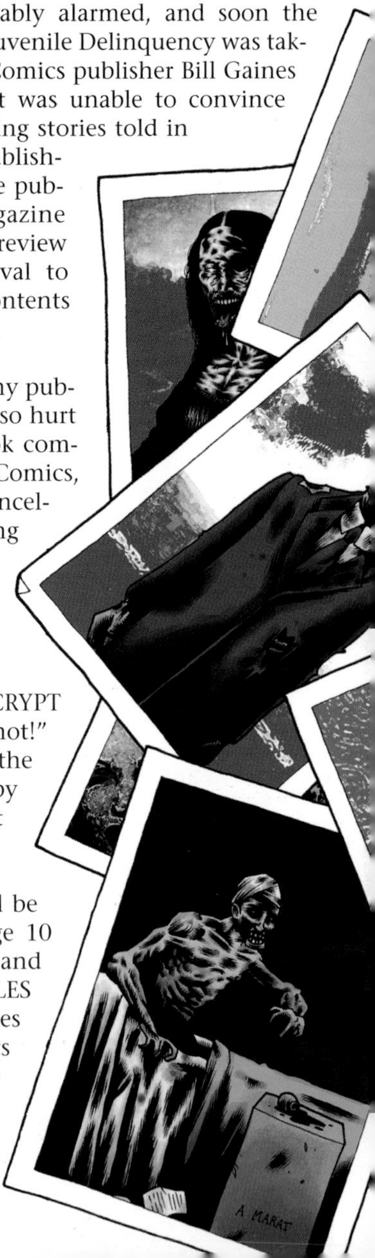

Unfortunately, it was too late for many publishers, as the negative publicity had so hurt sales of comics that many comicbook companies went out of business. EC Comics, tried to hang in there, but despite canceling their horror comics, and creating new titles such as "Valor" and "Psychoanalysis," only MAD comics, in a new magazine format, survived.

The question is, was TALES FROM CRYPT really all that bad? "Of course not!" Salicrup insists. "Ironically, many of the original stories would be approved by today's revised Comics Code, but sure, there were some stories that still wouldn't get by. The point here is that the stories that Papercutz will be creating will be aimed at readers age 10 and up. Instead of excessive blood and gore, we'll be sticking to the TALES FROM THE CRYPT tradition of stories filled with interesting characters, lots of dark humor, and of course, the trademarked EC "shock" endings!" The first TALES FROM THE CRYPT comic from Papercutz, which will be on sale in comics shops in June, features:

•"Body of Work," by horror author Marc Bilgrey (H.P. Lovecraft's Magazine of Horror, "And Don't Forget to Rescue the Princess") and Mr. Exes (Abra Cadaver). The story reveals how two nosy and somewhat murderous neighbors discover the shocking inspiration for Jack Kroll's creepy "outsider" artwork.

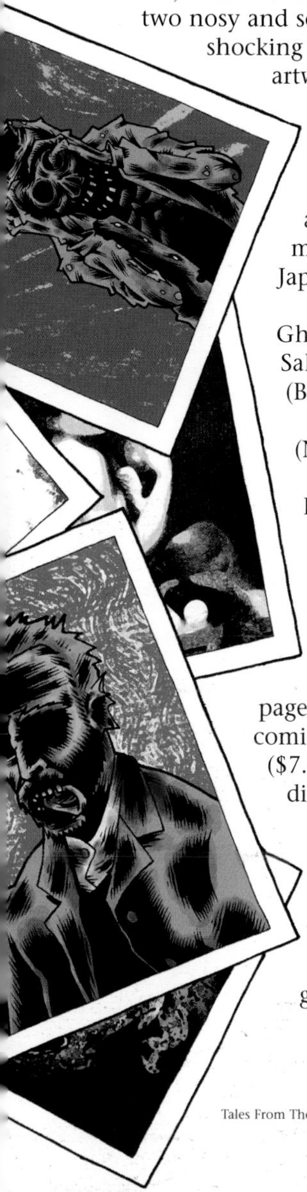

• "For Serious Collectors Only," by Rob Vollmar (Bluesman) and Tim Smith III (Teen Titans Go!). This tale explores how far Thomas Donalley— a middle-aged action-figure collector who lives in his mom's basement— will go for an ultra-rare Japanese figure.

•Introductory pages featuring the GhouLunatics are written by editor Jim Salicrup and drawn by artist Rick Parker (Beavis and Butt-Head).

• Cover by award-winning artist Kyle Baker (Nat Turner, Plastic Man, Why I Hate Saturn).

Future issues will include stories by Fred Van Lente (Marvel Adventures), Xeric Grant winner Neil Kleid, Stefan Petrucha (The Shadow of Frankenstein, NANCY DREW), Don McGregor (ZORRO), Sho Murase (NANCY DREW), and other great talents. Each bi-monthly issue is 48 full-color pages for an affordable $3.95. Naturally, the comics will be collected in the usual 112 page, ($7.95 paperback; $12.95 hardcover) full-color digest format, with the first volume, TALES FROM THE CRYPT *"Ghouls Gone Wild!"* available in bookstores everywhere in time for Halloween.

When reached for comment, the Crypt-Keeper said, "It's good to be back, boils and ghouls—and it's about time! Ahahahah!"

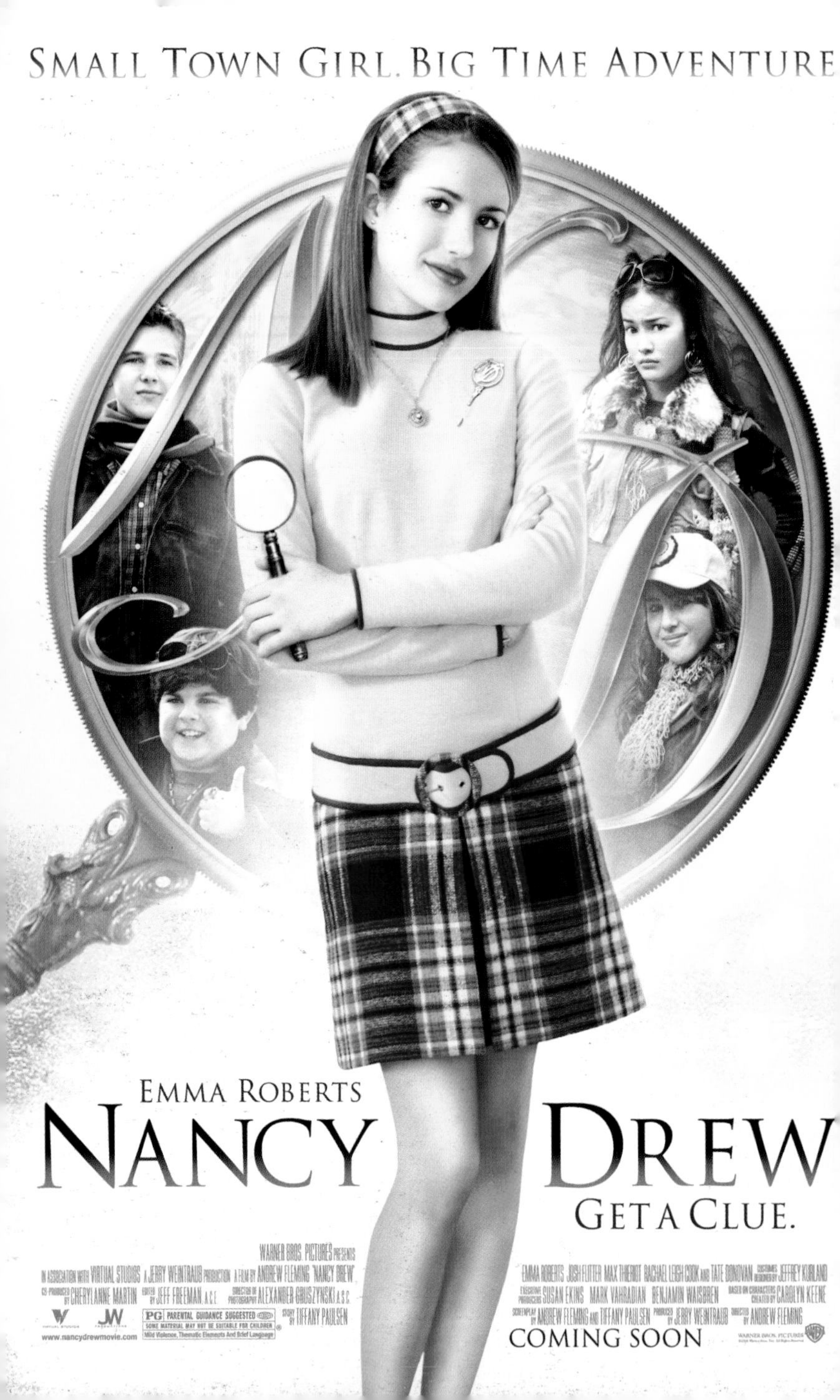

SMALL TOWN GIRL. BIG TIME ADVENTURE
EMMA ROBERTS
NANCY DREW
GET A CLUE.
WARNER BROS. PICTURES PRESENTS
IN ASSOCIATION WITH VIRTUAL STUDIOS A JERRY WEINTRAUB PRODUCTION A FILM BY ANDREW FLEMING "NANCY DREW"
CO-PRODUCED BY CHERYLANNE MARTIN EDITED BY JEFF FREEMAN, A.C.E. DIRECTOR OF PHOTOGRAPHY ALEXANDER GRUSZYNSKI, A.S.C.
STORY BY TIFFANY PAULSEN
EMMA ROBERTS JOSH FLITTER MAX THIERIOT RACHAEL LEIGH COOK AND TATE DONOVAN COSTUMES DESIGNED BY JEFFREY KURLAND
EXECUTIVE PRODUCERS SUSAN EKINS MARK VAHRADIAN BENJAMIN WAISBREN BASED ON CHARACTERS CREATED BY CAROLYN KEENE
SCREENPLAY BY ANDREW FLEMING AND TIFFANY PAULSEN PRODUCED BY JERRY WEINTRAUB DIRECTED BY ANDREW FLEMING
PG PARENTAL GUIDANCE SUGGESTED
SOME MATERIAL MAY NOT BE SUITABLE FOR CHILDREN
Mild Violence, Thematic Elements And Brief Language
www.nancydrewmovie.com
COMING SOON
WARNER BROS. PICTURES

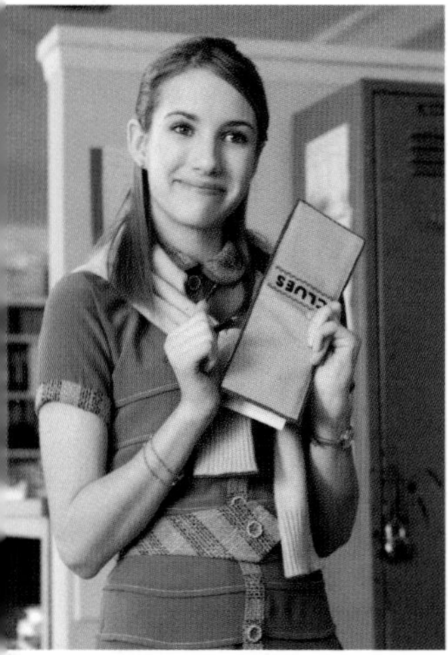

Nancy Drew (EMMA ROBERTS) in Warner Bros. Pictures' and Virtual Studios' teen drama action/adventure "Nancy Drew," distributed by Warner Bros. Pictures. Photo by Melinda Sue Gordon

The movie we've all been waiting for is almost here! To get a sneak peek, go online to: http://nancydrewmovie.warnerbros.com/ and watch the fun-filled, action-packed trailer plus a lot more. You'll get to see Nancy Drew in action, in lots of scenes from her soon to be released major motion picture!

The film follows Nancy (Emma Roberts) as she accompanies her father, Carson Drew (Tate Donovan), to Los Angeles on one of his business trips and stumbles across evidence about a long-unsolved crime involving the mysterious death of a beautiful movie star. Nancy's resourcefulness and personal responsibility are put to the test when she finds herself in the middle of the fast-living, self-indulgent world of Hollywood.

Top to bottom: Ned (MAX THIERIOT), Nancy Drew (EMMA ROBERTS) and Corky (JOSH FLITTER) in Warner Bros. Pictures' and Virtual Studios' teen drama action/adventure "Nancy Drew," distributed by Warner Bros. Pictures. Photo by Melinda Sue Gordon

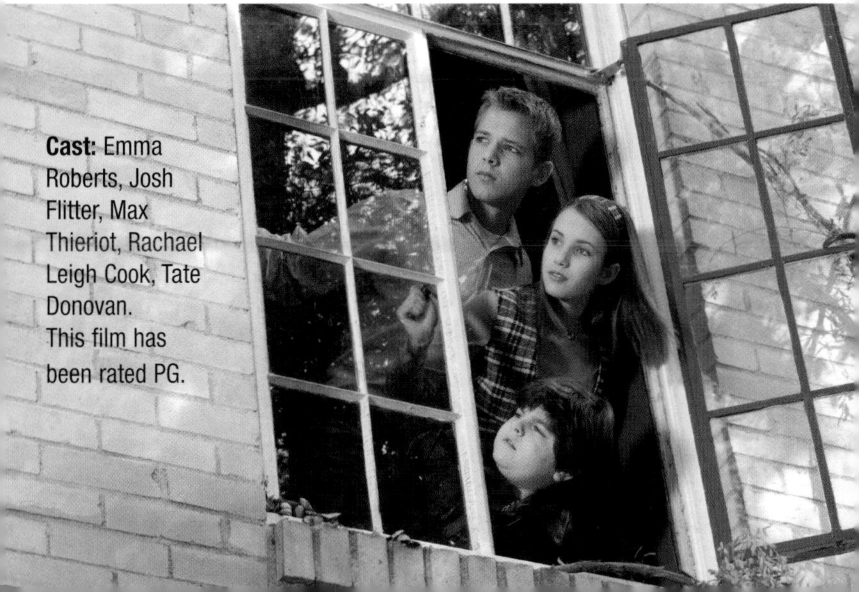

Cast: Emma Roberts, Josh Flitter, Max Thieriot, Rachael Leigh Cook, Tate Donovan.
This film has been rated PG.

Totally Spies!™

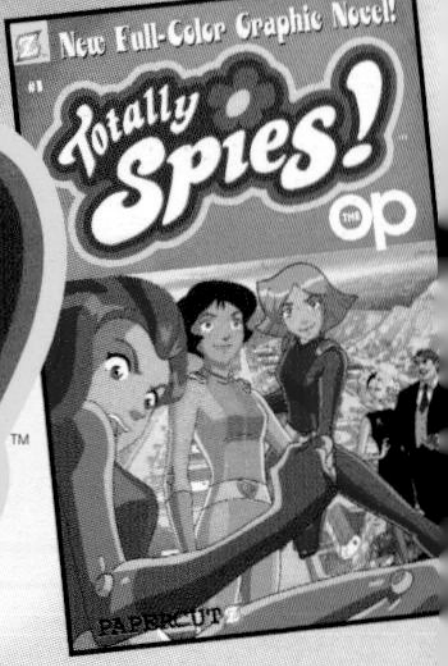

New Full-Color Graphic Novel!
#1
Totally Spies!
THE OP
PAPERCUTZ

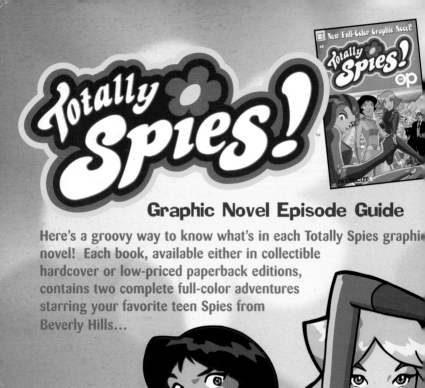

Graphic Novel Episode Guide

Here's a groovy way to know what's in each Totally Spies graphic novel! Each book, available either in collectible hardcover or low-priced paperback editions, contains two complete full-color adventures starring your favorite teen Spies from Beverly Hills...

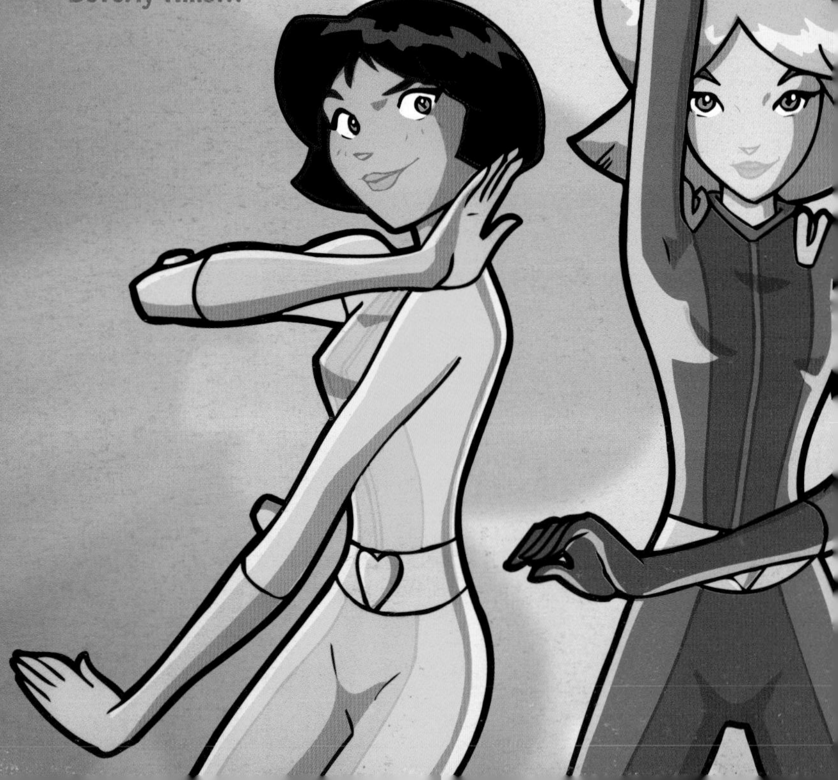

Totally Spies! Graphic Novel #1
"The O.P."

During a weekend road trip up the California coast, the girls' new car, a totally tricked-out, gadget-filled gift from Jerry to celebrate their recent success as super-spies, breaks down in a seemingly idyllic gated coastal town called Ocean Palisades – or "The O.P." for short. At first Alex, Sam, and Clover completely love it — the friendly, perfectly-tanned townspeople; the fancy, immaculate houses; the ridiculously scenic views – but, when they meet a few teens who seem to be too perfect to be real (they don't stay out after dark; they love spending time with their parents; they have sparkling teeth because they don't eat junk food), they start to get pretty weirded-out. Can the Spies find out what's really going on with the town's teens and save them from their crazy community – or will they be turned into perfect robot-like teens themselves and be forced to live in The O.P. forever?.

"Futureshock"

When the girls fiddle with Jerry's new time machine, they accidentally jet themselves 25 years into the future! At first they think it's way exciting – until they discover that Mandy is an all-powerful super villain who has control of all media! The spies are in awe when they see Mandy on the cover of every single magazine... starring in every single TV show and film... and dominating every single radio station – the whole time pushing her shallow Mandy agenda! And the worst part is, when the spies seek out their future selves, they discover that they're being held captive by Mandy! Desperate, present day Sam, Clover and Alex seek out future Jerry for help (he's the only one who knows how to work the time machine) — but to their shock, find that he's not exactly around anymore, he's had himself cryogenically frozen! The girls have to find a way to "thaw" him out, save the future versions of themselves from captivity, and stop Mandy before she totally "Mandifies" the planet!

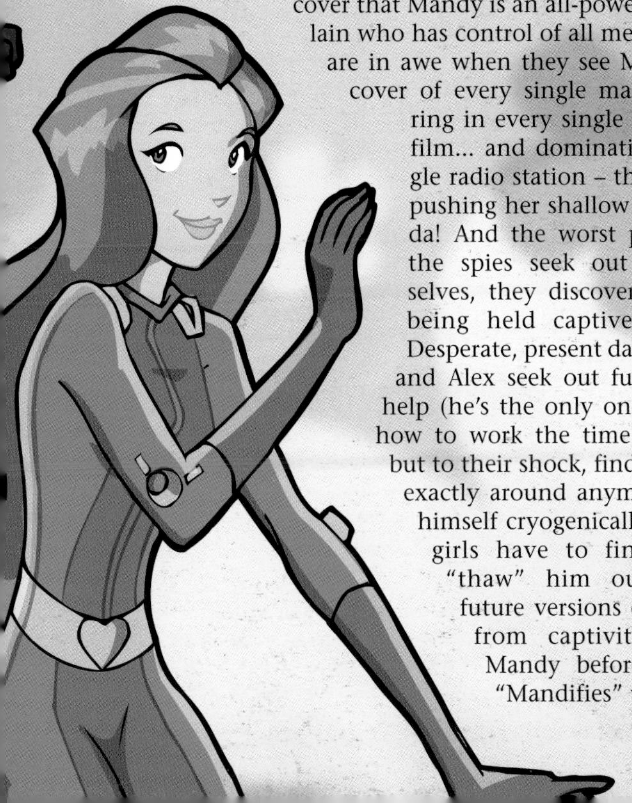

Totally Spies!
Graphic Novel #2
"I Hate The 80s!"

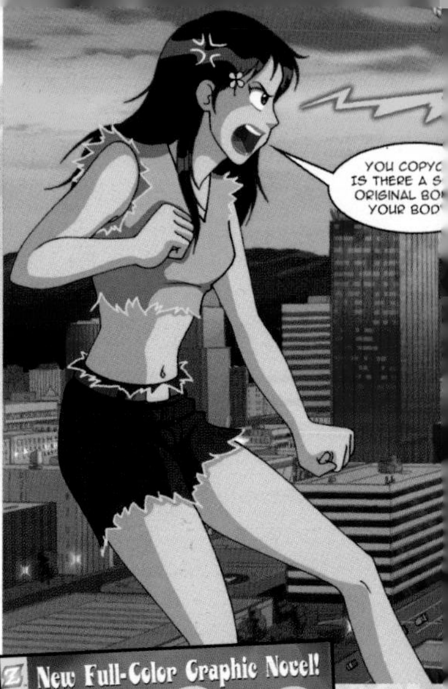

Boogie Gus has updated his look a bit — unfortunately, not for the better. No longer a worshipper of the 70s, Gus has gleefully discovered the 80s. And he's bent on using his new device – "The Eightifier" to turn Beverly Hills into the ultimate 80s paradise. Can the Spies stop Boogie Gus before their home town goes retro for good? Can the girls deal with their complicated-to-maintain New Wave haircuts? Can they deal with all the synth-pop music at their school dances? Can they stop Jerry from wearing robin's egg blue sports jackets with the sleeves rolled up and pastel pink t-shirts underneath?!

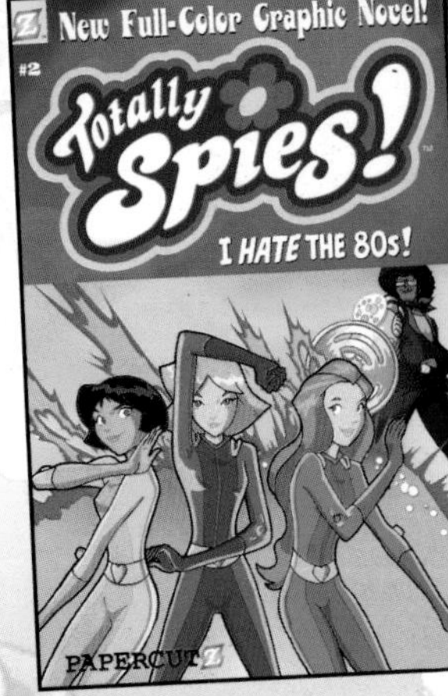
New Full-Color Graphic Novel!
#2
Totally Spies!
I HATE THE 80s!
PAPERCUTZ

"Attack Of The 50Ft. Tall Mandy!"
It's time to crown the new Miss Beverly Hills. Among this year's hopeful contestants are Mandy and Clover. In order to get that extra winning edge, they both unwittingly decide to get a special full-body makeover that promises to make their hair, smiles, eyes and even their attitudes bigger. Mandy: "And everyone knows that bigger is better when it comes to this type of competition." But as they are getting their treatment, both strapped into separate full-body machines, a shadowy figure sneaks into the spa and puts a microchip into Mandy's machine. Mandy is suddenly growing bigger in every way. As the Spies start to investigate a rash of disappearances among Miss Beverly Hills contestants, they find out that Mandy, who has now grown nearly fifty feet tall, is behind the crimes. They also discover that along with becoming bigger physically, Mandy's meanness has also become magnified. And in an effort to win the competition, she decided to take out the other contestants. Can the Spies stop this monolithic Mandy menace before it's too late?

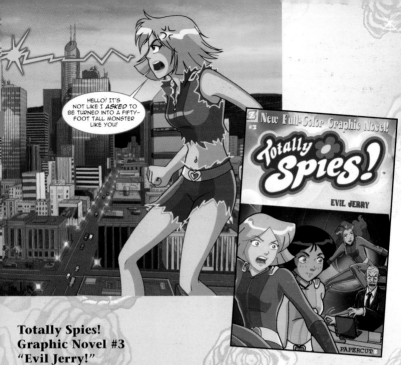

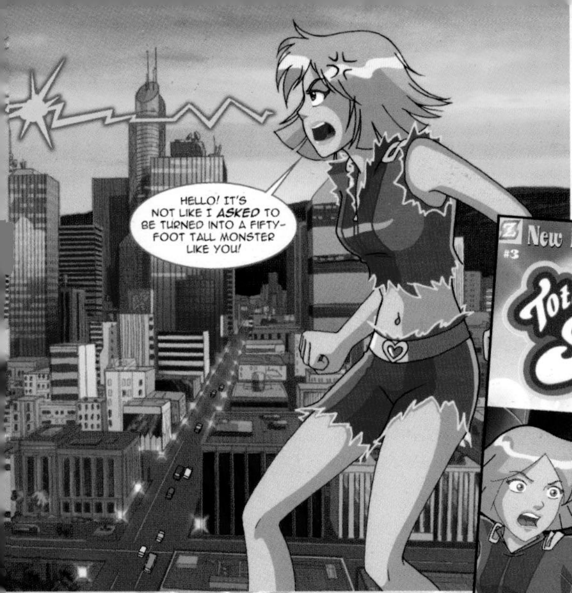
HELLO! IT'S NOT LIKE I ASKED TO BE TURNED INTO A FIFTY-FOOT TALL MONSTER LIKE YOU!

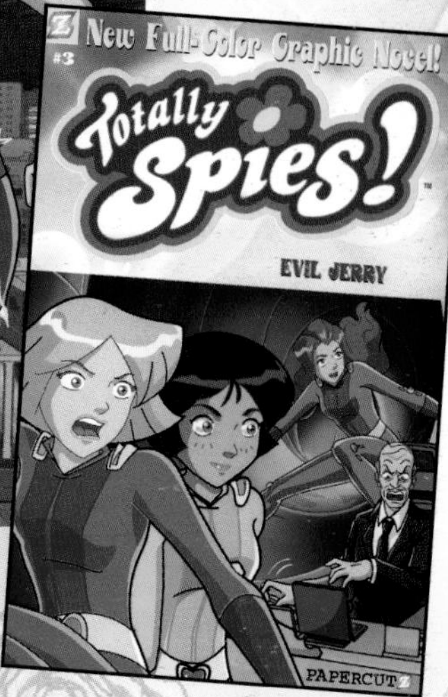
New Full-Color Graphic Novel!
#3
Totally Spies!
EVIL JERRY
PAPERCUT

Totally Spies!
Graphic Novel #3
"Evil Jerry!"

Jerry's sinister brother Terence is at it again – and this time, with the help of Tim Scam, he's created a crazy device that has the ability to gather half of the evil from him... and transfer it directly into Jerry! Luckily, the spies start to notice that Jerry's acting strangely. And even luckier, they figure out what's going on – Terence and a troop of ex-villains are to blame! Yes, the girls finally discover the LAMOS! Can the spies save Jerry and WOOHP before it's too late – or will Terence proceed with the rest of his wicked plan – moving himself and the rest of the LAMOS out of their submarine and into WOOHP (from which they can spread their evil all over the world)?

"Deja Cruise!"

The spies are totally psyched when Jerry informs them that he's offering them a little vacation on the new WOOHP Cruise Liner – a state-of-the-art, luxury ship designed to be a pleasure boat for overworked WOOHP agents! Once on the boat, the girls realize Jerry wasn't kidding, the ship is loaded with all sorts of amenities. Suddenly, the serenity of the vacation is broken as a gang of baddies, disguised as the ship's crew, take over the boat. Their plan: to destroy the ship with all of the WOOHP agents on it. The girls spring into action and try to defeat the villains, but their efforts only result in them accidentally causing the ship to sink. Or does it? The girls all wake up and find that things are back to normal. Was it all a bad dream caused by eating bad sushi? Suddenly, just as things seem to be back to normal, the entire incident happens again. The spies try to stop the villains, but again destroy the vessel. And yet, again, they wake up on the ship. The spies realize that they are re-living the same day over and over! And the only way to stop this vicious cycle is to defeat the bad guys. Can the girls figure out what to do, or will they be stuck on this boat forever?!

Totally Spies!
Graphic Novel #4
"Spies in Space"

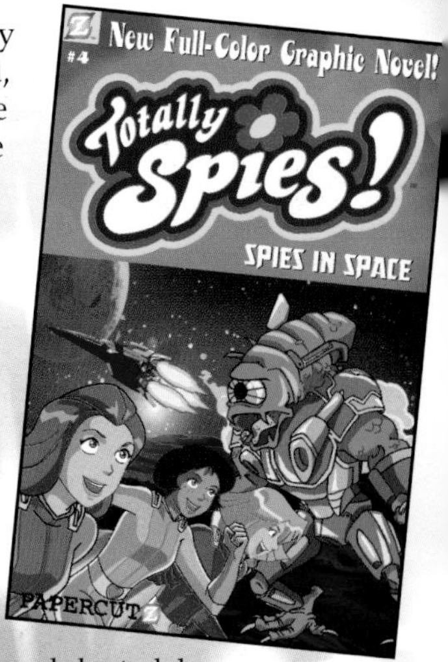
#4
New Full-Color Graphic Novel!
Totally Spies!
SPIES IN SPACE
PAPERCUTZ

The spies are way psyched when they find out that their favorite new band, The Alpha Centauris, are about to make music history. The band plans to be the first performers ever to broadcast a concert live from the moon. The only problem is, it's just days before the gig and the band is nowhere to be found. Apparently, their space transport has completely disappeared from WOOHP radar. Jerry puts the Spies on the case (as if they would have it any other way) and after GLADIS outfits them with cool intergalactic gadgets, including awesome space suits, the girls head off to find the band. After finding their abandoned ship, clues lead the Spies to believe the band was abducted by aliens. Can the girls save the band before they are evaporated by the sun?

"Spy Soccer"

It's the start of a new soccer season at Bev. High and Alex is psyched when her team gets a cool new coach. The only downside is that Clover and Sam feel a little snubbed because Alex is constantly busy with her team. Later, Jerry sends the girls on a mission to investigate a series of abductions. When the girls check out one of the crime scenes, they discover the place is totally trashed. And stranger still, one of the clues leads Sam and Clover back to... Alex?! When the girls confront Alex, she denies any wrongdoing, but can't explain or remember where she was at the time of the abduction. Then, seemingly out of nowhere, Alex's demeanor changes and she becomes very evil. She attacks Sam and Clover, and ultimately escapes. Sam and Clover discover that Alex's new soccer coach is using a special mind control ball to turn the Bev. High soccer team into her own private army – an army that uses their incredible, newfound, evil soccer techniques to get revenge on the coach's ex-teammates. Can Sam and Clover survive the final showdown – a death defying soccer match against the coach, Alex and her mind-controlled teammates?

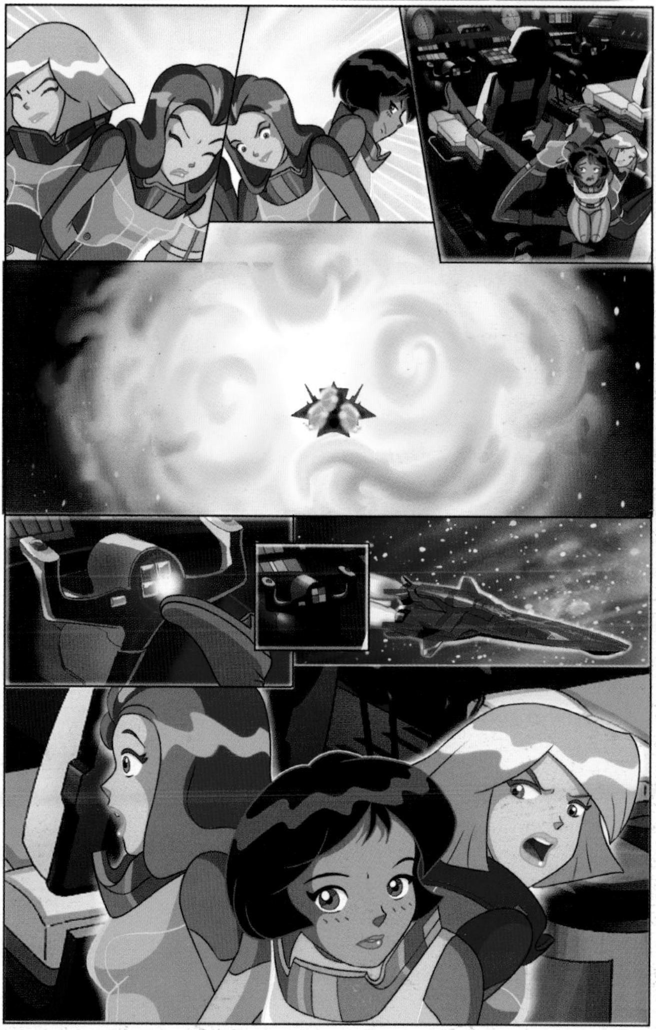

The Hardy Boys in Comics (and on TV and Vinyl)!

It's not that difficult to find an adult who remembers the late 70s live-action TV series, "The Hardy Boys Mysteries," with Shawn Cassidy and Parker Stevenson. And you can still find lots of Baby Boomers who recall the Hardy Boys serial, with Tim Considine and Tommy Kirk, which ran on the original Mickey Mouse Club TV series in the 50s. What's is almost impossible is finding anyone who might remember the Hardy Boys Saturday morning cartoon show from 1969. Like the Hardy Boys appearance on TV in the 50s, their animated TV series in the late 60s also inspired a four-issue comicbook series. But let's find out more about "The Mystery of The Forgotten Cartoon Series."

Back in the days long before entire cable networks were devoted to cartoons 24/7, the only place to see new cartoons on TV were on ABC, NBC, and CBS Saturday mornings. Back then Filmation Studios had a huge hit in the 60s with an animated series based on the Archie comicbook characters. Not only was it a hit on TV, but the songs performed by the animated Archies band became huge pop music hits — and you thought Gorillaz was the first cartoon band! But the technology didn't yet exist that could make it possible for a "cartoon band" to perform live on tour. The producers at Filmation decided to try to launch another cartoon series, based on characters loved by millions of children, but this time, they'd also assemble a live band made up of singers and musicians that looked just like the cartoon characters.

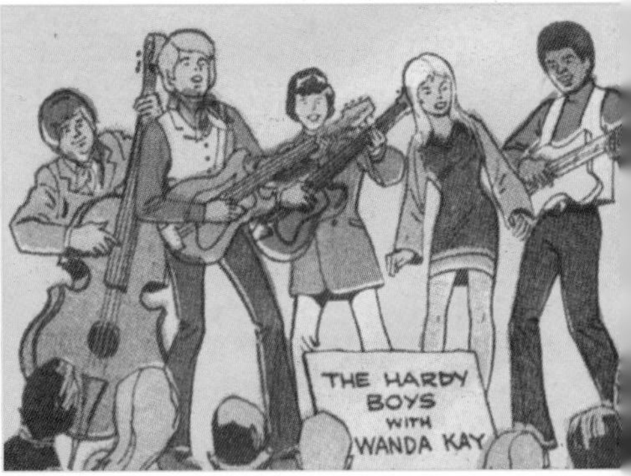
THE HARDY
BOYS
WITH
WANDA KAY

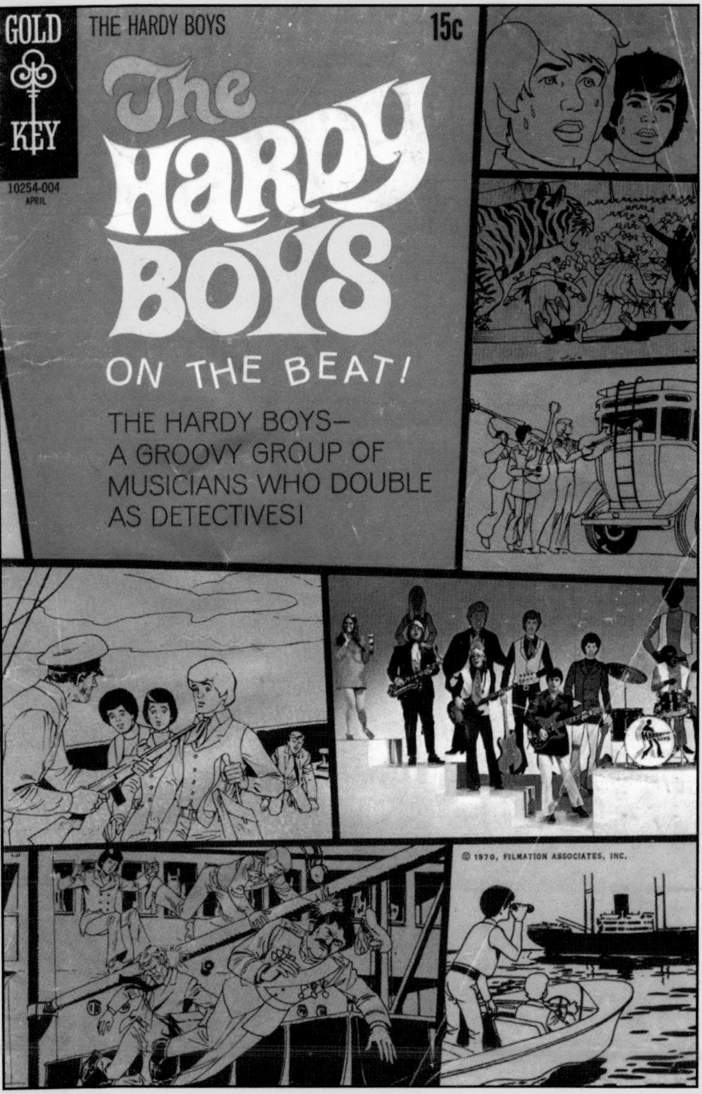
GOLD KEY
THE HARDY BOYS
15c
10254-004
APRIL
The HARDY BOYS
ON THE BEAT!
THE HARDY BOYS—
A GROOVY GROUP OF
MUSICIANS WHO DOUBLE
AS DETECTIVES!
© 1970, FILMATION ASSOCIATES, INC.

The Hardy Boys Gold Key Comicbook Checklist:

April 1970 – "Secret Of The Orinda Star," "The Dart-Riddle Rumble"
July 1970 – "Mystery Of The Catacombs," "Secret Mission"
October 1970 – "Mystery Of Wildcat Swamp," "The Headless Horseman"
January 1971 – "Paddle Wheel Peril" "The Guise Of Medusa"

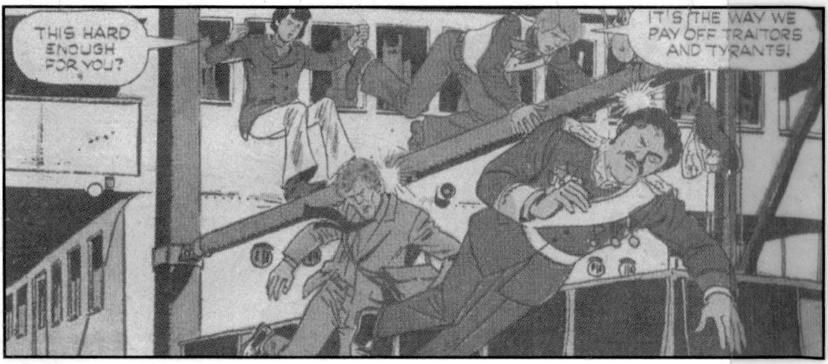
THIS HARD ENOUGH FOR YOU?
IT'S THE WAY WE PAY OFF TRAITORS AND TYRANTS!

The characters they chose to base this new show on was, of course, The Hardy Boys!

Filmation decided that in addition to solving mysteries, the Hardy Boys would be a touring bubblegum pop band. Joining Frank and Joe in this band, called The Hardy Boys Plus Three, were "Chubby" Morton, a character clearly based on Chet Morton, and new characters, Pete Jones (the first African-American character on a Saturday morning series*), and Wanda Kay Breckenridge.

For the non-singing parts of the show, actor Byron Kane provided the voices for Joe Hardy, Pete Jones, and Fenton Hardy; actor Dal McKennon did likewise for Frank Hardy and Chubby Morton, and actress Jane Webb supplied the female voices for Wanda Kay Breckenridge and Aunt Gertrude Hardy.

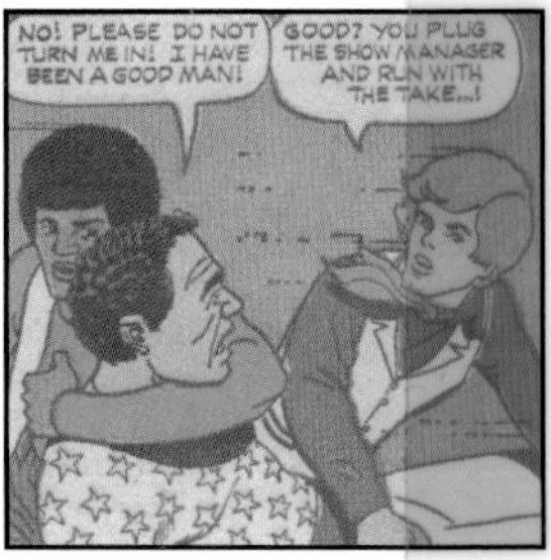
NO! PLEASE DO NOT TURN ME IN! I HAVE BEEN A GOOD MAN!
GOOD? YOU PLUG THE SHOW MANAGER AND RUN WITH THE TAKE...!

While the actual mystery/adventure stories were animated, the show did feature the groovy live-action band briefly at the end of each episode performing one of their songs. Two record albums were released, "Here Come The Hardy Boys" and "Wheels," featuring the musical Hardy Boys, and the first album even cracked Billboard's Top 200 Album Chart. About the only other place to "see" the live version of The Hardy Boys Plus Three was on the Hardy Boys comicbook's covers. Each of the four covers featured a mix of comic art and photos. The "live" band appeared most prominently on the second issue.

Oh, and the answer to "The Mystery of the Forgotten Cartoon Series" is that the show ran against the ratings blockbuster Scooby-Doo and everyone was watching the Scooby gang!

*While the prime time TV special, "Hey, Hey, Hey, It's Fat Albert," debuted in 1969 as well, "Fat Albert and the Cosby Kids" didn't become a regular Saturday morning series until 1972. Like The Hardy Boys it was also produced by Filmation Studios.